Crossroads

Crossroads

by

Schledia Phillips

THREE KEYS PUBLISHING

UNLOCKING WORLDS, HEARTS, AND MINDS

THREE KEYS PUBLISHING

Schledia Phillips

Like her on Facebook at Schledia Phillips, author

Or follow her blog at www.pinkyphillips.blogspot.com

Dedication

To Colby

Long ago two dirt roads crossed.
One was yours, the other mine,
And while we were yet children,
our lives were intertwined.
Along life's way,
we turned onto roads that led us worlds apart.
Despite the distance, despite the miles,
prayers for you were always in my heart.
Yet God's infinite wisdom caused our roads to turn
until once again they crossed.
My road had been long and rough,
and its darkness had me lost.
As I trudged forward through my darkest days,
I saw an intersection ahead.
I heard a familiar voice echo in my heart.
"Your prayers are answered," He said.
I am forever thankful for Our Crossroad,
our moment in time,
Choices were made that assured us I was yours,
and you were mine.
Our trails were merged,
those two dirt roads becoming one.
You are my path in life.
You've filled our journey
With love, laughter, and fun!
Colby, I love you,

Pinky

Acknowledgments

I would like to thank each and every individual who helped me on my journey in the creative concept, rough drafts, beta reads, revisions, edits, and cover creation. First to my husband, Colby Anderson, for inspiring me with the original idea that became Crossroads. This book would not exist were it not for you, my love. My daughter Trinity relentlessly listened to me read her chapter after chapter during the rough draft stage, giving me feedback. Thank you, Trin Trin. My Beta Reader, Lara Siedel. I cannot thank you enough for the amazing critique and the encouragement you gave me throughout the entire process. Crossroads is a better novel because of you! Thank you to Polished Pages for editing Crossroads. My photographer, Joy Colmerauer, thank you so much for the remarkable photography. Your photos made the cover what it is! A special thanks to Denny Bushman for agreeing to be the model for the cover. It was a pleasure working with you. You made a handsome model. Thank you to Dandy Art for taking Joy's photographs and creating the perfect cover for my novel.

Contents

The Dark Road
The Funeral

As Joshua Parker headed to the funeral home, low, dark clouds accumulated in the distance, blotting out the early afternoon sun. A gust of wind blew through the truck cab and ruffled his slicked-back hair. Breathing in the heady scent of the oncoming rain, he leaned forward over the steering wheel, narrowed his puffy gray eyes, and peered at the heavy wall of water rushing toward the truck. He swiftly jabbed the window switches and held them down, rolling up the windows to shield his children and himself from the approaching storm. As he drove into a dark gray cloud that seemed to cloak the road, fat droplets of rain pelted against the windshield of his truck. With the road concealed, apprehension coiled around his chest like a boa constrictor compressing his lungs. His heart muscles tightened, rapidly and vigorously pounding against his ribcage. Persistent swishing and splashing from the windshield wipers pulsed like a metronome in the back of his mind. The steady rhythm somehow soothed the aching in his chest as his heart caught onto the beat and slowed its pace to match the tempo of the wipers; music had been the key to many doorways in his life. It was the key that unlocked the door that led him to his wife, Isabella. Staring blankly ahead as he drove, his mind trailed after the music humming in his thoughts, taking him back to the summer of 2009 when Isabella sang her way into his heart...

Josh followed the music into his memories, finding his way to June 2009 at the community's gospel singing. The small town of Oak Ridge hosted the yearly event at The Trail, the town's community park. Anxious to perform, Josh had put together a quartet of men from his church. The harmonizing sounds of the bass blending with the tenors and the baritone delighted him, but more than anything, he cherished the camaraderie developed by night after night of practice. Samuel (the festival director) and Josh stood next to the pavilion, revamping last-minute changes to the schedule. The stark difference in the two men's stature made Josh (a man of average height) seem tall. Samuel flipped through the clipboard in his left hand and scratched through a timeslot. He tugged on his shirt collar, loosening it around his neck. The sweltering summer heat on the Alabama coast lingered as the sun inched westward and hid behind thick, puffy clouds.

Pressing his lips into a thin line, Samuel turned his mouth down in a frown. "I'll never get used to the humidity here on the coast," he grumbled.

Sweat beaded on Josh's forehead, attempting to cool down his rising body temperature. "Yeah, it can be tough to cope with...even for those of us who've grown up here." He chuckled as he wiped the sweat from his brow.

The sound crew set up speakers on both sides of the pavilion, the outdoor stage for the music festival. During the sound check, one of the microphones screeched, sending a shrill echo across the way. Standing on the far side of the grassy field, talking on her cell phone, Isabella Bennett cringed and planted her palm over her free ear. She snapped her head up as the noise shrieked from the speakers, sending the soundwaves throughout The Trail. Frustrated, Isabella snapped her cell phone shut with a forceful click and chucked it into her purse. Jutting out her thin bottom lip in a pout, she huffed, pacing back and forth past the funnel cake stand with her arms akimbo; the aroma of fried dough and sugar drew her in. With a sigh, she gave in to its allure and purchased her own. Munching on the delectable treat, she glanced around and soaked in the carnival atmosphere. She spotted three children tugging on their mom's arms (begging to play games or buy cotton candy) before she eyed Sam. She wove through the spindly pine trees, cut across the sandy walking trail, and marched onto the grassy field towards the pavilion. As she neared Sam, she eyed a dark-haired man standing beside him. Unwilling to interrupt their conversation, she held herself back, pacing back and forth over a small area, picking at her nails. Keeping her distance, she wrung her hands and waited for an opportune time to approach him.

Sam caught a glimpse of her demeanor from the corner of his eye. Her tiny frame nervously fidgeted, her ivory skin turning pallid. He patted Josh on the shoulder. "Give me a sec," he said, smiling.

"Sure thing, Sam." Josh watched his friend jog across the field and approached the panicky woman. He narrowed his eyes and admired her beauty from afar. The screech of an amplifier shifted his focus to the band members setting up the equipment. Stepping over to them, he introduced himself with a handshake and offered his assistance.

Samuel approached Isabella. "Everything okay, Isabella? You look a little nervous." His thick, salt-and-pepper-colored hair clung to his head, wet from the humidity.

Isabella frowned. "More like discouraged." Her cheeks puffed out with air as she blew out a heavy sigh. "Looks like my slot's gonna be free. My keyboard player just called. He's sick and can't make it."

Samuel shook his head and sighed. "It's been that kinda day." Rubbing his pudgy hand through his full beard, he raised his brow in thought. "I may have a solution to your dilemma. My friend, Josh, the guy I was talking to, plays the keyboard. Give me a sec, and I'll see if he can help you out."

Samuel hiked back to the pavilion and signaled Josh. Josh situated the stage monitor before meandering across the field to his friend and speaking with him discreetly. When Sam lifted his head from their huddle, he wore a huge grin and waved Isabella over. Her lemon-yellow skirt billowed around her as she breezed to his side. "Isabella, this is my friend, Josh. He's a musician. He said he'd help you out."

Josh stepped forward and offered his hand for a friendly shake. Isabella took his hand and peered into his eyes, studying his features. She found the flecks of yellow scattered throughout his slate-gray eyes fascinating. "I'm Josh," he said. "So, what are you singing?"

"Hmmm?" She scrutinized the shape of his face, trying to imagine his prominent jawline without the stubby beard that covered it.

A broad smile stretched across his face. He widened his eyes and raised his brow, cutting his eyes to Isabella's hand as it gripped his. He flashed his eyes back to hers, catching her in his gaze. "Sam said you were sing...ing and need...ed a keyboard player," he said, stretching his words out slowly and deliberately.

Isabella captured a glimmer of his eyes trailing toward their hands and realized (with a slight jolt) that her hand still clung to his. "Oh," she said, her voice shuddery as she yanked her hand free. "I'm sorry. Yes, well, I was going to be singing a song I wrote, but well, I wouldn't expect you to be able to learn it before my slot in forty-five minutes. Umm...I guess we should pick out an old hymn we can both handle?" She cringed, wrinkling her nose. She felt confidence seeping from her heart, leaving her feeling wretched and insecure.

The corner of Josh's mouth turned up in a half-smile as he admired the freckles scattered across her nose. Shrugging, he responded with a slight chuckle, "That'll work. Just pick one, and we can step inside the community center for a few minutes and go over it."

"Sure," she said, still holding his gaze. "I'm sorry, but your name is Josh, right?"

"Yep, sure is." He laughed and nodded.

"You remind me of a boy I knew when I was a little girl, but it was so long ago. I've been trying to picture you without the beard."

With his masculine hand, Josh stroked his prickly beard. "You caught me at a bad time on that. I don't normally have one, but my daughter likes the feel of stubble. She asked me to let my beard grow out last weekend. I'm not used to it." He dropped his hand and smiled, revealing his sparkling white teeth. "So, this boy's name was Josh?"

Isabella cast her gray eyes to the ground, eyeing her dainty foot as she kicked at the grass. "Yeah, his name was Josh. His mother was friends with my aunt. I'm sorry for staring. I just thought you might be him."

Tilting his head to the side, he raised his brow. "What's your aunt's name?"

Shuffling her feet, she answered in a small voice, "Ruth."

Josh squared his shoulders and nodded. "My mom did have a friend named Ruth. They went to church *together."*

A soft smile inched across her face, revealing a dimple on her right cheek. "Sounds like my aunt. She was a faithful believer."

Josh thrummed his fingers on the side of his chin in thought, stroking his well-trimmed beard. "Ruth had a daughter my age, Lyla. We went out a few times, and she had two sons. Dale was a couple of years older than me. He didn't like me too much—probably because I dated his sister. The other one was a good bit younger than me, though. Daniel?" He cast a questioning eye toward Isabella.

Isabella's countenance beamed. A smile flitted across her face as she glanced back into his eyes. "Yes, those're my cousins Dale, Lyla, and Daniel. Daniel was my best friend growing up. I practically lived at their house."

Josh shook his head. "I don't remember an Isabella, though."

Isabella cast her eyes to the ground and blushed. "Ummm...well." She scrunched her petite button nose. "You wouldn't have known me by my first name. I always went by Tink."

Josh's eyes widened, and his jaw dropped. He covered his mouth with his hand. "Tink? Oh, my goodness," he murmured through his splayed fingers. Dropping his hand, he continued, "I would've never recognized you."

Tink tilted her head and shrugged her shoulders. "Well, I was still practically a child when we saw each other last, so that doesn't surprise me. You're a lot different, too, but I could still see that same teenage boy in your eyes."

A lightning bolt cracked across the sky, shooting white, spidery flashes of electricity through the atmosphere. The brash rumbling jarred Josh and brought him back to the present. Shaking the memory that inundated his thoughts from his mind, he shook his head, craned his neck, and eyed his two youngest children sitting in the back cab of his truck. Twelve-year-old Josh Junior's bottom lip protruded in a pout, his broad chin trembling. Red veins surrounded his chestnut-brown eyes. His black suit jacket rose and fell with each shuddery breath he took. Crimson splotches covered his stepdaughter's (fifteen-year-old Ciara) narrow face, her emerald-green eyes filled with tears. Both children sat in the back seat with their hands folded neatly in their laps, watching the rain with blank stares. Ciara blinked, the tears flowing down her raw, swollen cheeks. Josh turned his head back to watch the road. Leaning over the steering wheel, he narrowed his puffy, red-rimmed eyes to peer through the storm.

Thirty minutes later, Josh stood at the head of his wife's pearl-white casket. Erected throughout the funeral home were sprays of flowers, and interspersed amongst them were framed photographs of Isabella during her life. Dazed, Josh acknowledged each friend and family member as they came to say their final goodbye to Isabella, the woman they all dearly loved. With each handshake and hug, the heaviness in his heart grew darker. He had never considered himself a cowardly man who feared the darkness, but this wasn't merely the absence of light; it was a stealthy shadow that slithered into his mind as he watched the light leave his wife's eyes when she slipped into eternity.

Josh had always heard that the eyes were the window to the soul, and now, Death convinced him of its truth; he had witnessed it for himself. When her soul departed its earthly home, black curtains descended over the windows of her eyes and concealed the hollow void behind them. Pain radiated through Josh's chest as his lungs emptied themselves of oxygen through his wails. Abandoning his body in search of its mate, his soul intertwined with the air expelled from his lungs. His body, an empty shell, sat next to their bed where he had just laid her body. He stared at her pale, limp hand as it slipped from her side and dangled off the side of the bed. He grabbed her hand, held it in his, and wept bitterly. Emptiness was all that remained.

Isabella insisted destiny brought them together. "We're soulmates," she would say to everyone, frequently reminding him of the vision God had given her. At the beginning of their friendship, Isabella dreamed of them standing outside a small, white church...

Josh followed behind her as she skipped around to the side of the building. Laughing, he held his hand out for hers and called her to come to him. Her laughter subsided, replaced with awe, as a magnetism she had never

experienced drew her to him. The force tugged at her belly, prodding deep from within her innermost being. Her spirit pressed through and poured from her navel like a silver stream. She watched as his spirit issued forth from his belly and intertwined with hers, wrapping around one another, mingling, and becoming one. It was that moment when she knew God had made her for Joshua Caleb Parker.

Josh heard the story so often that he knew it by heart. Isabella, the source of light in his life, always spoke of hope, faith, love, and healing. Now, with her life force gone, he was left to trudge his way through the blackness invading his heart and mind, and that darkness (the kind that crept into a man's spirit to consume him) was the darkness he feared.

Josh shook the hand of a grieving friend and realized he felt nothing. He found the numbness odd and wondered if he cut his flesh, would he even feel the pain? He suspected the blade would slice straight through to the bone without even causing him to flinch. Pain eluded him. Until now, he had never experienced the absence of physical pain, and he found himself longing for it to return. Pain assured him his wife was soon to arrive, as always, with her magical kisses.

Josh closed his eyes and envisioned Isabella. A distant memory rushed to the surface of his mind…

Chirping his early morning song, a red cardinal called to his mate as he perched in one of the oak trees hemming

the edge of the parking lot of The Trail. Isabella stood on the old wooden bridge at the beginning of the walking path. Although her back was to him, he could see she covered her eyes with her hands. Her soft brunette hair fell in waves down her back. Early morning sunlight pierced through the willowy pine trees that edged the path. Under the shafts of pale light, auburn hues glimmered in her hair. A light breeze ruffled through the trees, scattering pine needles over the sandy walking trail and blowing their scent across the parking lot.

He heard her alto voice call, "...forty-eight, forty-nine, fifty." She swept her hand across the nape of her neck and pulled her hair to one side. Glancing over her shoulder, she eyed Josh standing beside his truck and smiled.

Captivated by her beauty, Josh smiled in return and slammed his truck door. "Ah!" he yelped. Cringing, he drew his hand to his chest.

Isabella's smile faded, her eyes widening in shock. "Oh, no!" She rushed to his side. "Give me your hand." She held her hand out for his.

A crooked smile crept across his face as he stepped forward and stretched forth his bruised, throbbing hand. He raised a brow in jest. "Planning to smash the other one so it hurts worse?" He chuckled.

"Oh, hush, you silly man," she said as she winked, a glimmer shining in her eyes.

"Fifty, huh?" He winked back, staring into her large, almond-shaped

eyes. A hint of wild cherries brushed over his face. He breathed deeply, inhaling the scent. "Nice perfume," he uttered.

Isabella smirked. "Thanks." Shaking her head, she rolled her eyes. "And yes, fifty, that's what you said." She examined his hand. Looking up and gazing into his gray eyes (secretly searching for the yellow flecks she found intriguing), she smiled and drew his wounded hand to her lips. "My kisses are magical. They make everything better. Just ask my children." She brushed her lips over his injured fingers, gently caressing them. "See," she breathed. "Doesn't it already feel better?" Love and infatuation mingled together, shimmering in her gray eyes. It was there (in the location where they found each other after sixteen years) that she had given him that kiss, the first kiss she ever gave him.

The gentle tug of Josh's sleeve drew his mind back to his surroundings, freeing his mind from the memories. Desperation washed over him as the memory of Isabella's first kiss faded. Longing to hold onto the vivid pictures in his mind, he squeezed his eyes tight, stiffened his stance, and shrugged off the young boy, grasping his arm for comfort. Memories were the only place he could gaze at his wife's beauty. When he allowed himself to be drawn into his mind deep enough, he could even feel her touch him and imagine the scent of her skin. He needed to feel her near him, especially now that he had to gaze upon the empty shell that once held her beautiful spirit.

Grief worked its way into Josh's mind on the day

Isabella passed from this world. It immediately began working to build a barrier around him, drowning him in his own pain and preventing him from seeing anyone else's. Soft sniffles managed to make their way past it. Josh Junior's faint cries weaseled their way through the brick-and-mortar and drew Josh's attention to his side. Josh glanced down at his son and eyed warm, moist tears streaming down his round cheeks, saturating his plump lips.

"Josh, son. Hey, buddy." Josh bent over and wrapped his arms around his young son. "I'm sorry. Daddy's mind was elsewhere." He held his son tight.

"I miss Momma," Josh Junior cried.

Pulling back from his embrace of his son, he dug in his suit jacket, drew out a handkerchief, and patted his pudgy cheeks dry. "I know, son. I know. So do I, and Ciara, you know she misses Momma, too. We've gotta be strong for her. Caleb and Londyn, they miss her something fierce." He tugged on Josh Junior's tie, straightening it. "We've gotta be strong for each other, you know?"

Josh Junior nodded. "Yeah," he sniffled.

Josh ran his fingers through his son's light-brown hair. "You're such a handsome young man. You know, your mom was so proud of you."

Despite his quivering chin, Josh Junior forced a smile. "I know." A tear spilled over the dam created by his lower eyelid and ran down his olive-toned cheek.

With her graceful gait, Ciara entered the parlor where her mother was laid out. Her navy-blue dress hugged her narrow waist and draped below her knees. Her sleek, honey-brown hair hung past her waist. Grasping her mother's hand, she whispered, "I miss you so much, Momma. I promise I'll take care of Caleb and Josh Junior."

A tall, stocky man approached Ciara from behind. He wrapped his arm around her shoulder. "Your mom is still just as beautiful as ever," he said.

Ciara brushed the tears from her cheeks and glanced at her father, Dean Bennett. Shocked that her biological father would show up to his ex-wife's funeral, she knit her brow. "Hey, Dad," she said, her voice tainted with hesitance. She tilted her head and cut her eyes to peer around the room, searching for her stepmother. "Is Rebecca with you?"

"No, she couldn't get off work. She asked me to pass on her condolences to everyone." He shrugged. "I think she just felt it would be awkward to be the new wife at the ex-wife's funeral."

"Yeah, I didn't expect to see you here, much less my stepmom."

Dean's face twisted, an offended mask replacing the solemn countenance he sported only moments earlier. "Seriously, you didn't think I'd be here? Isabella was my wife and the mother of my children. Of course, I'm going to be here. You two need me. Even if you don't realize it." Anger swirled through his words and countenance like a forceful waterspout.

Fear that her father's anger issues may rip through the room surged through Ciara's tiny frame. A clip of her mom flinching at one of his outbursts flashed through her mind. Her face went ashen. Her blood drained from her extremities and rushed to her heart, causing her arms and legs to go limp. She grasped the arm of a nearby chair and seated herself. She inhaled a sharp breath and quickly gathered the words to diffuse the situation. "Sorry. I didn't mean to upset you. You and Mom weren't exactly on good terms, is all."

Dean's hardened countenance fell. "I know, but death changes things, sweetheart. I realize I made so many mistakes. I wanna make that right. I've been looking at bigger houses." A half-smile crept across one side of his face. He winked, leaned in close, and nudged Ciara's shoulder.

"Why?" Ciara raised her brow.

"So that you and Caleb will have rooms of your own. I know you don't wanna share a room with your stepsister. I'm no dummy."

Ciara sighed. "Oh, Dad, I'm not...I mean, I'm staying with Josh and Josh Junior. Caleb is in college. He lives in a dorm." She gently placed her hand on the side of his shoulder. "They need me. You, you have Rebecca and Cindy. Besides, you know Rebecca likes the *terrific trio,* as she calls it." She rolled her eyes and shrugged.

Dean's face flushed crimson. He clenched his jaw. "I guess I need to talk to Josh about this. You're my child, not his."

"Please don't cause any issues, not today. I love you, but I think you need to leave. We need to grieve without feeling animosity." She leaned forward, propped herself on her tiptoes, and kissed her father on the cheek. He huffed before turning on his heels and walking away.

Ciara inhaled a deep, cleansing breath. Slowly releasing it, she eyed her stepfather and stepbrother intermingling with guests on the far side of the room. Approaching them, she embraced them both. "The funeral...director...said...it's time for the guests...to enter the chapel." Her voice broke as she spoke. "He said...we will stay here with Momma...and pray...before we go in."

Josh nodded and signaled for Londyn and Caleb, his daughter and stepson, to approach. Londyn, Josh's eldest child, made her way across the room. She sidled up next to Ciara. Towering over her dainty stepsister, she grabbed Ciara's hand and squeezed it tight, signifying solidarity. The two girls were as different as daylight and dark in stature and personality, yet their bond was solid.

Tall, lanky Caleb stepped into the circle the children had formed with Josh. He wrapped his lean, muscular arms around his stepdad's shoulders and sobbed. "Thank you for making my momma happy. You're the best stepdad anyone could ask for," he cried. Tears rushed over his freckled cheeks.

Josh squeezed Caleb tightly. "You're not a stepson to me. You're my son. Always will be." Caleb stretched his thin lips across his face, smiling despite the aching in his chest.

The family stood in a close-knit circle, held hands, and prayed for God's comfort and peace.

The Rough Road Family Ties

Shafts of late afternoon sunlight broke through the light gray clouds moving across the sky. The heat expelled by the sun's rays soaked up the puddles left by the April rainstorm. A year had passed since Caleb laid his mother to rest, but rest had evaded those still living. Concerned for his grieving friend, Pastor Denison (along with his wife) arranged for the church to gather together at the Parker home on the anniversary of Isabella's funeral. Caleb Bennett sat in his car, thrumming his fingers on the steering wheel. Folding his lips over his teeth, he took a deep breath and gathered his emotions, hoping to suppress them as best he could. Stepping out of his car, he shoved his hands in his pants pockets and meandered towards his stepdad's front porch. Making his way across the yard, he kicked at the damp flowers poking up their flowery heads across the lawn. Narrowing his eyes, he glared at what he knew to be weeds. He hated them and all their deceptiveness. They popped up across the fields, flaunting lovely flowers that promised beautiful scenery but underneath grew invasive root systems weaving their way through the dirt and choking out the life of the flowerbeds his mother had spent countless hours tending. The image reminded him of her, his mother. She was a beautiful, elegant woman who exuded strength and courage. He never saw her as frail until he overheard her secretly weeping over her own prognosis. Despite her exterior beauty, an intrusive growth had weaseled through her body and strangled the life from her.

He glanced over his shoulder and eyed his sister and little stepbrother as they scrambled to climb out of his stepdad's truck. A shroud of darkness loomed over them. He wondered if he should withdraw from college and move back home. He turned on his heels and unlocked the front door. Patiently waiting, he stood, shoulders slumped, and held the door open for Londyn and Ciara; Josh had taught his sons to be gentlemen, opening doors for ladies as a sign of respect and honor. Isabella had taught her daughters to receive such gestures graciously, knowing the intention was to bestow reverence upon them, not to belittle them as needing a man to do such things for them. Isabella insisted a woman, a true lady, understood her value; therefore, she acknowledged the treatment as a gentleman's regard for her worth and importance in society.

As the girls crossed the threshold of their home, they passed through the spacious living room and made their way into the kitchen. Stopping short of the bar, Ciara stood ramrod straight. Her eyes pooled with tears at the abundance of food brought in by their church family while they had visited their mother's grave. A buffet of food covered the kitchen counters and the ten-foot-long island. The spectacular kitchen had seen its share of spreads, but it had never had such an abundance of food that any of them could remember. The aroma of freshly baked bread wafted through the house, reminding her of her mother.

Josh and Isabella built their home around their dual kitchen. The love of cooking and food was a source of income for them both. Josh (a chef who previously owned several restaurants) came up with the brilliant idea of creating a cooking show that featured them battling it out over their recipes. Isabella was no chef, but she knew her way around the kitchen. They filmed what grew to be a locally famous cooking show in their very own kitchen. They engaged weekly in Kitchen Wars, creating new recipes for their trendy line of recipe books.

A hard knot formed in Ciara's throat as she walked through the kitchen. She swallowed hard, pushing against the knot as it threatened to force its way out through cries; she didn't want to break in front of everyone. Grief was funny that way. Most days, she went on about life with a sense of normalcy, but today, she had to revisit the loss of her mom. Josh, her stepdad, wasn't coping as well as they were, so Londyn, Caleb, and Ciara had gone to their pastor, Clay Denison, with their concerns for their dad. He felt a gathering in his friend's home as a sign of support would do Josh some good, so here she was on the anniversary of her mother's death, standing in the kitchen surrounded by food. Brushing her long, slender fingers over the various dishes brought by their friends, she inspected the slew of casseroles. A tear rolled down her alabaster cheek. She stopped at the bacon-wrapped Brussels sprouts.

Adorned in a black baby doll dress, Londyn pranced across the room and came up from behind Ciara. Wrapping her arms around Ciara's shoulders, she squeezed her tight. "I'm sure they don't compare to your mom's," she said.

Ciara forced a strained smile. "No one makes Brussels sprouts like Momma. She won that kitchen war episode, hands down." She giggled and dried her cheek with her petite hand.

Straightening her posture, Londyn chuckled and rolled her large, crystal-blue eyes. "Yeah, Dad thought he had it, too! Boy, did he get blown away!"

Caleb came up from behind his sisters and wrapped his arms around them. "What are you two lovely ladies gabbing about over here? You trying to figure out where to hide the food from me?" He pulled away and ran his fingers through his nut-brown hair, tousling his fringed bangs.

Londyn brushed her large hands over her shoulders, flattening the wrinkles his grasp created. Shaking her head, she raised her brows and smirked. "Oh, no, we decided you can have it all. There's no way it'll be as good as Mom's anyway. Besides, you could stand to put on a few pounds." She wrapped her large hand around his wrist and lifted his thin arm out to the side.

Caleb flexed his arm, revealing the muscles hidden under his lanky build. Grinning, he said, "Just because you don't see the muscle doesn't mean it's not there."

Londyn dropped her arm and stepped back. "Wow, look at that!" She raised her brows in jest. "I bet girls are beating down your dorm room door." She chuckled.

Josh Junior skipped up to his siblings with a mouthful of cake. "Have you guys tried this red velvet cake? It's amazing." Small bites of cake spattered onto the floor as he spoke.

Londyn huffed, cocking her head to the side, and pushed his chin up. His teeth clanked together. "Josh, you know better than to talk with your mouth full of food."

Josh Junior turned his mouth down in a frown. "Sorry," he mumbled under his breath.

Caleb narrowed his eyes and shot a warning glare at his stepsister. He knew she tended to be a little bossy, but it wasn't time for that behavior. "Don't be so hard on him, El," Caleb interjected. "Not today. It's best if he's oblivious to the fact that we're all reliving Mom's death to try to help Dad through his grief."

Londyn exhaled a deep breath and shook her head. "Sorry, Joshie. I'm so used to *mothering* you." She cut her eyes to Caleb as she tousled Josh Junior's light brown hair.

A light knock resounded on the front door. *Tap, tap, tap.* Josh rounded the corner of the hall and opened the front door. Pastor Denison and his wife, Christina, stood waiting on the front porch. "Come in, Clay," Josh said, welcoming them into his home. "Thanks to you and the rest of the congregation, we have an overabundance of food. *Please,* help us eat it." He raised his brows. Holding the door open, he waved toward the spread filling his kitchen. Clay Denison turned his leaf-green eyes to his wife and stepped aside, allowing her to enter ahead of him. Her sage-green dress hung loosely over her straight, tiny frame.

Pastor Denison wrapped his arms around Josh. "You look good, brother."

Josh pulled back from their embrace, tilted his head to the side, and turned his mouth down in a frown. "Thanks. I don't feel so great. If I'm honest, I'm not coping very well."

Pastor Denison's children (twenty, sixteen, and eight) followed suit and stepped into the living room. "Wow, the congregation brought enough to feed an army, it seems." Pastor Denison chuckled as he intertwined his long, slender fingers in his wife's delicate hand.

Sixteen-year-old Christy Denison scanned the room and found Ciara. She gracefully moved across the room, finding her way to her best friend, her tall, willowy figure starkly contrasting with Ciara's short, hourglass shape. She wrapped her long, thin arms around her friend, seeking to comfort her. Ciara breathed deeply, feeling the warmth of a spring breeze across her face. Glancing across the room, she eyed her stepdad standing at the front door, waiting for other guests to enter. "Thank you, Christy." Pulling from her friend's embrace, she cut her eyes towards the front door. "I should go assist my dad."

"Of course," Christy said, nodding her head in consent.

Ciara strolled across the living room and came up from behind her stepdad. "Dad, I'll handle inviting our guests in. You go, be with Pastor Denison, and please make sure to eat. I fixed you a plate of food. It's on the table in your spot." She shooed him away. Smiling, she turned and greeted the family members as they stepped up to the front door. She stood with a gracious smile and waved each friend and family member through as they made their way into Josh and Isabella's home.

Charles Denison, the eldest of the three, cast his topaz eyes about the room and eyed Londyn. He flashed her a bright smile, squared his broad shoulders, and started for the kitchen. His crush on Londyn started at a kid's camp when he was twelve. At the age of seventeen, she attended camp as a counselor. Charles followed Caleb around the entire week of camp, eventually befriending him to gain access to his stepsister.

Candy, the youngest of the Denison children, skipped behind her brother into the kitchen. Her honey-blonde spirals bounced with each skip. She sidled next to Josh Junior and grinned. Pointing to the cake on the plate he held, she batted her round, topaz eyes at him and said, "That cake looks delicious."

Christy rolled her eyes and shook her head. "Candace, it's not appropriate to beg for food. Besides, the blessing hasn't been said yet." She breezed across the kitchen. Kneeling in front of her little sister, she straightened the bow wrapped around the waist of her dress and leaned in close, capturing her attention with the sincere gaze in her leafy-green eyes, and whispered, "Candy, it's not ladylike to flirt. Okay? I know you want to be a little lady, so...don't flirt with Josh. Today is about him remembering his mom. That's sad, don't you think?"

Candace's bottom lip jutted out in a pout. She nodded infinitesimally.

A smile crept across one side of Christy's oblong face. She squeezed Candy's pudgy cheeks between her long, slender fingers. "You're such a little lady. I'm proud of you."

Ciara shut the front door after the last guest entered her home. Pastor Denison stepped to the center of the living room; his dark blond hair was neatly combed back. "Ahem." He pushed his black-rimmed glasses up the bridge of his large, Roman nose and cleared his throat to quiet the crowd. "If I could have your attention, please. Josh has asked me to bless the food before we begin eating. I would like to begin by thanking those who brought an amazing spread to show love and support to this family. Isabella left us all a year ago today, and I know many may not understand why we all gathered around this family today; that's what families do. We surround each other in our time of need and show love and support."

Pastor Denison wrapped his slim arm around Josh's thick shoulder and looked him in the eyes. "Josh, your family has always been a blessing to our church. Y'all are loved. Isabella was loved and adored by so many. We are all praying for your family. Grief doesn't end the day we lose someone near and dear to our hearts. Grief takes time. The loss changes us. It becomes a part of who we are, and we want you all to know that we're there for you to the end."

Clay dropped his arm from around Josh and grabbed his hand instead. Everyone followed suit and grasped the hand of the person standing next to them. "Lord Jesus, our Heavenly Father, we come to You today seeking Your blessings upon the food brought here today by friends and family members. We ask that You open the floodgates of Heaven and pour out Your blessings upon all who worked to prepare the food before us. Touch the Parker family. Fill this home with Your Holy Spirit. Give comfort and peace where only You can. In the wonderful name of Jesus, the name above all names. The name of the One true God. Amen."

After thirty solid minutes of plate after plate piled with food, the line through the kitchen finally diminished. Pastor Denison sat at the table across from Josh and his children. He cut his eyes to the Italian dish sitting in front of Josh. "Looks delicious," he said.

"Hmmm...Yeah." Josh forced a half-smile. "I couldn't resist when I saw the roasted lamb and cannoli." Leaning across the table, he whispered, "Don't tell Ciara, but I wrapped up the plate she fixed me and put it in the frig." His smile stretched to his eyes, brightening them. "I took Isabella to Vita Sapori on our first official date, and we had roasted lamb, cannoli, and gnocchi with a superb butter sauce." He kissed the tips of his fingers as a sign of the meal's excellence.

Pastor Denison glanced at his wife and grinned. "We've never been there before. Christina has asked me to take her, but we just haven't taken the time to do it. What's it like?"

Josh's mind flashed back to that night nearly twelve years prior...

Isabella's face beamed (an excited glimmer in her eyes) as they approached the restaurant built to exemplify an Italian villa. Nestled throughout were small stucco cottages, perfectly accented with old terracotta tile roofing with a cobblestone pathway twining through the restaurant. Each Tuscan room (shaped slightly differently from the next) held four tables and accommodated eight patrons. Between them were well-lit patios with long tables for larger crowds. A brick fountain served as the center point of the villa. The rushing water and low lighting throughout the restaurant created an ambiance of romance.

Josh slipped his arm around her waist and pulled her close to his side. A young, attractive hostess grabbed two menus and guided them to one of the small cottages. A hot, muggy breeze wisped her short, fringed, red hair around her thin face. She seated them in one of the small cottages and bounced from the room. Flickering candles cast a yellow glow over Isabella's face, revealing her freckled nose. Josh gazed across the table, enraptured by her silhouette in the dim light. Isabella blushed and smiled at the table; her thick eyelashes fanned her pink cheeks.

Josh patted his pockets, his face falling as he sighed. Clearing his throat, Josh excused himself. "I'm so sorry to have to do this, but I forgot my wallet in the truck." He cringed. "I'll be right back. Don't order without me." He stood to his feet and shoved the chair back under the table. "I'm normally not this forgetful. I promise." He winked at Isabella as he rushed from the cottage.

Josh returned to the table as the hostess who seated him and Isabella escorted another couple into the cottage, seating them on the other side of the room. She returned after giving them ample time to review the menu and took their order, giving her professional input on the chef's most popular dishes.

"You know, I could have covered the meal," Isabella said.

"No way. My Momma raised a gentleman." Josh furrowed his brow, shook his head, and picked up the glass of lemonade, eyeing it suspiciously. He cleared his throat and set the glass down. "She also raised an honest man." His face flushed a bright red. He dropped his head and shoved his hand in his pocket. "I didn't forget my wallet, but I couldn't tell you what I did forget." He cleared

his throat. "I know this is technically our first date, but Isabella, I don't want you to slip through my fingers again. I mean, you were right there when we were children, and I missed it. I couldn't see that you were meant to be more than someone who was like family." Josh pulled his closed hand from his pocket and stretched his arm across the table, setting a small box in front of her.

Isabella's eyes grew wide. "What...what's this?"

A half-smile stretched across one side of Josh's face. "A gift...for you."

Isabella's eyes twinkled. A giggle slipped past her lips as she unraveled the bow neatly tied around the navy-blue box. Lifting the lid, she eyed a gold charm bracelet with a skate charm dangling from it. Laughter spilled from Isabella's lungs. "Oh, my goodness! You remembered."

"Of course, I remembered. Skating was my life back then, and yes, I remember you and Daniel following me around at the skating rink." He chuckled. "So, you like it?"

"I love it." She wrapped it in her palm and pulled it to her heart, hugging the gift.

The tantalizing smells of roasted lamb and cannoli wafted in the small cottage as the hefty server strode in with a bright smile and a chipper demeanor, carrying their meals. Her green eyes, surrounded by her chunky cheeks, lit up her face. She set their plates before them and poured their drinks. Excusing herself, she shut the cottage door behind her. Josh reached across the table and grabbed Isabella's hand, the bracelet dangling from her petite wrist. She closed her eyes and bowed her head. "Lord Jesus, bless this food and this evening. God, be with us and watch over us tonight. I pray that all we do glorifies You, Lord. In Jesus' name, Amen," he prayed.

"Amen," Isabella whispered.

The Italian couple on the other side of the room stood and approached Josh and Isabella. The man stretched forth his hand to shake Josh's. "Good evening," the man said. "My wife and I felt the Spirit of God move upon us to speak a blessing over your life."

Josh and Isabella both grinned. "Absolutely," they said in unison.

"How long have you two been married?" the woman asked.

Isabella's eyes lit up with eagerness to hear all God had spoken to the elderly couple standing before them. "Ummm, we're not married." Her slender face blushed a deep mauve. "This is actually our first official date, haha." A bashful chuckle slipped past her narrow lips.

The woman raised her brows and nodded her head. "You will be, but you already knew that didn't you?" She squinted her eyes, giving Isabella a slight wink, and tilted her head with a tsk-tsk. She grabbed Isabella's hand and looked her square in the eyes. "The Lord created Eve from Adam. She was a part of him from her creation. You, you were a part of this man from the moment God formed you in your mother's womb."

Isabella inhaled a slow, deep breath, closed her eyes, and prayed silently. The woman turned to look at Josh. "There are no coincidences for a righteous man because every step made by a righteous man is ordered by the Lord, so it wasn't happenstance when you ran into this woman." The woman spoke without removing her eyes from his. "If you two don't mind, can I ask you to hold hands and look at one another as my husband speaks over you both?"

Josh and Isabella nodded in agreement. Josh grasped her hand and intertwined their fingers together. The man placed one hand on Josh's shoulder, and with the other, he held his wife's hand. She, in turn, rested her free hand on Isabella's shoulder. "Lord Jesus, the Great I Am; the Everlasting Father; the King of kings, and the Lord of lords, we see Your anointing upon this couple. May You bless the joining of two hearts that You formed to fit together like pieces of a perfect puzzle. Where one lacks and falls prey to weakness, You have given great strength to the other so they may adhere in unity. May their bond be sealed by the glue of Your Holy Ghost. Link their hearts so they may feel the joys, the blessings, and the love flow from one to the other, continuously, just as they experience the heartache, the pain, and hurt together as one, no longer as two separate beings. Open the floodgates of Heaven and pour out Your blessings upon them both. Bless their children, bring them together, and bind them by Your Blood. In Jesus' name, I ask all these things, Amen."

Josh opened his eyes, pulling himself from the memory of their first date, and glanced across the table at Pastor Denison. Tears filled Clay Denison's eyes. He removed his black-rimmed glasses and dried the lenses with a cloth he pulled from his shirt pocket, patting his cheeks dry before replacing them. "That was a beautiful blessing spoken over the two of you."

"Huh," Josh huffed, shaking his head. Heat flushed through his body as his heart pounded against his ribcage, reddening his ruddy complexion. Silence filled the room momentarily as everyone cut their eyes toward him. "Yeah, it was," he started. His tone deepened, "But why, Clay, why?" He balled his hand in a tight fist and set his jaw, clenching his teeth, his taut muscles working underneath his skin. "Why would He have a couple who had never laid eyes on us before to speak such beautiful things, cause my heart to swell with faith and belief that I could finally have the love I had desired my entire life, just to snatch her away from me?" he seethed. His breath, along with the pent-up anger and frustration roiling in his chest, left him. "I have nothing left now. My desire to live left when she left me." Josh pushed his plate across the table, shoved his chair back, and rose to his feet. "I'm not hungry," he mumbled as he strode to his office.

Clay Denison turned to his wife. His mouth turned down in a frown. "I better go see about him." He gently set his fork on his plate and followed Josh's steps back to his office. Lightly tapping on his door, he requested entry.

"Come in, Clay."

The door swung open; Pastor Denison stepped in, shutting it behind him. "Josh, I know you're grieving, but you shouldn't say things like that. You have every reason in the world to live. Those children in there heard you say those powerful words, and you and I both know that if you were to lose them, then and only then would you be utterly alone, and even then, I would hope you would still cling to God."

Josh hung his head in shame. He sat silently, knowing he deserved the rebuttal. "Now, I'm your pastor, so I care about your spiritual well-being, but I'm also your friend, Josh. For crying out loud, our daughters are best friends, so I'm gonna say my peace, and then I'm leaving. I'm gonna ask you to take some time to yourself tomorrow or one day soon. Go to the cemetery and talk through your emotions with her and Jesus. Do it there, just you, her, and God. Please don't say such things in front of your children. They need you. I'm not asking you to be strong for them. Break right in front of 'em if you need to. They want real from you. They need to see you hurt, but they don't need to hear they're not enough to live for, Josh. I love you, brother, and I always will. Real love rebukes when a rebuke is necessary, but it does it in love, and I'm coming to you in love, brother. Take my advice, please." Clay Denison turned on his heels and shut the office door behind him.

The Broken Road
The Cemetery

Pebbles slapped against the underside of Josh's cobalt-blue truck as he turned onto a gravel road shrouded by a copse of live oaks. He cringed at the tings against the metal undercarriage (fearing some of them may ding his shiny, new truck), peeked through the windshield at the green canopy dripping with gray moss, and scoffed at the irony of their name. He knew it was time to heed Clay Denison's advice. Two weeks had passed since he had urged him to make the trip to visit Isabella—two weeks of only getting out of bed to go to the bathroom, but on this particular morning, Ciara barged into his room and demanded he get out of bed and eat something. Refusing, he hid beneath the covers. Ciara's chin trembled. She inhaled a sharp breath, attempting to hold back the deluge of tears pushing their way to the surface. At that moment, Josh knew he needed to comply with his pastor's suggestion.

Passing the cemetery sign serving as an entranceway, Josh immediately made a left onto what was known to the locals as ditch road. Tears filled his eyes, creating a colorful kaleidoscope of spring flowers and varying headstones as he drove past the rows of burial plots. He let off the gas and slowed his truck to a crawl as he approached the family plot. He parked at the end of the road and inhaled a sharp breath. Slowly releasing the air saturating his lungs, he exhaled and searched for the courage to face his fear—his new reality.

Josh clenched his jaw and glared through watery eyes at the lively bouquet of flowers in the vase next to Isabella's headstone. Ciara promised her mother she would keep her headstone adorned with her favorite flowers, yellow and white calla lilies. The flowers danced as a gentle breeze blew across the cemetery. They joyfully wisped, full of life and vitality. Their presence angered Josh. His mind screamed that she deserved to be the one dancing and laughing. Pushing the welled-up tears onto his cheeks, he closed his eyes. He wondered if he would ever run out of tears. He thought he had cried them all out, only to have them well up again from somewhere within him. It felt as if they rose from his throbbing heart, pushed their way over knots forming in his throat, surged through his cheeks, and finally poured from his eyes. The anger fueling them boiled in his chest, burning his lungs with each breath and making it nearly impossible to breathe. He grasped his chest, his face crumpling into a sob. His ribcage rose and fell in heavy heaves until the tears stopped and his breathing slowed. He pressed the heel of his hand against the sides of his temple, shaking his head back and forth, attempting to dispel the furious thoughts consuming him.

His hand trembled as he opened the truck door. Trepidation slithered in his mind like a snake, coiling around every glimmer of hope and smothering it. The gravel crunched beneath his feet as he stepped from his truck. A loud thud echoed through the empty cemetery as he slammed the door, reminding him he was utterly alone. Cringing at the clunking sound, he sauntered to her grave and collapsed, his knees burrowed in the dirt at the foot of her grave. The tears welled from within him again and surged forth. He covered his face with his large hands and wept.

"I don't know what to do with myself, Tink. You were the roadmap for our life. You navigated us through prayer and faith." He grabbed the nape of his neck and squeezed it. His knuckles turned white under the strength of his grip. "I can't do this alone. I need you, Tink." Letting go of his neck, he chuckled and threw his hand in the air. "And you know me...I can't find anything! You were the finder. Yep, you guessed it; we were almost late to your funeral because I couldn't find my truck keys." He chuckled and smiled. "But wouldn't you know it, our girl...she just slipped right in and filled your shoes.

She dangled 'em right in front of me and said, 'Just call me the finder.'" He wiped the tears from his cheek. "The children are trying so hard to help me get through my grief. You'd be so proud of 'em. They even helped Clay plan a big dinner at the house a few weeks ago. I got home from visiting you to find a house full of food, and our closest friends from church all came by to show their support."

Josh sniffled, rubbing his hand under his nose. "The children are great, Tink. It's like they were all able to go through the proper steps of grieving in record time. They still all have sad days and miss you terribly, but it's like they knew how to move on in life, and me…I'm stuck. I don't know how to get past being angry at how quickly you were snatched from me. The truth is, I don't wanna get past being angry or sad. I don't know how to live without you, and I don't want to." Josh pulled a folded paper from his pocket, unfolded it, and cleared his throat, "Uh, huh, I wrote a poem for you, my love."

And then he read:

"A DREAM OF YOU; IT PAINS ME SO.
A DREAM OF LOVE AND LETTING GO.
I'VE HELD YOU CLOSE BUT NOT SECURE.
I NURSE THE WOUNDS OF LOSS,
THAT OUR PATHS COULD RUN ALIGNED,
BUT ALAS, THEY ONLY CROSSED.
I'VE KNOWN THE SWEET CARESS THAT'S YOURS,
THE BEAUTY OF YOUR SMILE,
AND NOW THE STING THAT PLAGUES MY HEART,
WORSENS ALL THE WHILE.
A ROOM THAT'S YOURS SITS VACANT NOW,
THAT SPACE THAT'S IN MY HEART.
IT ONLY WAITS FOR YOUR RETURN,
TO MEND WHAT'S TORN APART.
LOVE ENDURES, SO IT'S BEEN SAID.
I HAVE TO SAY IT'S TRUE.
FOR IN DEATH AS IN LIFE,
MY HEART BELONGS TO YOU.
I LOVE YOU."

Crossroads

Josh eyed the bouquet of red roses and blue irises he had brought to give to his wife. He knelt forward, picked one of the irises from one of the headstone vases, and brought it to his face. Breathing in the sweet aroma, he sighed. He envisioned Isabella on their wedding day as she stood at the top of the staircase at Azalea Manor...

Isabella's elegant, white satin dress draped over her slender body, hugging her waistline. Her mother's pearls adorned her neck. She carried a bouquet of fresh yellow calla lilies and blue irises. Her brunette hair fell in soft ringlets down her back, cascading to her waist. A bright smile spread across her face as she glanced down at him (the man she loved) and mouthed, I love you. In a smooth stroke, the cellist pulled the bow across the strings, signaling the beginning of their wedding song and Isabella's descent down the staircase. Her breath caught, and nervous knots twisted in her stomach. Her thick, dark eyelashes fluttered. She closed her eyes to still them, released a slow breath, and whispered a prayer. Blinking her eyes open, she smiled at Josh and lifted her foot to take her first step into her new future. With each step, she drew nearer to him and one step closer to being his wife. Her heart pounded in her chest, sending a rush of warmth through her body, her cheeks flushing in response. She hesitated and inhaled a deep breath to reign in her emotions.

Josh smiled as he imagined waking up every morning for the rest of his life and finding her lying beside him. He stood, shoulders broad and straight, at the foot of the staircase dressed in a slim-fit black tuxedo. As Tink approached the last step, Josh stretched his hand out for hers. She placed her dainty hand in his and drew in a slow breath. Drawing her hand to his lips, he gently kissed it. Smiling, she stepped to his side. She gazed up at him with her bright eyes, leaned in close, and whispered, "You do know it's bad luck to see the bride before the ceremony, right?"

Josh knit his brow and narrowed his eyes. Tilting his head to the side, he turned his gaze on her. "Of course, I know that, but luck has nothing to do with us or our relationship. You and I...we are blessed."

The memory of their wedding day wilted like the flower in Josh's hand. He glanced down at the blue, withering flower. Tears spilled onto his cheeks. "Ten years wasn't enough time." Arching his neck, he gazed into the blue skies. "Ten years wasn't enough time, God. It wasn't. You're all-powerful. You raised Lazarus. Please, God." His voice broke. "Why couldn't you give her back to me? You could have healed her. You could have breathed life back into her body before we buried her." Casting his eyes back to the headstone surrounded by two bouquets of wilting flowers, he cried, "I'm so sorry, Tink. Please forgive me for...for not realizing you were the one meant for me when we were children. All I wanted was to be in love and be loved, and you were right there. You loved me with pure, innocent love, and I was too blind to see it. I should have married you when we were young, Tink. I was supposed to always be yours, and you were always supposed to be mine. Maybe...maybe if I had...maybe things would be different now. We could have saved each other from so much pain this world has inflicted on us both."

Josh shoved the flower back into the vase he pulled it from. "I wasted so many years, and now...now I've lost you, and I'm broken all over again. You found a shattered man when you approached me that day at The Trail. You always believed you were meant to put the pieces of my heart back together, and you did it. I didn't think you could...not at first, and then one day I woke up, and all the pain of my past was gone...just gone. All the mistakes I had made, and all the scars I had because of 'em...you made it all better. I was whole again, but now I'm worse than ever. It isn't fair, Tink. It isn't fair," he cried.

Josh buried his face in his large hands and wept bitterly. Tears saturated his cheeks. After several minutes of broken sobs, he wiped his eyes dry and sniffed, "I love you, my Tinkerbella."

A shadow moved at a slow clip across the headstones and hovered over Josh. Josh turned his head and peered up at an elderly man standing at the edge of the family plot. His shaggy, silver hair fell to his shoulders in frizzy curls. "Can I help you? Josh asked.

The man looked worn, rough around the edges, like old weather-beaten leather. His fair, thin (almost translucent) skin bore large, round age spots and was deeply cragged. He turned his mouth down in a frown and shook his head. "No, no, I don't believe you can," he said in his deep yet frail voice.

Confused, Josh furrowed his brow and scratched his forehead. "Do you need something?"

The scrawny silver-haired man cleared his throat. Wiry eyebrows framed his heavy-lidded, sullen eyes. "Oh, I have everything I need. I've learned to be content in whatever state I find myself. If we're to be honest, most of us express our wants as if they are our needs, but we can all get along with much less than what we often have."

Josh huffed and chuckled. "Yeah, I suppose you're right about that." He stood and patted his knees, dusting the dirt from his jeans. In a friendly gesture, he stretched forth his hand for a shake. The elderly man shoved his weathered hand into his pocket and pulled out a jeweled pendant. His hand shivered with age as he reached out to meet the hand extended to him. He grasped Josh's hand; uncurling his stubby fingers from around the pendant, he dropped it in Josh's cupped hand. A smile inched across his wrinkled face, and his green eyes lit up excitedly.

He clasped his free hand over their joined hands and peered into Josh's gray eyes. His grimy nails made Josh wonder if he was the cemetery's groundskeeper. "I came to help you, Josh."

Josh knit his brow. "How do you know—"

The elderly man waved, dismissing the question before he completed it. "Never mind that. That's not important. Don't go worrying yourself with how I came to know what I know. Concentrate on why I'm here." His voice cracked as if his fragile voice box were ready to shatter.

"Why are you here?"

"To remind you of Jeremiah 31:13, 'for I will turn

their mourning into joy, and will comfort them, and make them rejoice from their sorrow.' and," he raised his brows; a glimmer twinkled in his eyes, "to tell you that you can have her back if you so choose. It's all about your choices. That's what's important here. This token," he squeezed Josh's hand with all the strength his frail hand could muster, "can bring you to her if you believe."

Josh shook his head in disbelief. His nostrils flared as he tightened his mouth in a hard line. Anger churned in his gut, burning his stomach lining as it roiled and swelled, pushing to the surface. "My wife is dead," he spewed, releasing his pent-up anger. "How can a token take me to her?"

The old man's shoulders drooped. "You're angry. I understand. It's all part of the process we go through when we lose a part of ourselves. That's what's happened here, you know...half of you is gone...just ripped away from your soul." Discouraged, he shook his head, turned, and headed for the road. Looking over his shoulder, he said, "You'll find your Crossroads; time will reveal 'em. Remember, your grief will be turned into joy."

"I'll find what?" Josh hollered as the man disappeared behind a mausoleum. He tsk-tsked and shoved the pendant into his pocket. "Time will reveal 'em? Crazy old man," he muttered as he strode towards his truck.

The Crossroad
The Moonstone

K *nock, knock, knock. Knock, knock, knock.* The persistent rapping on Josh's bedroom door roused him from sleep. He tossed over in his bed, pulling the burgundy down comforter with him. A stream of afternoon light filtered through the blinds and pierced his eyelids. He squinted, slipped the comforter over his head, and groaned, "Who is it?"

"It's me, Dad," the voice muffled through the door.

Me? he questioned himself, sifting through his mind (fuzzy from the days upon days he had spent in his bed grieving), searching for familiarity in the voice but unable to find it. "Who's me?" Josh curled his body in the fetal position and hugged a pillow. Dark thoughts lingered from his dreams. His muscles ached as if atrophy had set in on him. His eyes rapidly moved beneath his lids as his mind searched for the time and the day. *How long have I slept,* he wondered?

The bedroom door screeched as it cracked open ever so slightly. A nose and lips jutted through the small gap. "Josh," he replied in a soft voice.

Josh's eyelids were heavy and weighted. They felt swollen shut, and they burned. He poked his head out from under the covers and unsuccessfully attempted to pry open his eyes. He gently rubbed his fingers over them and winced from the soreness of raw skin, and then he remembered the hours he had spent weeping into his pillow. Repeatedly drying his eyes with his bare hands throughout the night, he had chafed his eyelids. He managed to open them both into wafer-thin slits. The yellow sunlight poured through the small openings and stung his eyes. He quickly squeezed them shut and tossed himself over, shifting towards the sound of his son's voice.

"Dad," Josh called.

"What'd you want, son?" he mumbled from under the covers.

Josh Junior tiptoed through the door and shut it behind him. Soaking in the faint light filtering through the blinds, his pupils swallowed his dark, chestnut irises. He scanned the room, searching for courage and his voice. Wringing his hands, he chewed on his bottom lip.

He swallowed hard, pushing down the lump of disappointment rising in his throat. "It's Saturday," he started, finding his voice. "You said you'd take me to Grandma and Grandpa's today to work on the truck. You were gonna let me drive around the backfield."

Josh was clueless about what day it was until he heard his son say it. He had no idea how long he had slept. It felt like days to his aching body. He remembered shutting himself in his room after visiting Tink, and he vaguely recalled a conversation held through his closed bedroom door about going to his parents' home. Memories of the conversation flickered in his mind. He had given them his word, and their word was something they did not take lightly in their family. Ciara was due to take her driving test, and lessons were definitely a priority before allowing her on the streets of Oak Ridge.

Josh stretched his arms across his chest, pulling the knots in his back, and yawned. Groggily, he threw back the covers, sat upright, flung his legs to the floor, and rubbed his eyes. Prying them open, he blinked several times and set his focus on his son. Josh Junior stood a few feet away from him. Unkempt, his thick, light-brown hair was mussed on one side, and he was dressed in mix-matched, wrinkled clothes.

Josh shook his head and sighed, "Tell you what," He rubbed his hands over his face and stifled a yawn. "You go brush your hair and put on a nice pair of jeans and a nice shirt, and I'll get on up and get ready, too."

Josh Junior grinned. "Yes, Sir." He took off. The sound of quick, heavy footfalls slapped across the ceramic tile lining the hallway.

Josh rolled his neck, stretching the muscles to further wake himself. Every muscle in his body rebelled against movement. Picking through a pile of clothes at the foot of his bed, he donned a pair of jeans. His eyes skimmed over their bedroom. Piles of clothes and paperwork sat in mounds scattered over the floor. He knew Tink would be disappointed in how he had let things go. He grabbed a wrinkled shirt from the pile. Sniffing, he wrinkled his nose at the stench of dirty clothes saturating his room. Staring at the crumpled shirt he clutched, he pictured his son standing at the edge of his bed sporting rumpled, unmatched clothes. He tossed the shirt back onto the pile and willed himself to his closet.

Josh found a nice pullover shirt and slipped it over his head. Shutting the closet door, he viewed himself in the full-length mirror hanging on it. He traced his fingers over the scruffy beard covering his face and neck, scrutinizing his appearance. Tink preferred him clean-shaven. *You're much too handsome to cover that chiseled jawline and those plump, kissable lips, and please tuck that shirt* in, he heard Tink's voice whisper in his ear. He closed his eyes and imagined his wife standing next to him. Inhaling a slow, steady breath, he searched for her scent. "I miss you," he breathed. Her familiar aroma brushed over his cheek like a kiss from beyond before fading. He blinked and tucked in his shirt. Grabbing his keys from the nightstand, he shoved them in his pocket. He jammed his feet into his work boots and headed out the door.

Ciara and Josh Junior climbed into Josh's truck and waited. Ciara stretched her plump lips into a grin and muttered, "Finally." She clapped her hands, bouncing up and down in the passenger seat. "As soon as you two get that old truck rolling, I'll be able to get my driving lessons."

Josh Junior poked his big sister and winked. "I'll be sure to tell Dad to take his sweet, lovin' time, then. We don't really need the roads endangered right now." He smirked.

Ciara's smile fell into a pout. "Oh, shut up." She shoved him. "And stop poking me. Geez, you're...You know, why do you like to aggravate me like that?"

He shrugged his shoulders. A grin tugged on one corner of his full lips. "I'm your little brother. That's what we do."

Josh climbed into the truck, closed the door with a soft click, and turned to face his children. "You guys ready?" He turned the ignition, the engine sputtering to life.

Josh Junior sat ramrod straight, and Ciara buckled up. "Buckle up, buuuutterrr—"

"Please don't say it." Josh Junior waved her off and snapped his seatbelt in place. Craning his neck to peer out the side window, he mumbled, "That's mom's saying."

Mimosa bushes lined McMartin Road, partially hanging over the street from both sides, creating a hot-pink flowery archway. As Josh drove to his parents' home, he rolled the truck windows down (allowing the potent aroma to saturate the cab) and breathed in a deep, cleansing breath. Ciara's head lolled back onto the headrest. Her honey-brown hair fell in soft waves over her shoulder and past her waist. Shafts of early afternoon sunlight permeated the cab, bathing her face in warmth. Her golden highlights gleamed under the sun's rays. She closed her emerald-green eyes and hugged her torso, relishing the sweet scent flowing through with the warm afternoon breeze. Josh Junior squeezed through the small space between the back cab and the passenger seat, poking his head out the window. He squeezed shut his dark brown eyes against the blast of perfumed air blowing forcefully against his face. Basking in the warmth of the mid-spring sun, he grinned.

Josh turned at a four-way crossing onto Milner Road before veering into his parents' paved driveway. He eyed the worn paint and made a mental note to repaint the front door the following week. Throwing the truck in park, he turned off the ignition. "Okay, you two go see your grandparents for a bit while I get all the tools together to get started on this old truck out here."

The children bounded from their dad's truck and raced to see who could reach the side door first. Josh headed to the shop and gathered the tools needed to work on his dad's old truck. Shoving his hand in his pocket, he grasped the keys to the vehicle and fingered the token given to him by the strange, old man in the cemetery. Josh fumbled it with his fingertips and pulled it out to observe it again. As he piddled with it, he heard the old man's words, *You'll find your crossroads...time will reveal 'em.* The old man's voice trailed in his mind.

"Time will reveal 'em," he whispered, rolling his eyes and shaking his head. He folded his hand over the token and mumbled, "I have to *believe* this token will bring me to her." It was more of a question than a statement, but deep in his heart, he wanted desperately to believe that something within the universe was powerful enough to bring him into his wife's presence.

He was a man of faith, so the existence of God wasn't even a question for him. He knew God. He had a relationship with Him. He believed God was all-powerful, but he had placed Jesus in a box that assured him He would never intervene in humanity's affairs in such a manner. He simply could not fathom the omnipotent God he served concerning Himself with his grief. Why would God snatch him up and wisp him away to where Tink now resided? Jesus had the lost, dying world to reach. One man missing his wife was nothing compared to the darkness consuming so many others. For Josh, it wasn't a question of whether God could do it, but it was, indeed, a question of whether God would do it. If God wasn't interested in bringing him to his wife, there really was no other entity in the university with a power capable of creating a token capable of transporting you into the next world with your deceased loved one.

Josh opened his hand and stared long and hard at the jeweled coin in his palm. His mouth slackened as he eyed the moonstone, an iridescent gem set in the center of the pendant the old man referred to as a token. He spun the coin-shaped jewel through his fingers back and forth back and forth before folding his hand over it with a tight squeeze. Knots twisted in his stomach as he sought understanding. "God," he breathed. "Tink's with You now, so You are the only one who could bring me to her. I know You can, and the old man who gave me this thing said all I had to do was believe. I believe in You, but the idea of you—" He stopped mid-sentence and mumbled an incoherent argument with himself. A nervous laugh slipped past his lips. Doubt over the words he was about to speak riddled his mind. He shook his head and attempted to dispel the bombardment of angry allegations assaulting his mind. Dark, antagonist judgments curled in his mind, whispering to him. The hushed tones rose to a shrieking blare, pummeling his thoughts with accusations against the God he loved. He clenched his fists and paced back and forth down the concrete drive. "Shut up!" he seethed through a clenched jaw as he thrust his fist into the door of the old truck.

Josh's hand throbbed around the coin. Cupping his palm, he glanced down, inspecting his hand for injury. He stared at the token once again and eyed the moonstone. Sunlight glimmered off the iridescent stone. A glint within the stone caught his attention. He blinked twice to focus his eyes and examine it. He spotted a glimpse of numbers deep within the gem and narrowed his eyes. "Eighty-eight?" He knit his brow and squinted. He heaved a heavy sigh and mumbled, "This is nuts," as he shoved the token back into his pocket.

Josh popped the hood of the old truck and

skimmed over the motor with his eyes. He disconnected the battery and hooked the battery charger to it. A wave of dizziness swept over him, causing the cables to slide out of focus. He rubbed his eyes and shook his head. The pavement rippled beneath his feet, throwing his body out of kilter. Bracing himself against the truck frame, he held steady and began sorting through what he had eaten. He wondered if he was having a reaction to something he had for breakfast. His head swam with dizziness, black and white dots dancing before his eyes. His hands slipped off the hood as he stumbled backward a few steps. Shaking his head, he stepped back towards the truck and glared at the motor—a big mush of blur. He blinked hard several times, pulled his head from under the hood, and squared his shoulders. Inhaling deep breaths, he sought to clear his muddled thought processes. And suddenly, the world around stopped spinning; the dots faded, and everything slid back into focus. The green of the trees seemed different somehow. Josh buried his face in his large hands and rubbed his eyes.

Josh's ears perked up when he heard a faint voice echoing in the distance; the voice sang a song he remembered from childhood. He craned his neck, following the direction from which the voice came, and peered towards the McMartin and Milner roads crossroads. The road at the crossing warbled like he was peering at it through a thick haze of gasoline. A young girl rounded the corner on a yellow bicycle. Her fluorescent pink t-shirt brought out the pink triangles in her brightly colored jams. Her side ponytail bounced back and forth as she swerved from one side of the red dirt road to the other. Singing as she peddled, she headed for his parents' driveway. As she whizzed past the mailbox, she shifted back on the bike's peddles (catching the brakes) and skidded to a halt. Kicking the stand in place, she glanced over at Josh. She skipped toward the truck. Her eyes landed on him as he took slow, steady steps toward the back of the truck. As she approached him, she stopped and smiled. A sense of familiarity washed over Josh. He studied the smidgen of freckles covering the child's nose and cheeks. Unable to place the young girl, he searched his mind for mental pictures of children in the neighborhood.

"Is Josh here?" she asked, glancing up at him. The afternoon sun danced across her gray eyes in shimmering lights.

He recognized her; he knew he did, but he could not put his finger on when and where he had seen her. He knit his brow, cleared his throat, and asked, "You're looking for Josh?"

The sunlight pierced the girl's eyes. She wrinkled her nose and squinted. "Yeah, are you his dad?"

A proud smile stretched across Josh's face. He turned to face the house. "He's in the house, but I'll go get him."

He glanced down at the dirt driveway as he turned on his heels. "What?" He stared at the red clay covering his work boots. His eyes darted from the dirt driveway to the red-clay road and back to the house, now adorned in a fresh coat of paint. Confusion slammed against him with another wave of dizziness. He threw his hand out to catch himself on the tailgate. Glancing down at the old green truck his dad owned when he was a child, he heard the creak of the door of the house opening just before it shut with a clunk. Josh squeezed his eyes and blinked several times, attempting to bring the world back into focus.

He turned back to face the young girl. "Here he comes now." He pinched the bridge of his nose, trying to understand what was happening to him.

His mind spun in circles again. He closed his eyes and pressed the heel of his hands over them, willing the world around him to stop spinning.

"Hey, Josh," the girl called. "I rode down to see if you were going skating tonight."

"Yep."

Josh snapped his head up and around. His breath caught in his throat as he watched himself (at thirteen) approaching the young girl. He stepped backward and threw his hand over his mouth. "Tink," he breathed in an inaudible whisper. Tears rushed to the surface and spilled over onto his cheeks before he even had a moment to gather himself.

Thirteen-year-old Josh stared at him questioningly with narrowed eyes. "Who are you?"

Assuming her unanswered question had actually been answered by his reply, Tink folded her arms across her chest and took a step back, awaiting his response.

Josh rifled quickly through possible answers that wouldn't make him sound like a madman. "A family member," his voice trialed. Clearing his throat, he pieced together a better response. He knew Josh would know family members. "A distant cousin, but I'm a friend...a friend of your dad's," he choked out his response.

Thirteen-year-old Josh shrugged his shoulders. "Okay." He turned his gaze back to Tink. "Soooo...you and Daniel gonna be there?"

"Yeah, Aunt Ruth said she'd drop us off if you were gonna be there to keep an eye on us."

"She needs me to keep an eye on y'all, huh? Well, that's gonna cost you and Daniel both."

Tink's eyes widened. "Cost us?" She scratched behind her ear and fidgeted as the warmth of a flush rushed to her cheeks. She made a silent wish that his naming price would be couple skating.

Thirteen-year-old Josh gave a half-smile and chortled. "Yep, no Hokey Pokey for you two, and y'all have to let me teach you a few of my tricks."

Disappointed, she dropped her head and chewed on her bottom lip. "Umm...yeah, sure. You really think you can teach me a few of your tricks?" She glanced up at him with timorous eyes.

His light-brown hair (parted on the side) hung past his brows. He brushed his bangs back out of his eyes, squared his shoulders, and lifted his head with pride. "Of course," he tsk, tsked as he folded his arms across his chest.

Shaken, Josh had taken several steps back,

inching his way towards a copse of trees on the edge of the property line. Stepping into the shadows, he shoved his hand back into his pocket and retrieved the token. He rubbed his thumb over the moonstone and searched for the number he had seen. "Eighty-eight...I saw eighty-eight." He wiped the tears from his eyes and cleared his view. "Tw...tw..twenty-one," he stuttered, reading the number hidden deep within the gem.

Josh yanked his head up and peered across the yard through the rippled haze he had witnessed when Tink rounded the corner onto his street. Both children had vanished. They were gone with no evidence as to where they had disappeared. He glanced down at the red clay covering his work boots. "It was real," he cried. He swallowed hard against the lump in his throat (his heart, he assumed), pushing it back into his chest where it belonged. He needed it now that he knew he could have her back. Following a trail of red dust from his work boots, he strode back to where Tink had parked her bike.

With no sign of her in sight, he increased his pace to a brisk jog. Struggling to catch up to wherever she had gone, he broke into a full-on run, his feet pounding against the asphalt. "Tink," he hollered. Gasping for breath, he stopped in the center of the four-way crossing. Inhaling gulping breaths, he propped his hands on his knees and surveyed the roads in every direction, but all he found was emptiness.

Crossroads

The Road Taken
The Mentors

Drawn back to 2021, Josh headed east, racing down McMartin Road. As he searched for Tink, he prayed for a passageway—a wormhole—to the day he had just traveled to in 1988. Dark clouds rolled in from the west, smothering the afternoon sunlight. Unaware of how the coin had taken him back in time and clueless as to what had caused him to be sucked back to the present, his mind rifled through every possible scenario. He ran at a clipped pace down the road in the direction she had come from when she rounded the corner on her bicycle. As his feet pounded against the asphalt, his mind picked the old man's words apart and sought to use his wisdom to formulate a recipe that could be prepared to bring the desired results—multiple trips back in time! *Time will reveal 'em. Time will reveal 'em*, his mind chanted. *What did time reveal? Was it the crossroads he told me I'd find? And what does that mean anyway? Is it a literal place where roads cross? I mean, my parents' home is right down from a four-way crossing. If it is literal, does it have to be a four-way crossing? Is it even about a location? Is it just the token? Or is it the perfect combination of time, crossroads, and this coin*, he wondered?

Josh veered onto Westley Drive and looked straight ahead, lengthening his strides, hurrying towards Royce Road—the road on which Tink's aunt lived. Sweat poured from his head, flattening his dark brown hair to his forehead. Mopping up the beads of perspiration, he swiped his hand across his brow. "I need...to find...him," he told himself. Winded, he continued to debate himself, "I need answers. I need...to know how to blend...everything perfectly to...open up whatever...path was opened to bring...me back to her. I...can't believe it. I can't...believe this is real. I just...traveled back in time!" His eyes widened; he chortled at the thoughts and questions churning in his mind. "Either that...or I'm going...to wake up...in a mental insti...tution. I have to...believe. I simply have to. I can...have her back. I can...actually have her...back and be with...her every day. I...just have to figure...out how all this...works."

Panting, Josh stopped on the corner of Westley and

Royce Road. His calves burned, and his quadriceps tightened like cords. He stood, hands on his hips, sweat dripping down his brow. He patted his forehead dry with the palms of his hands and started back for his parents' home with a plan devised in his mind: to find the old man from the graveyard.

Scattered wildflowers poked their heads out from among the tall grass edging the road—painting the roadside with colorful arrays of yellows, oranges, purples, blues, and whites. Walking the familiar path, Josh reminisced and took a trip down memory lane, pondering the many excursions down the same road he'd made throughout his life...

Five-year-old Josh (attempting to outrun one of his favorite comic book characters) dashed barefoot up and down the road as speedily as his tiny feet would take him. During his adolescent years, he peddled through the country roads, meeting and entertaining his neighbors. His parents bought him a motorcycle for his thirteenth Christmas.

Josh stood at the edge of the road and envisioned the back wheel of his motorcycle as it kicked up rocks and spewed clay mixed with multicolored pebbles, filling the length of the road with a heavy cloud of red dust as he sped down the red dirt roads...

Things were significantly different in Oak Ridge when Josh was a small boy. Back in those days, most of the

streets were not paved. As a child, Josh never imagined that would change. Those old, clay roads washed out every time heavy rain swept across the coast, leaving chunks of missing road and massive potholes, making summers inundated with tropical storms full of bumpy rides. Oak Ridge (a farming community known for two things: watermelons and pecans) was a small town with most homes situated on ten acres or more. Pecan orchards lined the vast majority of the roads, and farmers grew the most magnificent watermelons in all of Alabama. Neighborly citizens readily shared their milk and eggs with anyone in need. Everyone trusted everyone during those days, so the children left home at daybreak and traipsed the roads (as well as the woods) until dark, and Josh was no different; he spent his childhood exploring the ins and outs of the small town he called home.

Josh (a vibrant child full of life, laughter, and words—lots of words) never met a stranger. Drawn to the elderly, he developed relationships with several of the aging widows in the neighborhood. His frequent visits were rewarded with homemade cookies, cakes, and pies, and of course, sweet tea or a cold glass of lemonade always accompanied his dessert.

A cool breeze, brought in by the coming rain, blew across Josh's face; the fresh, clean scent of honeysuckle and orange blossoms captured his mind, escorting his thoughts back to a particular time from his childhood.

Mrs. Lidington, an elderly widow, lived down the street from Josh on Westley Drive. One of his favorite stops, her house stood proud and strong with the

American flag flapping as her yard's centerpiece. When Josh was six years old, he took off bicycling down the red dirt road, exploring the neighborhood. Veering onto Westley Drive, he peddled with all his might as if he were in a race against an invisible foe, and Royce Road was their finish line. An angelic voice singing "Turn Your Eyes Upon Jesus" caught his attention. He kicked back on the pedals, skidded to a stop, and turned his ear toward the beautiful music. Josh followed the sound of the voice, peddling his bicycle as hard and fast as he could toward the source of the song. Out of the corner of his eye, he caught a glimpse of a gray-haired lady kneeling on a green cushion, pulling weeds from a flowerbed surrounding a flagpole.

"You have a beautiful voice," Josh called to her from the road.

At the sound of the small, young voice, Grace Lidington dug her small shovel into the flowerbed, bolted upright, and turned to see the young boy who called her. She had lost her only child when he was five years old. When her eyes landed on the clean-cut, light-brown-haired boy, a smile inched across her aging, wrinkled face, and her blue eyes lit up. "Why, thank you, young man. What's your name?"

"My name is Josh. I live down on Milner Road. What's your name?"

Grace propped her arms on her folded legs. "My name is Grace Lidington. Nice to meet you, Josh."

"Nice to meet you, Mrs. Lidington. I like the song you're singing. Whatcha doing?"

Crossroads

"Oh, I'm weeding my flowerbed, and what are you doing?"

"Racing down to Royce Road."

The sweltering heat of the Gulf Coast glistened Josh's forehead with sweat. Grace eyed his red face and the beads of perspiration. "Well, Josh, it's scorching hot out here. I'm going to head in for a glass of sweet tea. Would you like to come in, have a glass, and cool off before continuing your race?"

Josh swiped the back of his hand across his forehead, mopping up the sweat. A bright smile beamed across his face. "Yes, ma'am. I'd love a glass of tea."

Grace hauled herself to her feet, wobbling a bit as she did so. Josh pushed his bike up the drive and kicked the kickstand in place, propping his bicycle up, and with a spry step, he followed her inside. Once Josh stepped through the doorway, lively conversation replaced the peaceful atmosphere Grace had become accustomed to after the death of her husband of twenty-five years. Crossing the threshold of Grace's home unleashed a bridle that had harnessed Josh's tongue while outside; words spewed forth from his little mouth as if his words were water held back by a dam that broke when he stepped inside her home.

The smell of sweet bread saturated her home. Josh stood stock-still, closed his eyes, and breathed deeply. "Your house smells delicious."

"Why, thank you, Josh. You'll have to try some of my bread." Grace extended her arm and beckoned him to sit.

Josh eyed her hand as it moved to her recliner. He cut his eyes from the recliner to Grace, back to the recliner, and then to the floor, plopping down at the corner of her chair. Making her way to the refrigerator, she poured him a tall glass of iced tea while he filled her in on all the happenings in his home, some not so good. Josh stood to his feet and took the glass from her hand, seating himself gently so as not to spill a drop. Impressed by his well-groomed, clean-cut appearance and bubbling personality, Grace felt an overwhelming sense of pity for the boy. His father (as she learned from his stories) was a hard man, a man Josh feared in an unhealthy way. That, coupled with his adorable, friendly ways, opened Grace Lidington's heart; she immediately fell in love with him. With a graceful gate, Ms. Lidington made her way across the room to a bookshelf that covered the far wall. She skimmed through them and picked a book to share with her new friend. As she sauntered to her seat, she praised him for being well-groomed, hoping to foster continued cleanliness in him.

Nestling in her seat, she traced her long, slender fingers over the front of the book. "This book was Finley's favorite, so I'd like to read it to you."

"Who's Finley?" Josh asked, his voice muffled by the glass of tea as he slurped.

Grace's eyes lit up, and her face beamed with pride. A smile inched across her face. "Finley was my son. I lost him when he was not much older than you. We were in a car accident on our way to see my in-laws. My husband and I survived the wreck, but our little Finn wasn't so fortunate."

Sitting the glass on the fireplace's ledge, Josh gulped and pounced to his feet. Throwing his arms around Grace, he whispered in her ear, "I'm sorry." Tears rushed to the surface of his gray eyes. "I'll come visit you all the time if you want."

Grace sniffled, "I'd love that, Josh."

Josh sat back on the floor, crossed his legs, and gazed happily at Mrs. Lidington, giving her all his attention. Grace opened the book and began reading to him. Josh closed his eyes, breathed deeply, and imagined himself far away in the jungle she described in vivid detail. His heart pounded ferociously in his chest as he imagined the sleek, blank panther pouncing down in front of him and leaning back on his haunches, ready to devour him with his massive fangs. His roar sent chills up Josh's spine; he shivered and folded his arms across his chest, clutching himself so hard he left red marks on his arms. A frightened yelp slipped past his lips. The book seemed to come to life as Mrs. Lidington read to him.

After that day, Josh regularly rode his bike to Mrs. Lidington's house to hear more stories and enjoy sweet bread and iced tea. His favorite tale took him on a different kind of adventure, an adventure into belief and wishes. Within the pages, he learned that wishes could come true when made with an eyelash, and his childlike faith assured him it would work. He set his mind right then and there on the wish he intended to make the next time he lost an eyelash!

Mrs. Lidington, an educator, encouraged Josh to

focus on his studies, and she always insisted that Josh go to college and get a degree. An intellectual, she had collected a library of books for her own child. She held tight to them after she lost her son, never finding it in her heart to get rid of them. She often referred to Finley during her conversations with Josh. She told him how much he reminded her of her sweet boy, frequently pointing out how thankful she felt for keeping all his books. At one point, she had considered donating them to the local library. In fact, the day Josh stopped by for the first time, she had pulled out several boxes to pack them all away and take them to the new Oak Ridge Library. They were both grateful she had decided to work with her flowerbeds that day instead.

Folds of dark clouds swept overhead, hiding the sun and threatening another spring rainstorm. Glancing down at the mailbox that once towered over him, Josh stood at the edge of Mrs. Lidington's driveway and peered into the sky. The sunlight found its escape through short gaps in the cloud cover. He shielded his eyes with his hand and murmured, "You know, you only bring more beauty in the end." He wasn't sure where the comment came from. It had simply slipped past his lips without thought. He glanced across the yard, eyeing the old flagpole, and pictured the flowerbed Mrs. Lidington had been tending when they met. It was her; when he was a young boy, she had told him the rains of life only brought beauty in the end...

Josh remembered the sound of her voice as she hurried

him inside and glanced back through the glass door at the large rain droplets. "Run to the house," Mrs. Lidington called to him from behind. He glanced up and gazed at the smile on her aging face as she stared at the rain through the storm door.

"You look happy," Josh said.

"Oh, I am happy, Josh."

"But the storm is messing up your flowerbed."

Mrs. Lidington whimsically raised her brows. "Ah, it may seem so, dear boy, but the storm will only bring more beauty in the end, Josh."

Josh knit his brow in the confusion typical of a nine-year-old boy.   "How?" he asked.

Mrs. Lidington shrugged her shoulders. "Well, all we can see right now is how the rain has beat the flowers-down flat against the saturated ground, but," she grinned and tsked, "what we can't see is what's going on underneath the dirt where the roots are soaking in what they need for life." Her smile faded. She knelt down, bringing her eyes level with his.   "Josh, I need to tell you something."

"Okay," he said, nodding.

"I'm afraid I have to go away."

"What? Why? Where?"

"I'm dying, and I don't have much time left to spend with you. I want you to understand that just like this storm may seem to be damaging my flowerbed, the flowers will flourish after the sun returns. Death will not have the last say about me either. Death is like that storm; it only brings more beauty in the end."

Mrs. Lidington sat in her usual chair but did not pull out a book to read to him. Instead, Josh climbed in her lap, buried his face in her shoulder, and wept. While she held him in her arms, she assured him she would be better off. He refused to accept what she said to him. How could she be better off? His childish mind naturally rejected that as truth. He loved her; he didn't want her to die.

That afternoon, Josh raced home and locked himself in his mother's bathroom. When he finally emerged, his eyes were swollen and red, and he lacked eyelashes!

Mrs. Parker gaped. "Josh! What have you done to your eyelashes?"

Sniffling, Josh dropped his head and stared at the floor. He shuffled across the floor, shoulders slumped. His chest rose and fell in shuddery breaths. "I...made...one hundred...and...forty-four...wishes...that...Mrs. Lidington...won't die," he sniveled.

"Oh, Josh," his mother said in a soothing tone. She wrapped her arms around her son and comforted him.

Josh started down the street, glancing over his shoulder at the home that once belonged to his mentor, Mrs. Lidington. His old neighborhood brought back so many stories for him to reflect upon as he strolled back to his parents' home, where he lived growing up. Along with each painful thought from his childhood, there were memories filled with love, laughter, and relationships. Revisiting them during his present grief brought the sorrow he had buried deep in the recesses of his soul to the surface...

Crossroads

Mrs. Stevenson (one of the widows he often visited as a child) frequently required his assistance with opening jars and climbing up to retrieve items from the cabinet for her. As she aged, losing the ability to drive, Josh offered his driving services. He stopped in every Monday afternoon after school to retrieve the grocery list she had waiting for him; they always visited over a slice of cake, his favorite being lemon and blueberry with cream cheese icing (made from scratch). After their lengthy visit, Josh headed home to do his homework, and the following day (after school let out), he headed straight to the grocery store; his willingness to aid her in her requests led to her imparting talent and recipes. What started as him pulling out her ingredients so she could prepare her meals and desserts became her teaching him all her tricks in the kitchen. Josh developed a love for food and cooking, and that love followed him into adulthood and took him to culinary school.

Thunder rumbled in the distance, warning Josh of the storm rolling in from the coast. Picking up the pace, he jogged onto Westley Drive. As he passed the home that once belonged to Mrs. Stevenson, he thought of the recipe book—one of his prized possessions—she gifted him just before she passed away. He used several of her cakes and pies in the fine dining restaurant he owned in Emerald Creek, Florida. Josh left Emerald Creek and the restaurant to return to Oak Ridge in 2008 when his mother fell ill. While nursing his mother back to health, he decided to stay in Oak Ridge, initially living off the sale of his restaurant. Josh Junior had just been born when Beatrice Parker fell ill. Neither living in Oak Ridge nor selling the restaurant fell into Samantha Parker's plans, so she left Josh and the children and moved back to Florida.

Crossroads

The Fork in the Road
The Graveyard

Ciara's face flushed crimson. She hollered, "Where have you been?" She paced back and forth across the edge of the driveway with her hands on her hips. "We've been worried sick? We heard you call for Mom, so we rushed out here, and you were nowhere to be found," she huffed and threw her hands in the air.

Josh slowed from a steady jog to a speed walk. As he strode toward her, his chest rose and fell in deep breaths. "I...I thought I saw your mom," he gasped, "so I ran down the street to try and find her. I know it sounds crazy, but...well, it is what it is." He shrugged.

Crossroads

Ciara stopped dead in her tracks. Her jaw dropped, mouth agape. Raising her brow, she threw her hand over her mouth, mumbling under her breath, "Oh, Dad." She squeezed her eyes closed and pulled her hand free from her mouth. Blinking her eyes open, she inhaled a sharp breath and folded her hands, intertwining her fingers. "Dad, I...I'm really worried about you. Maybe you should see your doctor. He might be able to give you something to get you through all this."

Josh clenched, his jaw working under his skin and his face set in a hard mask as he darted past her. "I'm not going to the doctor. I'm fine. Go back in the house." He cut his eyes at her as he rushed past her. "I'll have the truck running in a few minutes, and then you can get your driving lessons."

Ciara bounced on the balls of her feet, folded her arms over her chest, and glanced at the dark clouds that hovered above them. Worry that her driving lesson would be put off once again wrinkled her forehead. She closed her eyes and whispered a prayer. "God, please delay the rain." The rumbling thunder distanced itself, moving farther to the east. Within thirty minutes, Josh had the old truck purring like a fat, happy cat; he was a great mechanic, but he'd rather be in a kitchen behind a hibachi grill cooking a feast.

Staying true to his word, he climbed in the passenger seat and coached Ciara through the basics of driving and the standard ritual all drivers should adhere to before cranking their vehicle. While most drivers ignored those standard rules, Ciara stuck to each one.

She sat nervously in the driver's seat, wringing her hands around the steering wheel. When the car took off down the road—heading toward the crossroad of McMartin and Milner roads—her palms poured sweat. Her heartbeat raced, and her breathing escalated as she neared her first stop sign.

"Alright, let off the gas and slowly press on the brakes. You want to ease into a stop," Josh instructed her.

Ciara lifted her right foot from the accelerator and sifted through the process in her mind. "Start slowing down now," Josh reiterated.

"Okay, okay," she mumbled. Her chest clenched; thoughts raced through her mind at such a rapid rate that confusion set in. She slammed her foot down on the accelerator rather than touching the brake. The truck lurched forward. Ciara screamed, "Ahhhh!"

Josh straddled the center console, grabbed the stirring wheel, yanked it to the side, kicked Ciara's foot away from the accelerator, and found the brake, bringing them to an abrupt halt just shy of the ditch. Josh Junior sat stock-still in the back cab, wide-eyed and mouth agape. Ciara covered her mouth with ˋ trembling hands. Her chest rose and fell with heavy, gasping breaths. Josh gripped the stirring wheel with such force that his knuckles turned white. Silence and shuddery breathing filled the small truck cab.

After several minutes at a standstill, Josh breathed deeply. Eventually mustering up the courage to finish Ciara's driving lessons, he directed her around the block.

Crossroads

Ciara pulled her torso close to the steering wheel, hovering just over it and clutching it with all her might, and narrowed her eyes to see the road clearly. She drove (at a snail's pace) around the block three times before Josh guided her back to her grandparents' home. Pulling into their drive, Ciara shifted into park and reluctantly released her vice grip on the steering wheel. Her widened eyes relaxed, and her cheeks puffed like a blowfish as she blew out all the air in her lungs. Tilting her head to face her dad, she shifted her body. A huge grin slithered across her face.

Josh folded his arms across his chest and turned the corners of his mouth down, nodding infinitesimally. "Not too bad for your first time, C."

"Thanks, Dad!" Excited, Ciara climbed out of the truck and skipped to the side door.

Josh Junior bounced from the truck and started after his sister. Josh grabbed his arm and pulled him back. "Leave her be. She's excited that she did it. Come on, son. Let's go to the backfield."

Ciara burst through the door, exclaiming, "Grandma, I did it!"

Josh and Josh Junior climbed into the truck cab and drove back to the backfield. Josh Junior clambered into the driver's seat, pressed the gas pedal, and took off. A natural behind the wheel, he drove around the pond. He wheeled around as if he had been driving his entire life.

Fading sunlight peeked through the nimbus clouds

as best she could, sending hints that she was losing her battle against the approaching darkness. Josh read her warning and dropped the children off at the house (firmly insisting to Josh Junior that he not gloat about his driving lesson). Racing off to the cemetery, he sped through the gravel roads and slammed on brakes at the edge of the family plot. He bounded out of the truck onto the rocks, his feet crunching into the pebble-strewn road. He slammed the truck door behind him. He paced frantically through the graveyard using the remaining light of the day to search for the wiry-haired man. He turned his head every which way, his eyes darting from side to side, scanning the area.

"Where are you?" he finally hollered. "It happened. I found one of those crossroads you mentioned. I have questions."

Josh walked over nearly every inch of the graveyard; the sun dropped low, casting orange rays and brown shadows over the headstones. He was about to give up when he rounded an aged sarcophagus (one he imagined had been there since the cemetery was opened to its permanent residents) and eyed the elderly man sitting on a bench whittling on a broken broom handle with a pocketknife.

"There you are! I was hoping I'd find you here. I've searched the entire graveyard looking for you. It happ—" Josh's eyes landed on the broom handle and the pocketknife cutting into it. Taken back, he asked, "A broom handle? Really? What do you expect that to become?"

Crossroads

The silver-haired man shaved a slice of wood from the handle before glancing up at Josh with staid eyes. "Oh, I expect it'll turn out to be what it's meant to be."

Josh raised his brows. "Are you telling me that piece of wood has a purpose, like it's meant to be something other than a broom handle?" He folded his arms across his chest and cast the frizzy-haired man a questioning eye.

"Yeah, once I picked it up in my hands and determined to give it a purpose beyond what it was originally intended to be and do, then yep, it was meant to be something besides a broom handle." Peering into Josh's eyes, the old man squinted against the remaining sunlight as it dropped closer to the horizon. His bright green eyes glistened. "You know, you and I and..." he cocked his head to the side and tutted, "well, pretty much every person ever born into this ole world came into this life a lot like this ole broom handle. It might be just a chunk of wood, but it had a purpose. We come into the world with a basic purpose, too. I'm sure you already know that purpose, but I'll remind you since most seem to forget." A half-smile crept up one side of his face.

The old man set the chunk of wood and the pocketknife on the bench. Squeezing his arthritic hands, he cracked his knuckles. Picking the items back up, he sighed, "Age. It can be a friend with wisdom and an enemy with pain, but that's not what you need to hear now. Relationship. It's all about having a relationship with our creator; our spirit man (the core of us all) is the part of us that has that relationship with the Lord. But there's so much more to it than that. You see, He didn't make us simply spirit beings; He made us in His image, so we are more than just a spirit. He placed that spirit in a body. It's just the shell for the spirit to live in, but the spirit alone doesn't reside there. Magic happened when He placed spirit into the shell of the man."

Josh sat on the bench next to the elderly man. The old man gave Josh a sidelong glance and smiled. "The magic of combining spirit and body created the soul. See, the spirit is kind of like the lignin (the oxygen-containing portion) that makes up this piece of wood, and the wood itself—the cellulose fibers—is like our body, but somewhere within this ole chunk of wood," signaling the body, he patted his chest, "is a soul. Still, we must whittle away at the body to see it." He held up the pocketknife and twisted it before slicing a sliver of wood from the broom handle. "The soul, my son, is the part of us that gets shaped and fashioned by the choices we make by those around us, and hopefully by the Lord." He winked.

The silver-haired man cracked a half-smile. The crags in his wrinkled face deepened. "You probably thought I was gonna tell ya the final product after all the carving is like our bodies, but it ain't so. Our bodies are just a lump of flesh like this lump of wood. What we look like (what we really look like)...that is seen in the soul. See, just like this ole broom handle in my hand, we start getting whittled on as soon as we're born. Our parents are usually the first to hold the knife and begin sculpting on us. Sometimes that's good, but sometimes that's bad, and then every circumstance in our life is used to mold us in some way, but there is more to it than that; how we respond to those circumstances determines how deep the cuts go and what they leave behind, and then, well, the people we encounter carve on us too if we let 'em."

The old man cut out a chunk of wood he hadn't intended to cut. "See here," he held up the piece for Josh to see, "I wounded this piece of art. I made a wrong cut. People damage us sometimes in the same way I damaged this carving of mine." He shoved his wrinkled hand into his pocket and pulled out a small tube of wood glue and some tape. He squeezed a small dot of glue onto the wood and placed the slice back where it belonged, and then he picked up the scotch tape from the bench and wrapped a piece around it to secure it before setting it aside to dry. "I'll have to sand that piece a little after it dries, but it'll be as good as new." He tilted his head to the side and huffed. "Well, almost as good as new. When I finish that piece, you'll be able to see where it was damaged if you look long enough and hard enough. We're a lot like that. Bad people and good people with good intentions can hurt us and cut out a chunk of our hearts, but if we allow Him, Jesus can glue us back together. He'll need to sand down the rough edges after that, and that part can be painful, but in the end, we'll be put back together like new."

The wrinkled man squared his shoulders and shifted his torso to a guarded position. "Sometimes the one holding the knife cutting into us is Death, and he hurts us in a different sort of way. Most blame God for sending Death, but Death doesn't always come because

He sent him. God even tries to warn folks that Death is near, but most don't understand his voice to be His. They've become accustomed to ignoring His voice, so they no longer recognize it." The old man pointed the tip of the knife to the taped-up chunk of wood sitting on the bench. "He can heal those places just as easily as He warns us of Death stalking us. Of course, the scar remains. Sometimes scars are hideous, and those scars remind us daily of the battles that left 'em, but sometimes scars are barely visible, and who we are (as a result of those wounds) is all that remains of the war. We forget the happening altogether. The process of healing both kinds of scars is the same, time and work. God must sand out the accusations, the hatred, the murder, the hopelessness, the desperation—all the emotions that come from being whittled on by the battles."

Josh threw his hands up in the air and shook his head. "Who are you? Are you like an Old Testament Prophet? You know they were always given these great words of wisdom to pass on to different men in the Bible." Barely audible, he mumbled, "Or are you just some crazy old homeless man living in a cemetery?"

The old man shook his head and guffawed. "Well, some might call me crazy, but I'm no homeless man, and I sure ain't a prophet of old."

Josh's eyes widened in shock. He hadn't meant for the old man to hear that part. The old man's green eyes shimmered when he stuck his hand out for the shake known by all as the official meeting. Shifting his eyes from the old man's hand to his face, Josh searched for malice within the man's eyes. He inched his hand forward and grasped the man's hand, giving it one firm shake. "My name is Chadok, and no, I don't live out here with those gone on. I come here quite frequently because *I* have a purpose. People tend to need me when they've lost someone, so I go to the best place to find 'em." He shoved his hand in his pocket, pulled out a fresh chunk of wood, and started whittling on it again. "So, you said you've been looking for me?" He shot Josh a quizzical look.

Josh exhaled a deep breath, his chest collapsing with relief. Breathing out the anxiety that had built up since seeing Tink, he prepared himself for answers. "I need to understand how it works." Josh pulled the coin from his pocket and held it in his cupped hand. "It took me back to 1988 when Tink was just eight years old and came to my house. I was there. I saw her, but it only lasted a few minutes, and then, I was sucked back to now." He folded his fingers over the coin, squeezing it, and closed his eyes. "What is it, and how does it work?" His chest tightened, rising and falling in quick, short breaths. "I need to get back to her. Please, help me find her again."

The old man carved notches in the piece of broom handle in his hands and sighed. With the back edge of his pocketknife, he touched Josh's fingers, willing them to open. Josh unfolded his hand. The tip of the blade touched the moonstone. "This is a moonstone set in that token. They say it bears truth within it. Some believe it symbolizes the passion between two soulmates who are meant to be one. It's said that if the passion and the love that bound the two together...if it is strong enough, then it still lives, and that means there is...well, there's a tie, a link if you will, to certain places on certain roads if you fervently believe."

"Certain roads? Like the street my parents live on?"

Chadok squinted, a slight grin sliding across his deeply cragged face, and blew across the piece of wood, sending tiny shards onto the ground at his feet. "You see, Josh, life is nothing more than a journey leading us all, hopefully, to the destination of Heaven, rejoining God in the place He prepared for us. Now, our journey requires a path—a road, if you will, and every person born into this world is set on a particular path the moment the first breath is taken. It's a road that begins their personal journey through life. Along the road of your journey (as well as on everyone else's path), there are special moments when one path crosses another."

The old man began carving lines around the cylinder-shaped piece of wood and cleared his throat. "These crossings are times of very significant moments in our lives when we have an opportunity to make decisions that will profoundly affect the remainder of our journey. I like to call them crossroads. They are moments in one sojourner's life touched by another traveler with purpose, faith, hope, or love. Believe it or not, there are times when all four powerful, supernatural elements are present in the crossing of those two particular paths." Chadok twisted the cylinder-shaped piece of wood and dug into the center of the carving, blowing the wood chips to the ground. "There are crossroads where the traveler meets aimlessness, doubt, despair, or hatred, but those aren't the crossroads I imagine you're searching for, now are you?" He winked at Josh. "When two roads that contain any of those enchanted elements cross, magic or mayhem is born. This magic is a special kind of magic. There are times when a crossroad contains so much power that it pulls a soul back to it—like a wormhole if you will, but if you hold on tight to that token, it will hold you."

Josh knit his brow, confusion twisted on his face. "How exactly does it hold me?"

"It holds you to see the truth within it, the truth in the element, whether it be a purpose, faith, hope, or love, or it can hold you to seeing the deception that confused you, leaving you aimless, full of doubt, despair, and even filled with seeds of hatred. When roads cross, there are either truths or deceptions present; the truths were meant to lead the traveler to his destination, and the enemy planted the deceptions to deter him from it. Sometimes, when traveling on the road, we miss seeing the truth altogether because we're blinded by the deception. The moonstone will open your eyes to see the truth you may have missed, the truth you were meant to see all along but didn't because of blindness, or maybe you simply ignored it, but then again, you may have seen it with both your physical and spiritual eyes and followed it." Chadok tapped the stone with the tip of his knife and stared into Josh's eyes. The intensity of his stare sent a shiver down Josh's spine. "Sometimes crossroads merge and become one. That's a powerful crossroad when that happens."

Josh knit his brow. Dropping his head, he stared at the grass under his feet and dug the toe of his shoe into the thick bed of blades. "So, I need to find moments from my life when my path intersected with Tink's? Like special times in our life?"

The old man nodded. He blew the dust off the piece of art he was still whittling on. "Now you're gettin' the picture. You gotta be in the place of a crossroad for it to work, and it holds better if you speak to it. You need to know what you're searching for and from what time of your life it's in. Now, don't ask me how to know what *all* of your crossroads are. I can't know them all. All I get is a flash, an image, only part of the picture. It's for you to figure out. Grief will help you if you allow it, but be careful; grief can be a foe as readily as a friend in your journey." Chadok shook his head. His frizzy, silver hair flapped side to side. "Grief is not meant to be your enemy, son. It's good at opening our eyes to see the truths we missed along the way, but it can take you down the wrong path if you allow the grief to guide you rather than showing you."

The old man stood and turned the carving around, observing his handiwork. Josh's pupils grew, soaking in the remaining light of the day. He eyed the broom handle. Carved within the four-inch-long piece of wood was a small bridge. Etched under the bridge, there was an outline of a cottage set on a cobblestone road. On the bottom of the carving was a staircase. The three pictures wound around it in a spiral.

Chadok handed the carving to Josh. "You should

keep in mind that every crossroad holds significance. Every decision made at a crossroads turns to a different path. The supernatural powers released within those moments possess the ability to either alter one's destiny or seal it with the healing balm of acceptance. If you choose a different road from before, well…it's not without cost. You need to know the choice is worth the price you'll pay." He eyed the carving he had handed Josh, narrowed his eyes, and nodded. "My help for your journey. My little flashes." He winked.

The old man shoved his hands in his pockets and stepped away, whistling an old hymn Josh hadn't heard since he was a young boy. He folded his hand over the token and shoved it back into his pocket. Lifting the carving in front of his face, he examined the things the old man named Chadok sculpted in it, and then he remembered their significance and how they intertwined with his crossroads.

84

The Road Not Taken
The Secret

Orange and brown hues painted the sky; the apricot sun hovered barely above the treetops. Josh glanced at the sunset, admiring God's artwork. Cutting his eyes from the horizon down to his hand, he eyed the wooden bridge carved in the four-inch hunk of broom handle Chadok handed him before walking away. "It's the bridge at The Trail. This," he squeezed the totem, "must be a guide to help me find my crossroads," he whispered to himself, glancing around to see if he was still alone in the graveyard. The Trail was significant to them and their relationship. After sixteen years of living separate lives in different states, they ran into each other at The Trail. They frequented it throughout their relationship, making their profession of love for one another there.

A moist breeze swept through the graveyard, sending a shiver down Josh's spine. Purple rain clouds rolled in with the winds. Josh tilted his head, observing the warning sent by the dark clouds. Determined to find her at the crossroad of The Trail and beat the rain there, he shoved the carving in his pocket and jogged back to his truck. He cranked the engine, threw the transmission in reverse, backed onto a side road, and sped forward. When he turned off Ditch Road, he spotted a young woman kneeling at a freshly covered grave. She arched her neck, looking up and off to the side. Slowing his truck to a crawl, he narrowed his eyes, watching her lips and facial expressions. She seemed to be speaking to someone, but no one was there. He wondered if it was Chadok since he had disappeared. Was he an angel? Was he the spirit of someone buried there? He didn't know the answers to the barrage of questions flooding his mind, but he knew he had to find a crossroads that would bring him to Isabella. He glanced over his shoulder at the grieving woman, smiled (a crooked smile), and veered onto the main road. Through the rearview mirror, he watched the graveyard shrink smaller and smaller until he could no longer see it.

Josh watched the sun disappear below the horizon. The purple, lavender, and navy-blue hues of dusk swallowed the orange and yellow streaked sky. A bolt of white light cracked across the evening sky, rumbling and warning of heavy rain. He drove, almost immediately, into a wall of water. The torrential rain pounded the asphalt, and fat raindrops beat against the windshield, obscuring his view of the road. Turning his wiper blades on high, he wondered if he should drive home and wait until daybreak to find her again, but he simply couldn't bring himself to turn onto the road that led home. He needed her. He longed to see her, touch her, and hear the sound of her voice. He flicked a knob on the backside of the steering wheel (turning on the bright lights) and leaned forward. Narrowing his eyes, he watched the road—doing his best to read the road signs as he passed them. Darkness overtook the narrow road that led back to The Trail. Nearly missing his turn, he slammed on the brakes; the tires squealed, and water splashed against the bottom of his truck with a loud swish and hundreds of small pelting splatters. His chest rose and fell in ragged breaths. *What am I doing? Am I losing my mind?* He exhaled a deep breath and shook his head. *It doesn't matter; it doesn't. I have to try. I need to see her, and this may be my only opportunity. If it doesn't work, I'll come back in the morning and try again,* he coached himself through what he needed to do.

Josh turned into the parking lot of The Trail and turned off his truck. As he waited for the rain to slack off, he drummed his fingers against the steering wheel to the beat of the song they sang together just three hundred yards from where he sat. He bounced his legs up and down in a nervous rhythm, closed his eyes, and said a prayer, waiting for the rain to abate before he stepped onto the pavement. As he shut the truck door behind him, he grabbed the token from his pants pocket and held it in his cupped hand. "Okay, he said it works best if I speak to it." He brought it close to his face and examined the moonstone, eyeing every facet. "Alright, moonstone, what kind of truth do you hold for 2009? That's the year I want you to return me to...2009." He watched the stone with a scrutinizing eye. From within the stone, tiny veins melded together, creating the number 09. Until they surfaced within the stone, pieces of the numbers filtered in and out of view.

Josh folded his hand over the token and walked in the dark of night towards the bridge carved into the broom handle. Thunder rumbled. Raindrops fell from the black cloud above him in small pelts onto the crown of his head, dripped off the ends of his hair down to his brow, and trickled down his cheeks. He swiped his free hand over his face and cleared his view. The previous, tenuous link between the times had sucked him back into 2021 rather quickly, so he set his heart and mind on 2009 and his first trip to The Trail with Tink. The ground beneath his feet shifted, and dizziness overtook him. Stumbling, he righted himself and took slow, cautious steps. Being careful not to falter and trip over shifting tree roots, he kept a keen eye out for footholds. As he neared the bridge, a pale sun poked through shifting cloud cover, the weak rays obscured by the dark, heavy clouds. He squeezed his eyes tight and shook his head, looking up at the sky in amazement, his face awash in the early morning light. The world around him warbled slightly, but it was manageable, much more manageable than his last trip back in time; the first trip happened so suddenly, sucking him back in time with extreme force. This journey to the past was smoother. He wondered if the further back in time he ventured, the more traumatic the trip. Josh fingered the edges of his face and glanced toward the sky. The rain had ceased, but the heavy blankets of clouds still filled the gray sky.

2009

The sweet scent of early morning dew wafted around Josh. The wooden planks creaked beneath his feet as he strode over the bridge and made his way to the back side of the property. A massive live oak stretched its limbs over a grassy field used for picnics. They often shared picnic lunches there while dating. The tree blurred and slid out of focus. He leaned against its trunk and steadied himself. The dizziness swirling through his mind convinced him he had traveled back in time; he prayed he was journeying to the correct year. He narrowed his eyes and skimmed over the tree trunk, searching for a carving from his childhood. Squatting, he traced his fingertips over the base of the tree, feeling the etchings carved into the trunk. "This. I'll show her this," he said to himself. He rubbed his thumb over the impression and smiled:

Josh jogged back up the trail that brought him to the live oak. He slowed his pace as he neared the bridge he had crossed earlier. His head spun, and his vision blurred again. He stopped and rubbed his eyes, willing himself to stay in 2009. When he dropped his hands, he eyed Tink standing on the bridge, watching the fish swim in the small creek. He cracked a half-smile and stood, gazing at her silhouette in the early morning light. A starburst of light broke through the green canopy and danced over her profile with an iridescent shimmer. Leaves rustled in the trees surrounding the walking path. Tiny wings flapped as Bluebirds chirped from within the trees and bounced from one branch to another, singing morning love songs to one another. Josh closed his eyes and listened to them, soaking in the beauty of the musical notes they chose for their conversations. He started forward again, anxious to be next to Isabella, his wife, his love.

"Good morning," he called as he stepped onto the wooden slats of the bridge.

Isabella tilted her head towards the sound of his voice and smiled. "Good morning to you. You're not supposed to get here for another thirty minutes, but it looks like you got here before me."

"Thirty minutes, huh? You assume I would be late?"

"Oh no, not late, but I didn't expect you to be early." Her smile stretched to her eyes. Josh loved that about her, the way her eyes glimmered when she smiled. "I come here in the mornings after I drop the children off at school. It's peaceful here. The birds sing the most beautiful songs. My house is next to the Interstate, so all I can hear is the sound of vehicles racing towards the next state," her words ran together without pause, "or wherever they're headed..." her voice trailed off. She caught herself and worried she was talking too much. It wouldn't be the first time someone suggested it to her. She knew she rambled when she was nervous. It was the trait she disliked about herself more than any other. Her bashfulness gave rise to nervous chatter, and her nervous chit-chat annoyed even her. Mental awareness was the key to preventing wordy conversations on her side. As soon as she became cognizant of her long-windedness, she always made a conscious effort to bring her sentence to a halt.

"Well, I'm sorry to intrude on your alone time."

"Oh, no, you're fine." She swatted at him, brushing his comment off with a shrug.

"So, how's Daniel?" he asked, sidling beside her and leaning against the bridge railing.

She glanced up at him. "Oh, he's great. He lives in Alaska now."

"Alaska? What took him there?"

"The Coastguard. He joined up right after 911. He fell in love with the beauty there, and now he only comes back once every two years for a week-long visit with his momma."

Josh rifled through his memories of the day he found himself in as quickly as he could. He needed to be cautious with his words and the topics they discussed, but no matter how hard he tried to find memories of their conversations from that day, his thoughts were scattered; their many trips to The Trail throughout their relationship ran together in a jumbled web of memories, so rather than bring up another topic of conversation, he simply stared at her profile. She was dainty and beautiful, and he desperately wanted to touch her. "Okay, okay," he started. "How about we play a little game?" He raised his brows twice in jest.

Tink folded her arms across her chest. "A game?" Her eyes went wide.

"Not really a game, but you'll be blindfolded," he tutted. He inched closer, untied the scarf around her neck, and stepped behind her. "Are you okay with this? I don't want to freak you out or anything. There's just something I want to show you. It's a secret I've held since I was a young boy—something I've never shared with anyone in my entire life."

Tink's heart raced. Warmth rushed to her cheeks, tinting them bright pink. "And you wanna share it with me?" She Felt as if her heart was going to beat out of her chest, so she crossed her hands over her heart. Her breath caught in her throat, and a small whimper slipped past her lips.

Josh lifted the scarf, holding it loosely in front of her face.

Tink inhaled a deep breath. "And it's something here?"

A crooked smile inched across one side of Josh's face. "Yes, it's something here," he said. He folded the scarf and used it to cover her eyes, tying it over her chestnut hair. "I have a feeling you've never noticed it before."

"Okay, what do we do now?" she asked, holding her arms out in front of her to feel her way around. A large chunk of her hair stuck out from under the blindfold, sticking to the side of her face.

A smile crept across one side of Josh's face. He stretched forth his hand and tucked her hair behind her ear, removing it from her cheek, and then he grabbed her hand and squeezed it tight. He closed his eyes and savored the moment. Being able to touch her was all he desired; he opened his eyes and took a moment to gaze at her smile as he held her hand in his. Rubbing the tips of his fingers over her soft skin, he remembered holding her in his arms on their wedding night.

Isabella bounced excitedly on the balls of her feet. A grin spread across her face. "Are you going to guide me to where this thing I've never noticed is?" She shrugged her shoulders and giggled.

Josh chuckled. "Ha ha, yeah, sorry. I just got caught up looking at you. You're so beautiful."

Isabella folded her bottom lip over her teeth and bit down. Her ears turned red, and she dropped her head as if to gaze at the ground despite being blindfolded. "Hmm..." she breathed.

Early morning sunlight broke through the treetops in slender shafts, streaking the trail with hints of warmth and exposing the roots weaving themselves across the path in myriads of directions. Josh pulled her up next to him and slipped his arm around her waist. "See, I've got you. I won't let you trip or fall." He guided her through the path, helping her step over every stump and root along the way. When they reached the tree, he gently grasped both her shoulders, bringing her to a halt. He untied the scarf and draped it back around her neck. Isabella opened her eyes and stared blankly at the tree she saw almost daily.

She raised her brows and widened her eyes. "So, what haven't I noticed about this tree?" She tilted her head to the side and tisked, drumming her fingertips against one another. "I've seen this tree regularly since I was a child, so I'm pretty sure I know all about its history and everything," she said, her tone filled with jest.

Josh inhaled a sharp breath. "Okay, so I'm sharing something with you that I locked away in the back of my mind years ago. I kinda need to know that you're not gonna laugh at me." He held his hand out for her to take.

"No, of course not. I'd never laugh at you, especially if you're sharing a piece of your heart with me." She placed her dainty hand in his and allowed him to lead her to his secret. With her hand in his, he guided her into the shadows on the backside of the tree. Directing her eyes toward the bottom of the tree, he pointed to a heart carved at its base. The initials JP were etched above the heart, and the initials TS were below it.

Isabella squatted and ran her fingers over the carving. "So, JP, that's you, Josh Parker, but who's TS?"

Bracing himself, Josh squeezed his eyes shut, scrunching up his face. "Umm...it's you, Isabella. I had a bit of a thing for you when we were young, but I—"

Isabella's eyes flew wide open in shock. She stumbled back and fell on her behind. "Oh..." she squealed.

Josh sprang to her side. "Are you okay?"

"Of course. I'm fine. I'm fine. Just injured my pride, is all." She shooed him off. "But, you...you liked me?"

"Yes, but I made myself get over it because you were so much younger than me, and Dale flat-out told me you were too young for me."

She threw her hand over her mouth. "I thought I was invisible to you," she mumbled under her breath, inaudible to Josh. Dropping her hand to her side, she turned to face him and peered into his eyes. "Whoa, wait a minute. You mean to tell me that you liked me when we were children, and my cousin Dale knew about it?"

Josh shrugged. "Dale never really liked me. I guess that had to do with Lyla liking me. We went on a couple of dates, but they were awkward. I thought she was pretty, but it just wasn't there. Then, one day, he showed up at my house and confronted me about you. He insisted I should date Samantha. I guess he decided he didn't want me dating his sister either." Josh scoffed, shook his head, and threw his hands in the air. Dale literally came up from behind me, shoved me, and told me you were too young to stay away from you." He folded his arms across his chest and tilted his head in thought. "You know, I guess I have Dale to thank for my children. His bullying and pushiness are what put me in the mindset of accepting that you were too young for me, and that very day, Samantha made a move on me, so I fell for his advice."

"But he knew, and he never told me? I can't believe

him." Isabella folded her arms around her knees.

"It's not like I actually admitted it to him. I never told anyone until now."

Tink glanced at the carving and then cut her eyes to Josh. "You're just messing with me, right? I mean, my initials were IS, not TS, so this isn't really me carved in this tree." She tried to reason it all out in her mind. Isabella was bashful. Of course, she talked to Josh when they were children because he was practically family. His mom was best friends with her aunt Ruth, so Josh was like another cousin, but she was head over heels for him as a child, and that fact alone made her bashful side rise up within her when he was around. Not only was Josh older than her, but he was gorgeous. Girls, including Lyla, pined over him at the skating rink, so the fact that he noticed her blew her mind. She understood his interest in dating Lyla because she was drop-dead gorgeous, but Isabella grew up believing Josh Parker saw her as an annoying child and nothing more.

"Your name. That's what I was starting to say earlier. I always thought your name was Tink; I figured your parents named you after Tinkerbell or something like that. That's all I ever heard anyone call you, so I carved a T for Tink." Josh stretched out his arm and offered Isabella his hand.

A shy giggle crossed her lips as he hoisted her to her feet. "You were partially right. Tink's my nickname, and it came from Tinkerbell. My brother called me Tinkerbella, and it eventually morphed into Tink." She shrugged. "You umm...you really liked me?" She smiled up at him, blushing.

With a nod and a tisk, he replied, "Yeah, I did."

Isabella wrung her hands together. "Wow, that really blows my mind."

"So, now you know my secret." Josh winked.

"Hmmm..." she breathed.

Josh pointed at the trail, glancing at Isabella with a questioning eye. Nodding in agreement, she fell in line next to him and matched his stride. They walked side by side back to the bridge. Josh glanced down at his wristwatch, eyeing the time. Remembering what Isabella had said when she arrived, he knew the Josh of 2009 would be there any minute, so he had to figure out what to do. His mind skimmed through possible scenarios of how to get away without her seeing two of him.

As they reached the bridge, he grasped her hands in his. "So," he said, giving her a wink. "Close your eyes and count to fifty for me."

"Another game that's not really a game?" She asked, smiling up at him with a gleam of flirtation in her eyes.

Josh shrugged his shoulders, stepping into a shaft of sunlight. "Hmmm...kinda, but not really." He grinned and winked at her again. The starburst of light danced over him; his gray eyes shimmered in its sway.

Isabella released a deep breath, closed her eyes, covered them, and began counting, "One, two, three..."

Crossroads

8

The Trail
Magical Kisses

Josh craned his neck and searched out his surroundings. Thin shafts of light poked through the treetop canopy, prancing through the woods to the rhythm of the wind's song in the leaves. He wasn't ready to leave Isabella but couldn't allow his 2009 self to see him, so he set his mind to watching their interaction from nearby. Allowing the dancing sunbursts to guide him to the wooded shadows, he darted into the woods, hiding under the covering of the trees and shrubs. Isabella stood on the old wooden bridge at The Trail counting, anxious to find out what Josh had planned. He found a comfortable spot in the woods and crouched in the shrubs, watching and waiting for his 2009 self to arrive. Pulling back a branch, he eyed his truck as it pulled into the parking lot.

The Josh of 2009 climbed out of his truck and scanned his surroundings. A warm morning breeze swept across his face, carrying the scent of honeysuckle and pine. He briefly closed his eyes and basked in the warmth. Flicking his eyes open, he resumed his search. When his eyes fell on Isabella, her back was to him. Her brunette hair fell in soft waves down her back. He heard her call, "...forty-eight, forty-nine, fifty." She swept her hand across the backside of her neck and pulled her hair to one side. Glancing over her shoulder, she eyed Josh (standing beside his truck) and smiled.

Captivated by her beauty, Josh smiled in return and slammed his truck door. "Ah..." he yelped. Cringing, he drew his hand to his chest.

Isabella's smile faded. Her eyes widened in shock, and her jaw dropped. "Oh, no!" She rushed to his side. "Give me your hand." She held her hand out for his.

A crooked smile crept across his face as he stepped forward and stretched forth his bruised hand. He raised a brow in jest. "Planning to smash the other one to make it hurt worse?" He chuckled.

"Oh, hush, you silly man," she said. Their eyes locked.

"Fifty, huh?" He winked and grinned past the pain.

Isabella smirked. She shook her head, rolled her eyes, and shifted them toward the ground. "Yes, fifty, that's what you said," she whispered as she examined his hand. Looking up and gazing into his gray eyes, she smiled and drew his wounded hand to her lips. "My kisses are magical. They make everything better. Just ask my children." She brushed her lips over his injured fingers, gently caressing them. "See," she breathed. "Doesn't it feel better already?" Her gray eyes shimmered with infatuation.

Isabella tugged on the bottom of his shirt. "Nice shirt," she said. "It has been pretty warm out already this morning."

Josh knit his brow in confusion; shrugging, he brushed off the oddity of the comment. "Yeah, Alabama summers are brutal. Thin cotton shirts are a must, so you mentioned magical kisses *and* children. How many children do you have?" he asked as he started for the bridge.

Isabella clasped her hands together and stared at her feet as she shuffled them over the sandy path to the bridge. Hesitant to respond, she chewed on her bottom lip. As she stepped onto the wooden planks, she grasped the bridge railing and leaned against it. Embarrassed, she turned to face him, shifting her eyes to the side to avoid being caught in his gaze again. "Two. I have two children. My daughter is five. She's a little princess." She laughed. "And my son is eleven. Actually, he just turned eleven on the tenth of last month."

"May 10, huh? And what are their names?"

Isabella blushed and dropped her gaze to the creek, watching the water rush over a ledge of large rocks and plunge two feet into the waters swirling beneath the bridge. "So, I suppose today's as good a day as any to share *my* secret," she said. Nervous, she wrung her hands, folded her lips over her teeth, and cringed. "Ciara *and*...Caleb." She finally managed to force the name off her tongue and across her lips.

Watching from the woods, the Josh from 2021 shifted his weight to his knees and cringed at the crunching of twigs and leaves. Isabella jerked her head to the side and peered into the woods, searching for the source of the rustling leaves. "That's why she emphasized *her* secret that day? And my shirt," the Josh of 2021 mumbled, glancing down at his baby-blue shirt. Tink bought him the shirt just before she got sick. "Has this already all happened?" he wondered aloud. "Was I here that day, hiding in the woods? I need to be careful about what I wear, I guess." He shook his head, narrowed his eyes, and set his attention back where it needed to be—on the interaction between himself from 2021 and Tink.

The Josh from 2009 grinned. His eyes brightened. "Really? That's my middle name."

Isabella dropped her head, gazed at the water, and chewed on her bottom lip. Her face flushed crimson. "I know," she mumbled, barely audible.

"My son is Joshua Caleb Junior. He's a year old." Josh's words ran together. It took him a minute for her soft response to register with him. "Wait." He stepped back, and (with a slight tilt of his head) he leaned around to look Isabella in the eyes. "You know...I mean, you knew my full name? Did you...did you name him Caleb after me?"

Isabella picked at her nails. She turned her head away from Josh and inhaled a shuddery breath. "Yes and no. I...I really liked the name Caleb, and well, the name did come from knowing you when we were young. I just really thought it was a pretty name."

Josh let out a short, soft chuckle. "Okay, so you got the name from me but weren't technically naming him after me? Okay." He nodded his head and tisked. "Well, thank you for sharing that secret with me." He leaned to the side and nudged her.

Isabella shrugged her shoulders. "Well, it only seemed fair— considering..." She bent over and picked up a basket sitting next to her feet. "I brought breakfast." She held the basket up and smiled. "I figured we could have a picnic breakfast under the oak tree at the end of the trail. Is that okay with you?"

"Absolutely." Josh extended his arm to escort her through the path to the live oak. She hooked her arm through his and followed the trail that curled through the park. As they rounded a bend, bright red amaryllis flowers poked their heads out from under the bushes, edging the sandy pathway. "So, Isabella, how long has it been? Sixteen years or so, right?"

"Fifteen...to be precise." Isabella stopped dead in her tracks and pointed at a blue bird splashing in a birdbath just off the trail. "Look, isn't she a beauty? I love watching the birds out here; they're so majestic."

"Yeah, I have an area in my backyard dedicated to feeders and birdbaths. I usually have my morning coffee out there."

"Wow, that's amazing," she trilled.

"You should come over for coffee sometime. We'll birdwatch."

Isabella's face brightened. "That sounds delightful!"

Josh cleared his throat. "What have you been up to over the last fifteen years?"

"I got married right out of high school and had my son a year later."

"Who'd you marry?"

"Dean Bennett."

Josh raised his brow. "Don't know him. Was he a Mississippi boy?"

"Yeah, he was, but we went to different schools; he was older than me. He worked at the same company as my uncle. He didn't really have any family. His parents pretty much abandoned him, so my uncle invited him over for Thanksgiving dinner with our family. He was twenty, and I was sixteen at the time. It was my senior year."

The path ended, opening into the grassy field with the massive live oak as its centerpiece. Sunlight peeked through the cloud cover in patches. Isabella opened the basket and pulled out a small blanket. She fluffed it and spread it out, setting the basket on top. "Senior year at sixteen?" Josh folded his arms across his chest and mouthed, *wow.*

Isabella nodded as she smoothed the wrinkles from the blanket. "Yeah, I graduated early."

"So, you guys got married pretty quick then?"

Isabella laughed a nervous, breathy laugh as she pulled two small plates from the basket. "Huh, yeah. It ended up being a whirlwind of a relationship. I cared deeply for Dean. More than anything, I felt sorry for him. His home life was horrible."

"And your parents were okay with you getting married so soon after meeting him?"

Josh settled beside Tink on the blanket she stretched out over the grass. She handed him a plate covered with fresh fruits and a warm biscuit. "I didn't really give 'em a choice. Dean enlisted in the Marines and wanted to get married before he was shipped overseas, so we eloped."

Josh widened his eyes. "Whoa, I can't imagine little Tink being a rebel."

"I was going through a tough time in my life, and I thought Dean loved me. I needed that; I needed to be loved."

"So, I'm assuming you're divorced?" Josh cringed at the sound of the word passing over his lips.

Isabella shook her head and sighed. "Nope, not yet anyway." She took a bite of her biscuit covered in plum jelly.

Josh leaned backward. His jaw dropped. "You're married?"

Isabella swallowed hard, forcing her food down, and inhaled a deep breath. "Yes, at least for the next three weeks."

"Shew," Josh sighed and sipped the coffee Isabella

had served him. "You scared me there for a minute. For a split second, I thought you were about to say, 'After meeting you here today, I'll be getting one.'" Josh let out a nervous chuckle. Isabella rolled her eyes and shook her head. The corners of her mouth turned up in a grin.

The Josh from 2021 stood frozen in the woods to the south of the clearing, clutching a low-lying limb. His knuckles turned white from his weight bearing down on his grip. He tilted his head, bringing his ear as close to the edge of the tree line as he could without being seen. His mind reeled from his conversation with Tink. He watched them (Tink and himself) from the cover of the trees as they got to know one another. "I forgot she was still going through her divorce when we first met. I just went out there before *I* was supposed to get there." He rubbed his forehead. "How dumb," he mumbled. "I revealed my secret about liking her when we were kids. I held her hand and slipped my arm around her waist. She probably thinks the me out there now is too forward. I hope I didn't just mess things up and change the past by interjecting myself into this day."

The Josh of 2009 squared his shoulders and braced himself for the answer to the question on his mind. "What led the two of you to get a divorce? If you don't mind my asking," he muttered.

Isabella's chest tightened, constricting her airway. She inhaled a slow, cleansing breath and calmly exhaled, releasing the tension inching through her chest. "Well, I didn't take too well to being a prisoner. Our house was more like a maximum-security prison, not a home. He was very possessive and controlling, and those traits eventually led to physical restraints. For example, if we were arguing and I wanted to remove myself from the situation, he would stop me, and those situations led to the occasional slap across the face. On top of all that, he didn't understand faithfulness, so I got a job as a teacher's aide, and after saving up over three years, I bought a small house here in Oak Ridge, and I left Mississippi and Dean."

"I'm sorry you had to go through all of that. You deserve better."

"So," Isabella started. She leaned back, propped her elbow on the blanket, and faced Josh. She sipped her coffee and savored the brisk taste as the warmth slid down her throat. "Tell me about yourself. You mentioned having a son named after you. Fill me in on the last fifteen years of your life now that you've heard my soap opera."

Josh pinched a piece of his biscuit and dipped it in honey. "I graduated high school, went to culinary school, and moved to Florida. I managed a fast-food restaurant and worked the second shift at a chemical company until I saved enough money for a down payment on a restaurant in Emerald Creek. It was a fancy, fine-dining restaurant. I met my ex-wife (Samantha) at church while we were in high school. We dated through my senior year. She came from a well-to-do family, so she loved the life we had as restaurant owners. We made a name for ourselves there. We were invited to the parties at the mayor's mansion. You know that sort of life, but it wasn't for me. On the other hand, Samantha loved the lifestyle, and I think she really liked the mayor. When I moved back home to help my parents, she wanted to go back to Florida and live a life of luxury, so we divorced. I kept the children. We have a daughter named Londyn; she'll be thirteen in September, and of course, we have a son, Josh Junior; he turned a year last week. He was an infant when she left. I've often wondered if postpartum depression had something to do with her decision." He shrugged.

Josh popped the honey-dipped biscuit in his mouth and swallowed, following it up with a swig of coffee. "Staying in Florida wasn't an option for me. My mom fell ill right after Josh Junior was born; she needed me. I came home to take care of her. Samantha was resistant to coming back here at all. A week after I told her I wanted to sell the restaurant and move back to Oak Ridge, she filed for a divorce. She loves the children but said she couldn't do it alone, so she gave me full custody. So, here I am."

Isabella smiled up at Josh. "So, here we are."

The Drive
The Date

Streaks of varying shades of green swirled past Josh's eyes in a blur; the woods around him spun madly, causing him to lose his balance. For a moment, he lost all sense of which way was up and which was down. He toppled to the side. Clinging with both arms to the tree limb he had grasped earlier (when he found his spot in the woods outside the clearing), he held himself from tumbling amongst the moss and twigs. "*No*," he hissed, but the world around him continued in upheaval as the moonstone yanked him back to 2021. Realizing his time with Tink at The Trail had lapsed, he surrendered to the vortex and was swept back to the present.

When the world settled, Josh found himself crouched (his hands planted palms down in the mossy bed beneath his feet) in pitch blackness. He steadied himself and then drew his hand to his face, unable to see it until it was right on his nose. His eyes had yet to adjust to the stark difference in light. The world had shifted from the morning of 2009 to the night of 2021. He knew he was in the woods outside the clearing at The Trail, but he would have to feel his way around until he found the live oak.

Josh inched his way to standing, careful not to hit his head on any branches. Managing to creep slowly through the woods, he lifted his feet and warily padded his way through the brambles and underbrush. As he fumbled through the darkness, briers snagged his pants legs, catching him unaware and slowing his pace. Yanking himself free, he stumbled from the bushes and found himself in the clearing with the live oak. The moon reflected the sun's light, casting a soft glow over the clearing and lighting Josh's path. Following the moonlit path to the parking lot was a breeze for him. Flustered at being yanked to 2021 so abruptly, Josh shook his head and sighed. Despite his frustration, his heart swelled with joy and love over his visit with Tink. Being able to touch her and hear her voice was worth it all.

Josh unlocked the front door and eased in to find Ciara asleep in the recliner, her head lilting to the side and the television on. He felt guilty that she had apparently tried to wait up for him. He knew she was worried about him, but there was no need...now that he had Isabella back, there was no need at all to worry about him. Cringing at the sound of the door creaking, he twisted the knob and edged it closed. He tiptoed across the room and snatched the cream-colored throw draped over the back of the couch. Kissing his stepdaughter's forehead, he covered her with the warm, fuzzy blanket and turned off the television.

Josh shut his bedroom door and leaned against it. Relief washed over him. He found her; he found his way back to her, and now that he had the power of the token, he would never be without her again. Stripping off his clothes, he lumbered towards the bathroom and turned on the shower, anxious to wash away the filth and grime of the day. Standing under the shower nozzle, he recounted the day's events as steam rose from his bare back, and oh, what a day he had!

Twice in one day, he had traveled back in time, seeing Isabella on both occasions. Stopping at her dressing table, he traced his fingers over the brush she used each night before grasping her favorite perfume and making his way to the bed. He lightly sprayed her pillow and set the bottle of Chanel on her nightstand. As he crawled alone into their bed, he breathed in the sweet scent he had become accustomed to during their time together, and a sense of peace washed over him. No longer did he feel crippled with grief as he had since the day she left him. He nuzzled his head in his pillow, shifting until he found that sweet spot of comfort, and fell fast asleep.

Early morning sunlight bathed Josh's room in the warmth of spring. It seemed as if he had just closed his eyes when they blinked wide open, squinting immediately from the thin shafts of light piercing through the cracks in the blinds. Rest. Josh had slept through the night; he attributed the peace and restfulness he sensed to the gift of time travel given to him by Chadok. He felt sincerely rested for the first time since losing Isabella. "I never have to go another day without her," he mumbled to himself as he swung his legs over the side of the bed.

Moaning, he stretched the kinks from his muscles and stood to his feet. "I need to find Chadok again and thank him," he said, his voice muffled through his shirt as he pulled it over his head. Once dressed for the day, he made his bed and tidied up their bedroom. He grabbed the carving Chadok had made for him and eyed the cottage on a cobblestone road. He knew the place well. It was the restaurant, Vita Sapori; he had taken Isabella out to eat there on their first date.

Shutting the door behind him, he shuffled to the living room, rifled through the bookcase under the television, and pulled out a scrapbook Isabella had made titled *Our Story*. She had made the album from photos and keepsakes of their time together, including their time together while they courted and their wedding photos.

He flipped the album open and landed first on a picture of patriotic lights and fireworks. It was how their night had begun. He traced his fingers over the words she had written as he studied the pictures. His mind replayed the night in its entirety…

Josh pulled into Isabella's driveway. The tiny house, nestled against a wooded area covered with bushes and shrubs, sat in a neighborhood built originally for the Navy. The term Navy house was attached to them and remained even after the Naval Station was shut down in the early nineties. He glanced in the rearview mirror of his truck and patted his hair, ensuring it held in place. When he stepped out of his vehicle, he tugged his shirt and straightened it before stepping onto her porch. He wanted to make a good impression on her children. Isabella invited Josh in to meet her children (Ciara and Caleb) before they ventured out on their first date. They had been friends for a month and a half, and this was their first official date night.

Isabella started for the door handle, but before she could open it for herself, Josh quickly lifted it and tugged open the door. "Thank you," she said. "I'm so used to having to open doors for myself. My ex-husband wasn't a gentleman in the least, so I got used to doing it for myself all the time."

"Well," Josh said, smiling down at her. "As long as I'm around, you'll never have to open a door yourself." Isabella climbed in; he shut the door before making his way around to his side and settling behind the wheel. As he cranked the truck and pulled out of the drive, he faced her and said, "My momma raised me right. She taught me to always open doors for a lady because ladies should be

Crossroads

treated like royalty, and a princess never has to open her own doors." He smiled and winked at her, clicking his tongue on the roof of his mouth for emphasis. "And she instructed me on how to properly escort a lady down the street in a manner that enabled me to protect her if need be." He shook his head and waved his hand at her. "Not saying you couldn't protect yourself. I've seen a fierce side of you since we've been friends, but if I can protect you from an oncoming car or even an attack, I will."

Isabella grinned impishly. "You'll get no arguments from me." She blew across her nails. "I wouldn't want to break a nail decking anyone." She chortled. "So, where are we going?"

"Have you ever been to the stadium in Fair View?"

"No," she said, shaking her head, "I've never even been to Fair View."

Josh raised his brow. "Seriously, you've never been?"

"Nope. Dean kept me close to home, so I haven't experienced much."

Okay, wow...experiencing things with you will be so much fun! The stadium in Fair View has a patriotic drive-thru light show for the entire month of July. It's amazing. It's almost like a Christmas light spectacular, but it's patriotic with red, white, and blue lights flickering to "The Star-Spangled Banner," "America the Beautiful," and "God Bless America." The lights display several patriotic symbols: The Washington Monument, the Liberty Bell, the Bald Eagle, The Lincoln Memorial, the Statue of Liberty, and the American flag. It's pretty amazing." A huge grin

114

spread across his face as he realized he had the incredible privilege of introducing her to many firsts in her life. He couldn't fathom her never encountering things like the lights at the stadium, but he was thankful he was chosen to be the one to experience them with her.

Glimmering stars and a half-moon filled the navy-blue sky. Isabella leaned forward and tilted her head (looking out the front windshield) to search the skies and admire God's handiwork. The trip to Fair View took an hour, so—along with her stargazing— they filled their drive with conversations of childhood events.

Josh set his mind on broaching the topic heavy on his heart. His chest tightened, and his heart pounded. A half-smile slid across one side of his face. Turning to face her, he cleared his throat and said, "So, yesterday was our what? Twelfth trip out to The Trail?"

Tink stared off in the distance and chewed on her bottom lip, calculating the weeks since they first met for their morning biscuit at The Trail. "Ummm...yeah," she stuttered, "It's been six weeks now, and we've managed to hang out and share breakfast there twice each week."

Josh playfully raised his brows. "Yesterday's visit was pretty intense, huh?"

Isabella's face flushed. "Yeah," she said, dropping her head and diverting her eyes to see the trees out the side window. "Confession day," she mumbled. Her breath created a circle of fog on the window, and she etched a heart in it.

Josh shook his head. "Confession day; I like that." Josh stretched his arm over the seat and wrapped his hand around hers. Isabella smiled and cut her eyes to their joined hands. "You know...yesterday, I told you I love you, and yeah, you admitted to naming your son after me for more than liking—" He briefly released her hand and the steering wheel, making quotation signs as he uttered the word 'liking.' "My middle name. You also said you were crazy about me when we were children but never told me how you feel about me now."

Isabella's eyes flew open wide. Her jaw dropped. "But I did. I admitted it all to you. Did you not hear me? I told you, yes, I named my son after you. I liked your name, but I was also crazy about you when I was a little girl; then you told me you loved me and asked me how I felt about you, and I told you that I've loved you since I was a little girl."

"But you were a little girl. I wanted to know how you feel about me now. I'm crazy about you, Isabella."

Isabella blushed and glanced up at him. Stroking the back of his hand with her free hand, she said, "I've loved you since I was a little girl means that I loved you then, and well, I never stopped loving you. You were always in my heart."

Josh's face beamed; he squeezed her hand tight. "Really? You love me?"

Isabella met his eyes with hers. She studied the tiny flakes of yellow in his gray eyes. "Yes, I do."

"Thank you. I really needed to hear you say it. My mind has been reeling since yesterday, and I keep hearing this voice telling me that you liked me when we were children, but that doesn't mean anything about now. I just *really needed to hear you say it."*

A green arrow glowed, signaling Josh to go; he turned off the highway onto a service road that took him down to the stadium. Dropping Tink's hand, he paid the entrance fee. The female attendant directed him to turn his radio to 104.2. He followed her instructions, pressed the accelerator, and inched the truck through the obstacle course of lights. Patriotic music filled the truck cab. Isabella's eyes gleamed with excitement. Catching glimpses of every dancing light in his line of vision, Josh turned his head from side to side. The truck swerved, slightly veering towards the rope barrier. As they neared the end, "God Bless America" blared through his speakers. Tink clapped and giggled, following the lights with her eyes as they flickered to the beat. She leaned forward, staring out the front windshield, and soaked in the spectacular show celebrating the birth of the great nation of America.

Isabella stretched her hand across the cab, grasped Josh's hand, and intertwined her fingers with his. Scooting to the center of the front seat, she laid her head on his shoulder. "Thank you for bringing me here. It's beautiful, and it's nice to know we share a love for our country."

As they rounded the last turn through the maze of lights, he pulled to the side of the road, leaned over, and kissed her forehead. "Oh, there's more to come," he said as he pulled back onto the highway and headed south towards the coastline.

Josh parked in the public square at the beach.

Crossroads

Isabella rolled down the door window. Folding her arms across the opening, she nestled her head in the crook of her elbow and eyed the waves crashing beyond the shore. The peaceful sounds of water lapping onto the sandy beach swept Isabella back to her youth. She closed her eyes and breathed in the salty air, sighing. Josh slipped off his socks and shoes. Holding up the towels he brought to clean their feet before putting their shoes back on, he encouraged Tink to take her shoes off as well. Isabella slipped off her strappy dress sandals. Climbing out of the truck, Josh pounced onto the sandy asphalt. He made his way to Tink's door, opening it for her. Extending his hand to her, he helped her from the cab, grasping her hand in his. They walked side by side onto the beach. Her stomach twisted in nervous knots. With every touch of his hand, hot, tingly feelings rushed through her body—warming her heart. Blushing, she glanced towards the water. The gulf stretched to the horizon, and cumulus clouds drifted like heaps of rounded, fluffy cotton candy in the navy-blue sky. The stark difference in the atmosphere from the shoreline, where clouds drowned out the stars, compared to the starry night sky she had witnessed an hour north of the coastline, amazed Isabella. She dug her toes into the wet sand as they edged along the waterline. The sound of crashing waves with their rhythmic motions calmed her nerves. She breathed in the salty smell of the heavens and exhaled, uncoiling the knots that made it difficult for her to breathe. Finding a wooden bench close to the pier, they sat together and stared at the waters, watching the waves break in the distance. The moon reflected soft light that danced upon the waves in shimmers.

Josh gazed into Isabella's gray eyes. Her thick, dark lashes brightened them, causing them to glimmer like diamonds. He tilted his head (touching her forehead with his) and closed his eyes. Slipping his arm around her waist, he inched himself closer to her. Isabella's breath caught in her throat. Warmth spread through her face, turning her complexion a glowing mauve. She longed to brush her lips against his. Her heart pounded in her chest, and a hard knot twisted in her stomach. Pressing his hand firmly against the small of her back, he pulled her body next to his. He tilted his head close to hers. With his lips inches from hers, he breathed, "Kiss me."

Crossroads

10

The Intersection
The Villa

Josh inhaled a deep breath and closed his eyes, relishing in the memory of their first real kiss. When he opened his eyes, he found his fingers tracing a picture of the beach at Fair View. He eyed the shirt he wore in the picture fastened above the beach scene and shut the album. Darting across the floor, he made his way to his bedroom. He rummaged through his closet, searching for the clothes he wore on their first date to Vita Sapori. As he sifted through his clothes, thankfulness welled up within him. Isabella had stayed on him for years to donate his clothes, but he refused, insisting the older they were, the more comfortable they were. Inhaling a deep breath, he held it in and prayed he would find what he needed. He shoved a stack of clothes to the side and pulled out a hanger sporting the dress shirt he wore that night. He blew out the breath he held in his lungs and sighed in relief. "Thank you, God, for me not listening to my wife when she pestered me to throw all this out."

As evening neared, Josh readied himself to travel back in time. The savory smells of roast, carrots, and potatoes wafted into Josh's bedroom. His stomach gnawed within him, reminding him he hadn't eaten all day. He shimmied into the pants he wore that night back in 2009 and slipped his arms into his shirt. Buttoning it up, he walked through his plans to find the crossroad etched in the carving. He picked it up, along with the token, from his nightstand and shoved them both in his pocket before grabbing his keys. Turning to see himself in the mirror, he realized he had a few strands of gray that would be recognizable. "Good thing she didn't notice them yesterday when I went back," he mumbled, running his fingertips through the sides of his hair. Stepping into the bathroom, he tugged open Isabella's drawer, where she kept her makeup and stuff for her hair. Rifling through it, he found a spray bottle of root cover-up. He had never used anything of the sort, so he cautiously read every word in the directions twice! He covered his face with a washcloth and did his best to hide the twelve years of aging that had taken place since their first date. Once he finished, he admired his handiwork with a curt nod. Shoving the drawer back shut, he inhaled a deep breath and made his way to the living room. Willing his growling stomach to hush, he started for the front door.

Ciara called from the kitchen. "Hey, Dad, where are you going all dressed up?" She opened the oven, pulled out the roast, and basted it with the rue.

Stopping in his tracks, Josh breathed deeply and turned to face her. "On a date to see Tink. Oh, smells delicious, honey."

Ciara dropped the baster she held in her hand. Her jaw dropped. "You're just leaving without sup...Ummm...ummm..." she stammered. "Did you just say you're going on a date with mom?"

Josh's stomach growled, gnawing at him and demanding he give it samples of the smells saturating the kitchen. He snatched a fork from the counter and jabbed a carrot and three potatoes, shoving it in his mouth to temper his insistent stomach. He closed his eyes and reasoned through his explanation. He swallowed hard and cleared his throat. "Oh, my goodness, you inherited your mom's ability in the kitchen. Sorry, I won't be here to eat it, but be sure to make me a plate."

Ciara stared wide-eyed with her hands on her hips, awaiting his response.

Josh rolled his eyes and shrugged. "I'm going to the place we had our first date, Ciara. That's all."

Ciara released the breath of worry she held, her eyes relaxed; she knew everyone grieved differently, so she settled quickly in her mind that maybe this was his way of grieving and coping with his loss. "I waited up for you last night. Did you put the covers on me when you came in?"

A crooked smile crept across his face. "I did."

Josh Junior bounced from his room. "Hey, Dad, thanks for the driving lessons yesterday. Can we do it again next Saturday?" He scurried across the living room floor and wrapped his arms around his dad. Josh returned his embrace.

"Of course, son," he said, cutting his eyes to Ciara, "we'll all head back down to grandma and grandpa's next Saturday and have another round of lessons. Sound good to you, Ciara?"

Openmouthed, Ciara nodded. "Yeah, sounds good. Go enjoy your dinner, but don't fill up. There's plenty here, okay." She forced a weak smile through the worry creeping up in her heart again; she couldn't help herself. Something was off in his demeanor. "Did he color his hair?" she whispered under her breath.

Josh Junior bolted out the front door and hollered, "Riding bikes with Blake."

Ciara stepped on the porch. "Listen for the horn, Joshie!" she yelled. Tears rushed to the surface of her eyes, and her face crumpled as she shut the front door with a loud clunk.

Josh parked down the street from where he parked in 2009. He knew he needed to be able to get away without being seen. He pondered that night all those years ago, wondering how he might interject himself into their date. His thoughts drifted back in time, recalling the nervousness that consumed him, twisting his stomach into knots...

They had just professed their love for one another and kissed on the beach. Their relationship was new and fresh. He remembered hearing his heart thrumming as it pounded against his chest wall. The twisted mass in his stomach had forced its way into his chest. He felt as if his heart might burst. He had excused himself to run back to the truck to get the gift he had brought her, a gold bracelet with a skate charm. It may have seemed silly to some for him to have purchased her something meaningful so early on, but he was completely and totally head over heels in love, and he remembered all too well how determined he was that she would not slip through his fingers again. "Dorlan," he muttered, remembering details from the evening. On his way back to the cottage at the restaurant, he ran into an old high school buddy. He pinpointed the memory of his conversation with his friend, remembering how Dorlan had held him in a lengthy discussion, reminiscing about their senior year.

That's it, he said to himself.

Dorlan had always been a chatterbox, and pulling away from him was never easy, so he plotted his entrance. His trip to get the bracelet and running into Dorlan would present the perfect opportunity for him to slip in and replace his 2009 self. He would use the time his other self was held captive in conversation to see Isabella.

While waiting to cross the street, Josh stood at the intersection, shoved his hand in his pocket, and fumbled the etched broom handle between his fingers and thumb. Whistling, he craned his neck and watched the stars flickering in the night sky. Red, yellow, and green lights flashed off and on down the long strip of highway, catching his attention. He cut his eyes to the street. Cars and trucks rushed past him in both directions. Fidgeting, he ran his fingers down his jaw and tapped his foot impatiently. When the intersection cleared, the crosswalk flashed green. Josh hurried across onto the cobblestone sidewalk. He dropped the totem and grasped the token. Opening his palm, he pulled his cupped hand close to his chest and skimmed his eyes over his surroundings. Whispering, he spoke to the moonstone, "2009...I need you to take me back to 2009 to the restaurant Vita Sapori."

The colors of the moonstone wavered, and the numbers 0 and 9 came to the surface. Josh's head swam with colorful dots of lights. The cobblestones beneath his feet shifted. He bent his knees to keep himself from being thrown off balance by the swirling madness around and under him. Greens and browns and reds zipped past him, sending him off kilter. Stumbling forward, he threw his arms out to brace his fall, catching his balance before he faltered.

As the spinning came to a halt, he found himself standing on a cobblestone walkway. It twined through the restaurant (Vita Sapori), designed as an Italian Villa. Colorful lights were strung over the outdoor patios, creating a romantic atmosphere. Several small cottages were nestled throughout the villa, built to resemble an Italian estate from Roman times.

Josh started forward, being sure to stay in the shadows and keep himself hidden. He found the cottage the hostess would be seating them in. He looked through the window and found it empty. Turning his head from side to side, he searched for a place to hide until his younger self and Isabella arrived. He found a dark corner with a tall table for two facing the cottage—their cottage. Seating himself, he held up a menu and waited, occasionally peering over and around it in an attempt to catch them approaching.

Laughter echoed across the street. Josh recognized the voice to be Tink's. He tilted his head to the side and eyed himself and Isabella, crossing the road and stepping onto the cobblestone walk. Isabella's face beamed with excitement, and her eyes glistened. A smile inched across one side of Josh's face as he savored the sound of her laughter and how happy she had been that night. She was in love with him despite his nervous reservations. Josh wanted desperately to be loved, but his heart had been so shattered by a woman who loved his money and the support he provided more than she loved him that part of him always wondered if he deserved to be loved the way he wanted. A romantic at heart, he wanted to love someone unfettered. He wanted to be loved in the same manner.

Hiding behind the menu, Josh watched as the Josh of 2009 slipped his arm around Isabella's waist and pulled her close to his side. The red-haired hostess guided them to the cottage across from his small corner table. Josh peered over his menu, staring hard through the window, awaiting his opportunity. Flickering candles cast a yellow glow over Isabella's face. Her eyes cut to the table. Then, the Josh of 2009 scooted his chair back and excused himself. As he rounded the corner, heading to his truck, the Josh of 2021 glanced at his watch and waited for several minutes to pass. He knew Isabella would catch on if he bounced back into the cottage immediately, so he patiently waited until he knew he would have ample time to make it to the truck. As soon as the second hand on his watch clicked into place, he laid the menu on the table and made his way to the cottage, taking advantage of the small portion of time he was being given with Tink.

Josh strode into the cottage, sitting directly across from Isabella. "Sorry," he heaved as if he were out of breath. "How do you like the place?" He craned his neck, scanning the rustic dining area with his eyes.

"It's really nice." Isabella smiled and eyed her menu.

Josh stretched his hand across the table and grasped Isabella's hand. Intertwining their fingers together, he peered into her eyes and said, "I can honestly say that for the first time in my life, I feel an overwhelming sense of thankfulness for an individual getting sick."

Isabella narrowed her eyes. "Really, who?"

"Your keyboard player. Sam wouldn't have guided you to me if he had not gotten sick, and I may not have run into you." He rubbed his thumb over hers, petting her.

Tink winked. "Oh, our paths would've crossed eventually. Don't forget we both happened to be helping the same outreach. We just hadn't seen each other there. I was serving meals to the homeless on Saturdays, and you served on Mondays, but eventually, I think we would have bumped into one another at the soup kitchen."

The corners of Josh's mouth turned up in a tight smile. "Yeah, I suppose you're right," he shrugged, "Our paths seemed to have been meant to cross one way or another. Well," he cleared his throat, "I'm thankful they crossed when they did, and I'm still thankful he got sick that day," he winked, "You have an amazing voice, by the way." He cleared his throat again, tugging his tie and stretching his collar.

Isabella's face flushed. Warmth radiated through her bright pink cheeks. Casting her eyes to the table, she drummed the fingers of her free hand against the table. "And you are an amazing keyboard player. Thank you for the patience you showed me that day. I'd really like to sing with you again."

"I have a feeling we'll be doing a lot of that in our future." He smiled and winked. "Tink...Isabella, you're the most beautiful woman I've ever known in my entire life."

Isabella blushed and cast her eyes at the menu again. A chunky waitress entered the cottage. Her thin, black hair was pulled in a tight bun on the top of her head. She held her head high, quickly running through the spectacular wine list like a professional vinter before asking, "Would you like anything from our wine list tonight?"

Josh glanced across the table at Isabella. "Would you like a glass of wine?" he asked.

"I think I'll have a sweet tea," she whispered across the table to him, making it clear she hoped he'd place the order for her.

Josh squared his shoulders. "She'll have a sweet tea, and I'll have a lemonade," he said, glancing up at the waitress.

"Alright, I'll be right back with those," the waitress stated before turning on her heels and leaving the cottage.

"Does it bother you that I call you Tink?" Josh asked.

Isabella shook her head, straightened her shoulders, and cleared her throat. "No, not at all. Why?"

"Well, Isabella is such a gorgeous, graceful name, and Tink is a bit childlike. I worry that it may offend you as an adult being called a name from your childhood, but it was how I knew you, so it rolls off my tongue more naturally than Isabella."

Tink grinned. "I'm Tink. It's who I am. I've always been Tink, and if I'm going to be completely honest with you, it sounds weird to hear you call me Isabella. I mean, you were like family when I was a child. Granted, I was head over heels crazy about you, but all my family called me Tink, and so did you. To hear you call me Isabella? Classmates and business associates call me Isabella. It endears me to you when I hear you say Tink." She bit her bottom lip, stared at the table, piddled with the silverware, and smiled a half-smile.

Their waitress returned with their drink order; she placed the sweet tea in front of Isabella and the lemonade next to Josh. "Are you two ready to order?"

"No," Josh glanced up at the waitress. "I'm sorry. We've been so busy talking that we haven't even looked at the menu yet, so we need a few more minutes."

"Not a problem," the waitress said, excusing herself from the room.

"I'm sorry, Tink," Josh started. "I need to excuse myself again. "I'll be back in a jif."

Tink raised her brows and grinned in a teasing way. "Sure thing. I'll be going over the menu."

Josh scooted his chair back, exited the cottage, and returned to the corner table. He knew that he (the he of 2009) would soon get away from Dorlan, so he held up the menu and waited. Josh eyed his younger self return as the hostess who had seated them escorted an Italian couple into the cottage; she accompanied them to the far side of the room. Entering the room behind them, the Josh of 2009 pulled out his chair and seated himself across from Isabella.

"Is everything okay?" Isabella asked, wide-eyed.

"Yeah, yeah, sorry about that," Josh cringed. He picked up the glass of lemonade and eyed it suspiciously, rattling the ice around. "Ah, I sure do love a cold glass of lemonade." He didn't remember ordering it before he left or informing Isabella that lemonade was his favorite drink.

Sitting in the shadowy corner, Josh peeked over the menu, his eyes following the waitress. She entered the cottage and stood at the end of Josh and Isabella's table, smiling and jotting down their order. As soon as she exited the dining area, the Italian couple on the other side of the room stood and approached Josh and Isabella. Josh remembered the night well. They had prayed a blessing over them, but the interaction held a slightly different perspective from his point of view, looking through the window. There seemed to be an aura surrounding them both. The man stretched forth his hand to shake Josh's. Josh tried to remember each word spoken during that encounter as we watched their mouths move.

Isabella's eyes lit up with eagerness, and her slender face blushed a deep mauve. The woman raised her brows and nodded her head. The Josh of 2021 narrowed his eyes to read her lips. "You will be," he uttered. "She just spoke a prophetic word to Tink. She said You will be." The woman winked at Isabella, grabbed her hand, and looked her square in the eyes. Josh leaned over the table, jutting his head over the menu even farther, and squinted, trying to see every word form on the woman's lips. For a brief moment, the woman glanced out the window, making eye contact with him. One corner of her mouth turned up in a half smile that shook Josh to his core. Then she turned to look at the Josh of 2009. Josh watched himself grasp Isabella's hand and intertwine their fingers together. The elderly man edged over and placed one hand on his shoulder. With the other hand, he held his wife's hand. In turn, she positioned her free hand on Isabella's shoulder. As their mouths began moving, the aura around them grew, and suddenly, it was as if Josh was back in the cottage with them all, hearing every word they prayed that evening. He closed his eyes and allowed himself to bask in every word prayed over them that night.

His eyes blinked open as soon as he heard the word *amen.* "I...I think...did we encounter angels unaware that night?" He sat in disbelief and awe.

The tantalizing smells of roasted lamb and cannoli rolled past him, lingering around him as the waitress rounded the corner and entered the cottage. His hands shook violently. Dropping the menu, he clenched his fists and stared at them, seeing six hands shaking before him. He kicked the stool out from under himself and fell back against the brick wall. Muffled voices echoed in his ears, and the colorful lights draped over the cobblestone path seemed to rush across the villa, streaks of colors blurring in their wake. He placed the heels of his hands over his eyes, hoping to regain some semblance of normal vision. Stumbling, he made his way back to the street. He shoved his hand in his pocket and pulled out the token. The number 21 floated to the surface of the moonstone, and then it disappeared into the gem as quickly as it emerged.

Crossroads

11

The Path to Love

Azalea Manor

2021

The sun inched its way across the heavens, moving westward. Josh held his hand above his brow and squinted, staring at the late afternoon sky streaked in burnt orange and purple hues. As the sun dipped closer to the horizon, Josh studied its proximity to the land and figured the time to be near five in the afternoon. He had just traveled back in time, witnessing a star-filled night, and now, he was in the present, admiring an early-evening painted skyline. It amazed him, yet it boggled his mind. As he shoved the coin back into his pocket, he grasped the carving and shook his head to cast off the confusion of the change in time. He pulled his closed fist into his line of sight, unfolding his fingers from around the totem, and searched for the third carving. He immediately cast his eyes to the staircase; he knew it was the staircase at Azalea Manor—the mansion where they were married. He rubbed his thumb over the four-inch hunk of the broom handle and recognized a stark difference in the wood; the first two carvings he used to find his crossroads were missing. He searched for them to no avail, twisting and turning the chunk of wood in his hand. He wondered if it meant the crossroads back to those days and locations had disappeared along with the carvings. Knots twisted in his stomach and pushed their way to his throat, threatening to spew acid and bile on the sidewalk. He couldn't lose his way to her; he simply couldn't. Panic and confusion crept into his mind.

Lurching forward, he darted across the street and sprinted back to his truck. He needed his tux from their wedding day and knew where Tink kept it. He slammed his foot on the accelerator and raced back to their home. The front door slammed behind him as he rushed through the living room.

"Hey, Da—" Ciara stood with her hand in the air (the beginnings of a wave), mouth agape.

Josh shut his bedroom door with a loud thud. He knelt before the cedar chest at the foot of their bed and popped the locking mechanism. The smell of pent-up cedar brushed across his face as the hinges on the lid creaked open. His eyes fell on the black bag holding his tuxedo. Lifting it from the chest, he unzipped the bag to be positive it was, in fact, his tuxedo. From the corner of his eyes, he saw Isabella's wedding dress. His breath caught in his throat, and tears rushed to the surface of his eyes, threatening to spill over.

Josh traced the tips of his fingers over the white satin gown embossed with pearls. Closing his eyes, he pictured their wedding night as they stood on the sidewalk at Azalea Manor, waving goodbye to their children...

The children smiled and waved from the backseat of their aunt's van. Isabella slipped her arms around Josh's trim, muscular torso. Standing together, they watched as the vehicle gained speed, the taillights disappearing into the darkness. Isabella peeked up at Josh. He gazed into her almond-shaped eyes—reflective pools of desire tinged with apprehension. She longed for him, yet nervousness twisted in the pit of her belly. They had waited for this night. Their friends thought it silly of them to hold off until marriage, insisting they were both consenting adults, but Isabella and Josh both desired to lead their children by example. Isabella tilted her head to gaze at the sky. She swept her hand at the expanse of stars. "Isn't it amazing?"

The waxing moon reflected pale light into the atmosphere along with the multitude of glimmering stars illuminating the night. Josh glanced at the sky before casting his eyes upon Isabella. A gentle breeze tousled her long brunette hair, sweeping it across her button-nose and high cheekbones. "It is," he began in a rich, tenor voice, "but it doesn't compare to your beauty."

A smile twitched at the corner of Isabella's perfectly shaped, thin lips. She bit her bottom lip and stared intensely into Josh's eyes. She shifted, facing him, and inched forward, pressing her body next to his. He wrapped his arms around her thin waist. Sliding his hands into the small of her back, he held her tightly. He leaned over and brushed his full lips over her cheek. "Would you like to go to our room now?" he whispered in her ear.

The warm tickle of breath on her ear sent shivers over her body, raising the hairs on the nape of her neck. Their eyes connected; her pupils swallowed her gray irises, and her heart quickened. "Yes," she breathed.

Josh scooped Isabella into his arms and carried her (with her arms wrapped around his broad shoulders) back into the manor. Slipping her slender hands up the back of his neck, she cradled his head, tracing her fingers through his coffee-brown hair. Josh stopped at the base of the stairwell and pressed his lips against Isabella's. Her heart pounded in her chest, and her breathing escalated. Pulling herself free from his embrace, she stooped to the floor at the foot of the staircase and gathered the train of her gown around herself. Holding her hand in his, Josh led the way up the stairs.

Josh unlocked the honeymoon suite and swooped Isabella into his arms again, carrying her across the threshold of their room. He cradled her in his arms and laid her gently on the king-sized bed. She ran her fingers along the contours of his chiseled jaw, admiring his ruddy complexion and smooth skin. *"You're so handsome,"* she breathed, a smile inching across her face. She cast her eyes about the room. *"Can you draw the curtains, please?"* she asked, her voice shaking.

"Of course, sweetheart." Josh ambled across the room and drew the drapes overlooking the balcony. Isabella's eyes followed his movements as he strode to the window, regarding his stature. His muscular chest and abs enthralled her senses. Her heart raced within her chest, and warmth rushed through her body.

A nervous smile inched its way across Isabella's face. She bit her bottom lip (her face blushing) and dropped her feet to the floor. She tiptoed to the dressing table on the far side of the room and stood in front of a full-length oval Cheval mirror, brushing her hair. Tilting her head to the side, she eyed Josh as he dropped his hand from the drape and turned to face her. She wound her hair into a French twist, revealing her long, slender neck. Josh stood at the edge of the bed and watched her, his gaze lingering. She unlatched her pearls and placed them beside the brush on the dressing table. Soft light played over her silhouette. With her back to him, she glanced back at her husband. Her eyes spoke to him without so much as a whisper passing her lips. Josh breezed across the room and slowly unzipped her gown. As it dropped to the floor, she turned towards him, put her hand to his lips, and gently brushed over them with her fingertips. *"I love you,"* she breathed, pressing her lips against his.

A sharp pain shot through Josh's chest as the

memory of their wedding night slipped from his mind. He flicked open his eyes, clutched Isabella's gown, drew it to his face, and breathed deep, searching for the scent of her lingering perfume. "I'll see you soon, my love," he breathed.

The lid of the cedar chest snapped closed with a soft click. Josh threw the black garment bag onto his bed and slid his tuxedo off the hanger. More determined than ever to find Tink, he quickly donned what he wore on their wedding day. He shoved his feet into his dress shoes, grabbed the token and the carving, curled his fingers around them, and shoved them both in his pocket. He snatched his truck keys from the bed and headed for the door. Yanking the door open, he found himself nose to nose with Ciara, her fist raised, ready to knock on the door. Startled, she gasped for breath, jumped back, and yelped, "Ahh...," Her heart hammered so hard against her ribcage that she threw her hand over her chest, senselessly attempting to slow it down. "Shoo, you scared me, Dad."

Josh chuckled. "Sorry, Boogley, I didn't mean to scare you."

The corners of Ciara's mouth turned down as she exhaled her pent-up breath. "Uh...," she uttered, "don't you think I'm a little old for that nickname?" She tilted her head to the side, scanning his attire with narrowed eyes. "What's going on? Why are you wearing the tux from—"

Interrupting her midstream, Josh explained, "Boog...," he started, harrumphing. "Ciara, sweetheart,

I'm simply trying to connect with your mom, that's all."

Ciara folded her arms across her chest, lifted her pointy chin, and arched her brow. "By wearing what you wore when you got married? How's that supposed to help you grieve?" Flustered, she threw her hands in the air. "I'm really worried about you." She furrowed her brow and huffed. "I don't understand what's happening?" Tears rushed to the surface of her emerald eyes, bathing them in a deep pool of frustration and worry.

Josh gently grasped his daughter by the shoulders and peered into her eyes. Her pouty lips and chin trembled. "I can't explain it, not yet, anyway. Don't worry, sweetheart. I'm fine. I truly am." Shifting her petite frame to the side, he added, "But I need to go now. I'll be home in a few hours, and we can watch a movie together. How's that sound?"

With a deep sigh, Ciara conceded, dropping her arms to her side.

Josh parked down the street from Azalea Manor. Stepping out of his truck, he tilted his head, searching for warmth from the sun, but the setting sun and its light disappeared behind the tree line ahead of him. A bouquet of pine intermingled with magnolias and honeysuckle guided him to the wooded area on the back side of the manor. Walking across the paved road, he started towards the woods. He pulled the coin from his pocket and spoke to the moonstone, instructing it to take him back to 2010 when he married Isabella.

The pine trees swayed back and forth, yet the wind did not blow. Woozy, Josh stumbled forward, nearly tumbling onto the pavement beneath his feet. Catching himself, he stooped forward and propped his hands on his knees, allowing the dizziness to pass. Blinking hard three times, he tried to focus on his surroundings. He wondered if he'd ever get used to the swirling maelstrom of time travel. The crossroad beckoned him, drawing him towards it like a strong magnetic force. He gave in to the power of its tug on his heart and followed it into the woods.

Stepping off the road into the tree line, he wove through the trees and undergrowth. Dead leaves and twigs crunched and snapped under his heavy footfalls. Josh blinked twice, adjusting his eyes to the darkness of the woods. The canopy of trees blocked the burnt sienna blend of light, casting purple shadows before his feet. Careful not to snag his tux on the briers, he hiked (slow and steady) through the underbrush. The sun continued its descent, draping the woods with a cloak of dark shadows. Deep orange hues of sunlight pierced through the gaps in the trees here and there, revealing stumps and brambles and giving Josh hints at a path. With every shaft of dim light breaking through the darkness and illuminating his path, he thanked God for His unfailing love and presence.

Josh stepped out from under the green canopy and turned his head from side to side, searching for the path through the gardens to the main mansion. Dusk took hold of the skies, painting the clouds with shades of navy and deep purple. Twining around flowerbeds and bushes, Josh strode through the gardens of Azalea Manor, winding through the rose garden and brushing past rows of gardenia bushes interspersed with hydrangeas, camellias, and hibiscuses. With each step he made toward the old, restored mansion, his feet sank into the cushiony, green carpet of the grassy knoll. Eyeing the white rod-iron bench under the massive oak growing on the hill, he picked up his pace, anxious to see his love. Spanish moss dripped from the hundred-year-old tree's limbs, casting grape-clustered shadows on the grass. Josh made his way to the back entrance. Grasping the knob, he leaned his ear against the door and listened for the sound of the Josh of 2010 stirring around in the groom's dressing room. Being assured the coast was clear, he turned the knob. The door creaked open, and he sidled to the back stairwell.

Slowly inching his way to the second story, he took soft, deliberate steps up the spiral staircase. Tiptoeing down the hall, he stopped at the bridal suite. He glanced around him and eyed the blue irises and yellow calla lilies adorning the mansion. The sweet aroma of the flower mixtures floated through the hallway. Breathing deeply, he inhaled their scent. He grasped the doorknob and hesitated. Leaning his head to the door, he listened for voices in the room. As soon as he was confident the coast was clear, he turned the knob, anxious to see and kiss the woman he loved. He eased the door open and stepped into the room, shutting the door with a soft click behind him.

Crossroads

Isabella stood on the far side of the room behind a dressing screen made of white chiffon. Regarding her features in the full-length mirror, she ran her dainty hands over her bodice, smoothing out the wrinkles in her wedding gown. The light from the wall sconce cast a soft sepia glow over her face. Her gray eyes danced in the subtle light beneath a thick fan of lashes. Her long, brunette hair hung in a curtain on one side of her face. Enraptured by her silhouette behind the sheer curtain, Josh longingly watched her as she primped and readied herself to marry him. A pang of sadness swept over him. *Was this his last crossroad? Would this be his last trip back in time?* Watching her with rapt attention, he pushed aside his thoughts and breezed across the room.

A light breeze of Channel drifted across the room. Josh breathed deeply, inhaling it. Isabella brushed her fingers through her long tresses and turned away from the mirror, approaching the dressing table. She picked up the blue garter and piddled with it. Taking delicate steps, Josh eased closer to her. Approaching her from behind, he slid one hand around her waist and the other over her mouth, and in a hushed voice, he shushed her. Isabella's heart pounded. The blood rushed to her heart, forcing adrenaline through her veins. Her eyes grew wide, and her body stiffened.

Releasing her, he moved into her line of sight. "It's me," he whispered.

Gaping, Isabella threw her hand over her mouth and paused to catch her breath. She tipped her head to one side and scolded him, "What...what are you doing here, Josh?"

Josh wrapped his arms around her waist and shrugged. "I needed to see you."

Isabella rolled her eyes and shook her head. She slipped her arms around his neck. Josh slid his hand to the small of her back and pulled her body next to his. Leaning his forehead against hers, he breathed, "I love you, Tink. Marrying you is the best decision I've ever made in my life. I only wish I had ignored our age difference and that idiot cousin of yours. If I could go back, I'd confront you when you were fifteen and ask how you feel about me."

Tink dropped her head and cast her eyes to the floor. A smile tugged at one corner of her mouth. Blushing, she fidgeted with his lapel and cut her eyes back at him. "Well, if you could go back and confront me, I would hope I would have the courage needed to be honest with you and tell you that I loved you, and if I did, what would you say?"

"I would tell you how beautiful you are, and I would tell you not to be afraid to tell me how you feel, and I would acknowledge to you that we couldn't be together right then because of our age difference, and then I would ask you if you would wait for me."

"I think it would be you needing to do the waiting." Isabella ran her hands down Josh's chest, caressing him.

"Oh, I'd let you know up front that I was gonna marry you when we got older and that I would wait for you to grow up, so all I would need to know is if you would be willing to save yourself for me."

Isabella's heart rate increased. Warmth rushed through her body, and her stomach fluttered. She stretched her arms and grabbed the back of his head. Pulling herself to him, she pressed her lips against his. Their kiss lingered. When she finally pulled herself from his embrace, she gazed into his eyes and breathed, "You better get going. Our wedding is about to start, and the girls will be here soon to help me finish getting dressed."

"Okay, but one more kiss," he said as he cradled her head and drew her lips to his, caressing them gently. Isabella stood with her eyes closed as Josh slipped out of the room.

Josh eased down the staircase. The doorknob to the groom's dressing room twisted. Josh yanked his head toward the sound of its rattle. Muffled voices spoke behind the door. Josh scurried down the hall and hid in the closet, leaving the door inched barely open. The Josh of 2010 stepped into the hallway, followed by his minister and friend, Clay Denison.

"It's hard to believe I'm getting married here, of all places."

"Why's that?" Clay Denison asked, scanning the elegance of the foyer with his eyes.

Josh chuckled. "You might not believe me, but when I was a young man, maybe sixteen or so," he grasped his chin in thought, "Sixteen, yeah, I was sixteen, and I always hoped to be able to purchase this old mansion and restore it to its former glory." He stepped to the staircase and ran his hands down the banister, patting it. "It may seem silly, but I kind of feel like that hope has become a reality, and that's what faith is, isn't it...the evidence of things hoped for?" He shrugged. "I know I'm not the one who did the restoration, but it was done, and that's what my hope was about all along."

Clay Denison patted Josh on the shoulder. "Sounds like a sermon might be brewing in your spirit."

Josh scratched his cheek and nodded. "Yeah, what's weird about it all is I hoped to see a building restored, and it was, and now God is restoring me in that very building I hoped to see made new. He's making my life new and complete for the first time in my life." Tears welled in Josh's eyes. He rubbed his fingertips over them, soaking up the tears.

The front door opened, and a young woman poked her head through the opening. "Hey, guys, I need you two out here for pictures," she said.

The Josh of 2010 and Pastor Denison exited the mansion through the front door. The Josh from 2021 inched the closet door open and peeked through the crack to be sure all was clear. He edged across the room and eased open the back door; it shut behind him with a soft thud. The gardens whirled as he hobbled unsteadily through them. Black and green dots danced before his eyes, and the world around him spun into darkness as he tumbled into the woods. With a backward glance, he watched the mansion twist and turn, the colors of the shutters shifting back to the colors of 2021. He clung to the trunk of a tree as the spinning vortex came to a halt. Still woozy from the pull of the crossroad, he curled his fingers around the smooth chunk of wood that once held

Crossroads

the etchings of his three crossroads.

The Detour

The Intervention

Ciara eyed Josh Jr. as he peddled his bike to his friend's house. Cutting her eyes to the left, she watched the taillights of her stepdad's truck disappear down the road. The mask of composure she held her face in as she saw her stepdad off on his *'date'* with her deceased mother crumpled. The front door closed with a loud clunk. She brushed her fingertips under her eyes, wiping away the hot tears stinging her cheeks. Inhaling a shuddery breath, she gathered herself, marched into the kitchen, and grabbed her cell phone from the countertop. With the swipe of her finger, she dialed Londyn's number.

"Hey, Sis," Londyn answered, her voice muffled and her cheeks puffy from the chunk of pizza she chewed. Swallowing hard, she asked, "How's dad?"

"Not good, El...you need to get over here now. Please," she begged, her voice breaking into sobs.

Londyn took a swig of root beer and smacked her plump lips. "I'm leaving now, but it's an hour's drive."

"Okay, I think Caleb should be here too." Ciara lifted the lid of the crockpot to check the roast.

"Oh, umm...okay..." she paused, "it's that bad, huh?" Her round face fell, feeling the weight of the worry heavy in her heart.

"I'm afraid so." The crockpot lid clanked as she replaced it. "Oh, I'm making one of Mom's roasts, so come hungry."

"Too late," Londyn said, raising her brows and widening her eyes. "Just finished a pizza, but I'm sure Caleb will scoff it down. See ya in a bit."

"See ya soon," Ciara responded. She tapped the phone, hung it up, and immediately dialed her brother's number.

Caleb hung up the phone with his sister; his tall, lanky body loped across the room. Pulling his suitcase from under his bed, he tossed it on the cedar chest. Snatching clothes from his closet, he quickly freed them from their hangers and shoved them in his suitcase.

"Dude, where you going?" his roommate asked.

Shaking his head, Caleb flung open a drawer on his

chest of drawers and snatched up a pile of shirts, socks, and underwear. "I've gotta get home. That was my sister. My stepdad hasn't been handling my mom's death...apparently at all."

"Didn't you guys just get together to try and encourage him that he isn't alone or something?" the short, stocky guy asked.

Caleb shrugged. "Yeah, the church made a big meal on the anniversary of her death; we all got together and ate and hung out. We did that all because we knew he wasn't moving on. It's like he's stuck, but this is worse. My sister just said he's pretending she's still alive."

His roommate's eyes grew wide. "Wow, that...that sounds serious." Glancing out the window, he pondered what Caleb had told him.

Caleb zipped his suitcase and set it on its rollers. "Hey, man," his roommate started. "Isn't denial a part of grief? I mean, I never lost anyone close to me, but it seems like Mrs. Pilkington taught something about that in my psychology class." He shrugged. "I'm no genius or anything...my grades clearly reflect that," he said, chortling, "but maybe you should google grief. See what you find."

Caleb stopped and stared at his friend, his almond-shaped eyes heavy and weary. With a curt nod, he replied, "Thanks, I'll do that. I hope that's all it is, but in the meantime, my sister is going out of her mind with worry right now. She needs me. I'll be back before finals."

Ciara stepped onto the porch with her mom's air horn in her hand. The honk blared through the neighborhood. Within two minutes, Josh Junior peddled his bicycle onto the driveway. "Roast is ready," Ciara hollered.

Josh Junior's light-brown hair (drenched with sweat) clung to his head and the sides of his face. At the sound of roast for supper, he sported a huge grin, especially his mom's recipe. When Tink found out she had stage four cancer, she bought an extra deep freezer and cases of canning jars. She spent weeks in the kitchen cooking her family's favorite meals, freezing or canning them. Their pantry was large, and one entire wall (from ceiling to the floor) was made of shelves filled with her cooking, canned and ready to heat. Josh Junior knew his sister had pulled pre-marinated roast (with precise, handwritten instructions from their mom) from the freezer and put it in the crockpot. He dashed through the front door and rushed to the bathroom to freshen up before eating.

Josh Junior jabbed his fork in a carrot and potato; he dipped them in the gravy, shoved them in his mouth, and chomped down. Ciara glanced at him. Making eye contact, she started, "Josh, I need to talk to you about something before El and Caleb get here."

Josh sat up straight and turned his head from side to side. His right cheek protruded like a chipmunk's due to the large hunk of roast he chewed on. "El and Caleb are coming over?" he asked, his voice muffled by the meat and potatoes. He swallowed hard, pushing as much food down his throat as possible. He grabbed the glass on the bar in front of him. Sliding his plump lips over the straw, he slurped down half his root beer.

Ciara placed her hand on his shoulder. Josh Junior noticed the red blotches that tainted her alabaster complexion. Gulping, he asked, "C, is everything okay? Why have you been crying?"

"That's what I need to talk to you about, Joshie. El and Caleb are coming over for a meeting."

"A meeting?" The quizzical look in his eyes wrinkled his forehead.

Ciara nodded. Her mouth turned down in a frown. "Yeah, it's called an intervention. I didn't want you to be thrown off by it because you've been going about life as normal, but Dad's not doing so great."

"What do you mean?" He dropped his fork and turned his chunky body to face her.

"Well, he keeps talking about mom like she's still alive, and when I call him on it, he shifts things around like it's how he is grieving, but I'm worried that it's more than that. Something's not right. I feel it. When Dad gets home tonight, we're gonna talk to him. You don't have to be in the room if you don't want to. He may get upset with us. If you want, you can stay in your room, or if you prefer, you can spend the night with your friend down the street."

Josh knit his brow and looked up at Ciara with his chestnut-brown eyes. His light brown hair tufted around his face. "I don't wanna be treated like a child. Mom and Dad always treated me like a grown-up, so don't start treating me like a baby now. I wanna be there. He's my dad, too."

Ciara dropped her head and sighed. Her waist-length hair slid forward over her shoulder, draping her face behind a curtain of honey-brown tresses. "You're right. I'm sorry, Joshie. I worry about you, that's all. I guess I have been treating you like a child lately." She placed her hand on his shoulder and looked him in the eyes. "Forgive me?" she pleaded.

A small smile crept across one side of his plump, oval-shaped face. "Sure." His olive skin flushed deep mauve.

Ciara grinned, stretching her pouty lips over her narrow face, and tilted her head towards the hall. "Good. Now go get your bath before they get here." She wrinkled her button nose and waved her hand in front of it, suggesting he needed a bath.

Ciara sat, her shoulders slumped, wringing her hands. Her feet bounced up and down on the hardwood flooring of their living room. Londyn inhaled a deep, clearing breath through her long, thin nose, slowly releasing it as she sat next to Ciara on the couch. With a click, the doorknob turned. Caleb fidgeted with the pictures situated on the mantle, straightening them. His freckle-smattered nose and cheeks flushed at the sound of the door opening. Wide-eyed, Josh stood with his hand on the knob. He turned his head, looking from one child to the other, and gulped twice as he shut the door.

Flummoxed, he cleared his throat. "Hey...guys. What's going on? When did you two come into town?"

Londyn straightened her broad shoulders, making her stance firm. Swallowing the lump forming in her throat, she started, "Dad, we all came together tonight because we're worried about you."

Josh waved his hand distractedly, shooing her. "I'm fine, El."

Londyn's gaze flashed to Ciara. Her shoulders slumped, the wind being taken from her lungs. She widened her eyes (raising her eyebrows quizzically) and shrugged. Caleb inched to the couch, seating himself—his posture rigid. Ciara nodded as though she understood her sister's signal.

Anxious, Ciara leaned over her knees and tapped her fingers on the coffee table in a nervous rhythm. "Huh Huh..." she cleared her airway and mustered the courage she needed. She sat up ramrod straight and squared her shoulders. "Dad...you've been talking about Mom like she's still alive, and you're going on *dates* with her." She stretched forth her arm and pointed her hand towards him. "I mean, come on...you're wearing the tux you married her in. Did you go to Azalea Manor?" she asked, her voice quivering from nervousness.

Josh frowned at Ciara. "I told you earlier that this," he swept his hands over the tuxedo he wore, "is my way of grieving over her," he said. With gentleness in his tone, he corrected her; nevertheless, he enforced his seriousness with the intense glare of his piercing gray eyes.

Caleb and Londyn exchanged amused looks. Arching his thick, bushy eyebrows, Caleb chimed in, "I know neither El nor I have been here, but Ciara has filled us in on a lot of odd stuff, and we think she's right."

Nervous, he changed positions on the couch several times and shook his head back and forth in bewilderment. "Will you sit down here with us?" He patted the empty spot on the couch.

With a curt shake, Josh huffed and rolled his eyes. Folding his arms over his chest, he paced back and forth over the floor on the opposite side of the room, refusing to sit. His eyes flared. The yellow flecks in his gray eyes seemed to glow with anger. He whirled around and shot Ciara a warning glare. She shrunk back under his intense stare. "I'm shocked at your behavior. I've done nothing to deserve this kind of treatment. For crying out loud, my wife died, and I'm sorry if it upsets you, but I have found hope, faith, love, and purpose at every crossroad I've been to, but don't worry..." He shook his finger at them. The blood rushed to his face, turning it crimson in color. "I think tonight's crossroad was the last one anyway," he spewed all the anger and frustration roiling in his belly.

Tears rushed to the surface of Ciara's eyes. She buried her face in her hands and sobbed. Londyn fumbled through her purse and pulled out her cell phone, typing crossroads in the search engine. "What's a crossroad, Dad?" she asked.

Josh Junior wiggled back into the armchair and hid behind two large throw pillows. Cutting his red-rimmed eyes towards his daughter, Josh rubbed his face with his hands and sighed. "Huh, you'll think I'm crazy."

"No, we won't," Londyn responded. *We're already wondering about that*, she mouthed.

Throwing his hands in the air, he spit, "A wormhole."

Ciara's wet face popped up out of her hands. "What do you mean a wormhole?"

"You know, a wormhole, a portal," he threw his hands out in front of him and shrugged. "Y'all watch Sci-fi stuff. It links you to a place and time in the past. You know...time travel." Josh inhaled a deep breath and blew it out (hard), suggesting he had given up. "I've been seeing your mom—as in—I've been going to our crossroads and traveling back in time and seeing Tink." He pulled the coin and the chunk of wood from his pocket. "This is how it works." He held up the piece of the broom handle and twisted it in front of them. "It used to have carvings, but they're gone now. I think they disappear after the crossroad is used up or something. There were three of 'em, but I actually went back in time four times. I didn't have this when I found the first one." He rubbed his forehead. "I don't know if there are any more, but I'm going to try to find 'em if I can." He paced back and forth across the room. Harrumphing, he added, "The fact that I found the first one without the totem...it gives me hope that there's more out there."

Josh found the courage to look at his children. Londyn dipped her head in thought. Caleb shook his head in bemusement while raking his fingernails through his sideburns. Ciara sat, mouth agape and eyes wide. Tears streamed down her porcelain cheeks.

Anger rushed through Josh's veins as he realized his children thought him insane. He snatched his keys and stormed out of the house, slamming the door behind him with a loud thud. Anger and denial battled for his thoughts as he stalked back and forth next to his truck. Wheeling around, he slammed his fist into the truck door and screamed!

Ciara shifted gears, putting her body in motion, and scrambled to her feet. Pacing back and forth over the living room floor, she cried, "Do you guys see what I'm talking about now? We have to do something. He needs help."

The Winding Road
The Journal

The full moon cast a dim light on the fist-shaped dent left in the door of Josh's truck. Clutching his injured hand, Josh cringed in pain and gritted his teeth. He shook his hand and hollered, "Great! Just great!" with a clenched jaw. Climbing behind the wheel of his truck, he sped off with no idea where he was headed. All he knew was he had to find another crossroad. Thrumming his fingers on the steering wheel, he scanned his mind for the memory of his talk with Chadok in the cemetery. Chadok explained crossroads—significant moments in life—to him that day.

159

Crossroads

He combed through memories of their life together. "That's it. Our honeymoon. That was as significant as you can get." Gripping the steering wheel, he swerved onto the Interstate ramp and headed to the small cottage edging the bay in Fair View. As he drove over the bridge, he stared at the night sky. Cirrus clouds streaked across the purple heavens, hiding any glimmer of starlight, yet the full moon lit the road ahead of him.

Josh parked in front of the reception lodge and entered. He exited with the key to the cottage they stayed in on their honeymoon. Twirling the keys around his fingers, he stepped onto the wooded path that led down to the bay. When the light of the lodge disappeared, he pulled out the token and called, "Two-thousand and ten." Laughter echoed from around the bend in the pathway. He quickly ducked away into the trees lining the sandy walkway.

Watching from the tree line, he eyed four teenagers turn onto the path from the branch that led to cabin two. Waiting for them to pass, he leaned against a sturdy weeping willow, being sure to keep still as stone. As soon as they passed, he lurched from the woods and took the last leg of the walk at a sprint, confident he would find a crossroad at their honeymoon cottage. Slamming into a root stump, he stumbled forward. Righting himself, he faced the white, sandy shoreline of the bay. He darted for the cabin door, the keys jangling in his hand. Racing from one room to the next, he searched for Tink, but the cabin was empty. A wooden wall calendar hung next to the front door. His face fell, his mouth turning down in a frown, as he eyed the month of April and the year 2021. Despondent, he slammed the door shut behind him as he rushed towards the bay. His thick chest rose and fell in quick, heavy heaves as he stopped at the water's edge. Hot tears stung his almond-shaped eyes. A deep groan surged forth from his belly. Bending over, he collapsed to his knees in the wet sand and wept. "Take me back, God, please," he cried.

Josh buried his face in his large hands and wept. The water lapped merely two feet in front of him. Scrambling to his feet, he dusted off with as much dignity as possible. He straightened his back, drawing himself to his standard height, and raised the moonstone to the moonlight for examination. Squinting, he searched for the number 10 in the gem. "Twenty-one? No, no, this *has* to be one of our crossroads!" he yelled. "This is where we spent our honeymoon." He folded his hand into a fist, enclosing the moonstone in his palm. "This place is important." He shook his fist. "Why isn't it working? Did I only get so many shots at it? I don't understand," he spit, curling his plump lips. "Please, God, please," he begged through a clenched jaw.

Morning sunlight peeked through the blinds in Josh's bedroom. He yawned, stretched, and dropped his feet to the floor with a thump. He glanced at the nightstand and eyed a notepad with a list of possible crossroads scribbled across the front page. Each possibility had been scratched off the list. He had spent the last week searching (to no avail) for crossroads at every possible place of significance for the two of them. He made several trips to the cemetery searching for Chadok without as much as a peep from him. He had nearly given up hope. Dropping to his feet, he strode across the room and opened the blinds, allowing unfiltered sunlight to bathe the room. A starburst of light glimmered on Tink's nightstands; Catching Josh's eye, streaks of color created a rainbow on the wall. Curious, he ambled to the nightstand and found her diamond earrings in a handmade trinket box Londyn had made for her on their first Christmas together as a family. He picked them up and held them in his cupped hand.

Dropping the diamonds back in their home, Josh tugged on the draw of her nightstand and found a red, glittery gift box the size of a large shoe box. Lifting the lid, he rooted through the colorful gift-wrapping paper and eyed Isabella's journal. When he flipped open the diary, he landed on Thanksgiving of 2019:

November 28, 2019

Jesus, today is Thanksgiving. It was silly of me to write that sentence since You know everything. I'm thankful for so many things in my life. You have given me the perfect husband and family. I am blessed beyond measure, but I feel overwhelmed and anxious and flat worn out. I know I'm probably being ridiculous, but I'm scared. I don't feel well, and I know I'm getting older, but I lost all the weight I had gained, so I thought I'd feel better and have more energy, but something is not right. I can feel it. I believe that something is not right in my body. I'm going to make an appointment, but I don't want to worry my husband. I'm sure it's nothing, and I'm probably just being a little paranoid. Anyway, enough of my ramblings. Thank you for the wonderful life you've given me, God.

Mrs. Joshua Parker,

Isabella

Josh flipped the page.

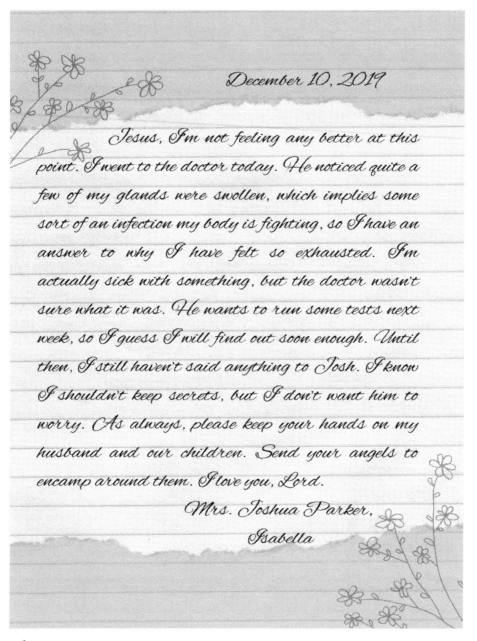

December 10, 2019

Jesus, I'm not feeling any better at this point. I went to the doctor today. He noticed quite a few of my glands were swollen, which implies some sort of an infection my body is fighting, so I have an answer to why I have felt so exhausted. I'm actually sick with something, but the doctor wasn't sure what it was. He wants to run some tests next week, so I guess I will find out soon enough. Until then, I still haven't said anything to Josh. I know I shouldn't keep secrets, but I don't want him to worry. As always, please keep your hands on my husband and our children. Send your angels to encamp around them. I love you, Lord.

Mrs. Joshua Parker,
Isabella

Why didn't she tell me," he said, his voice breaking as he turned the page.

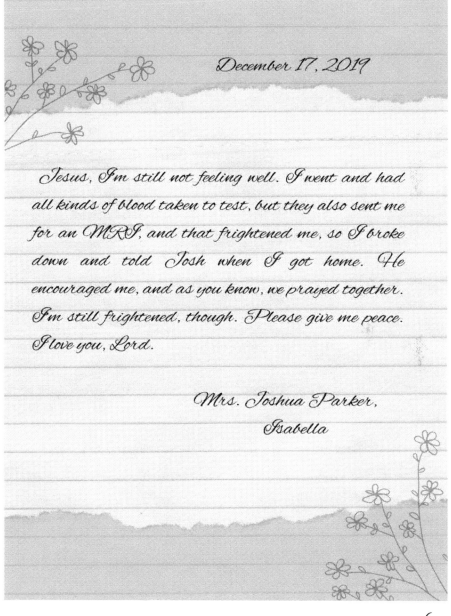

December 17, 2019

Jesus, I'm still not feeling well. I went and had all kinds of blood taken to test, but they also sent me for an MRI, and that frightened me, so I broke down and told Josh when I got home. He encouraged me, and as you know, we prayed together. I'm still frightened, though. Please give me peace. I love you, Lord.

Mrs. Joshua Parker,
Isabella

Crossroads

Josh thumbed through the pages and landed on January 15, 2020. He remembered the day without having to look at what she had written...

Small, round spice bowls covered Josh's side of the prep counter. Filling them, he precisely measured each seasoning for his pineapple chicken, Tink's favorite recipe. He longed to do something within his power to make her feel better and rescue her from the quicksand of depression she had fallen into; he hoped to at least make her smile with her favorite dish. She had struggled with depression, stemming from worry over her health for the last couple of months. Unable to make her physically well, helplessness had been eating away at Josh. He was anxious to do something to make her feel better, so he opted for his Pineapple chicken; it always made her smile. During their kitchen wars show, she quickly conceded that he made the best!

As he cut the chicken into small cubes, Isabella's phone rang. "It's the doctor's office," she said as she pressed the green phone on her screen. Her hand shook as she brought her cell phone to her ear. "Hello," she answered, swallowing the lump rising in her throat. The shaking in her hand increased, and her face blanched, all the color leaving her face and extremities. "I understand," she mumbled, pulling the phone from her ear. Unable to hang it up, she stared at it as it shook in her palm. Her knees gave out from under her. Josh abandoned his project and raced to her side, wrapping his arm around her to catch her.

Holding her steady, he took the phone from her and gave her his undivided attention. "What is it? What's wrong?" he pressed.

Isabella glanced up at Josh with a blank stare, her face pale. "They...they didn't say." She inhaled several quick, shuddery breaths. "It's bad, Josh. It must be. They want us to come to the office at 4:00 today for the results. They emphasized both." She covered her mouth with her dainty hand and whimpered. "Oh, Josh, I'm scared. They want us both there. That's not good," she cried. Hot tears rushed over her ivory cheeks.

Josh closed his eyes and pulled Isabella to him, holding her tight. She buried her head in his chest. "It's gonna be okay," he breathed. "I'll be right there with you, Tink."

Josh held her until her crying subsided. After what seemed an hour, she pulled herself free and dried her face with her hands. "I'm going to get dressed," she sniffled.

Sterile white walls surrounded Josh and Isabella. A stream of classical piano music trickled into the atmosphere through surround-sound speakers anchored in each corner. Josh sat on the edge of the waiting room chair and gripped Isabella's hand. Despite the peaceful sensation intended by the music, Isabella rocked her torso back and forth over her knees in a nervous rhythm. A lonely-looking lady sat on the far side of the room, her face solemn. A scarf covered her round head, and deep, dark circles edged her green eyes. She clutched her purse to her chest and stared at the floor. As the day came to a close, Josh, Isabella, and the lonely woman sat silently in the waiting room. The persistent tapping of Josh's foot against the blue-mottled ceramic tile echoed through the room. Isabella glanced around at the sterile white walls surrounding her, closing in on her like a funhouse. The waiting was driving her mad. Another fifteen minutes passed, and then they were alone in a room filled with only their thoughts and the sounds of Beethoven. Neither of them dared speak any of the words inundating their minds.

The door creaked open, and Nurse Barbara, a tall, big-boned woman, stepped into the room. Her short, gray hair lay against her head in tight curls. She glanced down at the clipboard cradled in her arm and then looked across the room, her brown eyes landing on Isabella. "Mrs. Parker, if you two will follow me."

Josh stood to his feet, stretching forth his hand for Isabella's. He helped her to her feet, and they walked hand in hand into the hallway. Nurse Barbara guided them down a long hallway to the doctor's office. Isabella had never been in the doctor's actual office before. Her eyes skimmed over the room, and she gulped, swallowing her pent-up nervousness before crossing the threshold. She proceeded through the door being held open for her and inched her way to the chair, seating herself—her posture rigid. Josh settled in the seat next to his wife, scooting in next to her. As the arm of his chair butted against hers, he grasped her hand and squeezed it tight.

Isabella tilted her head to look at her husband. The soft music pervading the room twisted in her ears, turning dark and loathsome. A dreadful feeling sank to the pit of her stomach; despite the ghastly churning in her innermost being, she tugged on the corners of her lips and forced a smile. Josh smiled wanly and squeezed her hand again. It was the only way he knew to say he was there without using his words. He wasn't certain words were something he could manage to say at that moment in time. He feared that if he opened his mouth to say anything, all that would come forth would be cries. Tapping out the rhythm of one of their favorite hymns to play and sing together, Josh drummed the fingers of his free hand against the arm of the chair—despite the classical music permeating the office.

Isabella felt the sickness invading her body more and more daily, sucking the life force from her. They both sat (silently awaiting the doctor) and braced themselves for the news. Dr. Whitman shut the door behind him with a soft click. He eased across the room and sat in his high-back, leather chair. His short, blond hair was neatly combed back. Scattered gray hair had been hidden under mousse, attempting to cover their presence and conceal his age. Remarkably, his smooth, fair skin hinted at youth. Isabella had only seen Dr. Whitman a few times, so she was unsure of his age, but his weary eyes expressed the field of oncology and the long hours he worked.

"It's been a long day, as I'm sure it has for the two of you," he said, tugging open his desk drawer, "so let's get right down to why I asked you both to come in." He shot his blue eyes across the desk at Isabella. A slight smile in his eyes gave her hope. As soon as he made eye contact with his patient, he shifted his eyes to the stack of

files scattered over his desk.

He pulled out a file and thumbed through it, his eyes turning grave. Isabella swallowed hard, pushing down the hard knot forming in her throat. Dr. Whitman deeply inhaled and looked across his desk at his patient, this time locking his eyes with hers. Squirming under his sincere gaze, Isabella shifted in her seat, inching her way to the edge. With his free hand, Josh reached across and grabbed her arm.

Dr. Whitman grimaced. "Your test results came back this morning, and I wanted to get the two of you in here as soon as possible. Isabella," he started, his eyes shifted from hers to Josh's and then back to hers, "you have an aggressive form of pancreatic cancer. If we begin treatments immediately, I can give you a month or two longer than without it." He sighed and prepared himself for the maelstrom of questions sure to follow his statement, but (rather than a barrage of questions) silence engulfed the room.

After several minutes of muted silence, Dr. Whitman broke the quietness. "Mrs. Parker," he called, leaning over his desk and locking his eyes onto hers, "did you hear what I said?"

Isabella nodded as though she understood, but her mind struggled to piece the doctor's words together in a way that made sense. She blinked twice and glanced at the floor, folding her bottom lip over her straight teeth and biting down. Her dazed eyes skimmed from the floor to her shoes to the window on the far side of the room. Finally, she lifted her head, her gaze falling on the doctor. She formed words with her thoughts and opened her mouth to speak to them, but they stuck in her throat. She swallowed hard, freeing the words caught in her throat. "You…you just told me I'm…I'm going," she gulped, "to die."

Dr. Whitman nodded sympathetically. Isabella's face crumpled. Tears threatened to push past her resolve. Awareness punched Josh in the gut, knocking the wind from him. Frantic, his eyes darted from Dr. Whitman to Isabella. He shot out of his chair, sending it screeching over the wood flooring, and hollered, "No, no! I can't accept that. I won't."

Isabella stood and stretched out her arm to grab her husband. Her legs protested and buckled. She threw her hands behind her and reached for the arm of the chair to catch herself. Josh caught her before she made it into the chair. "Are you okay?" he breathed.

Isabella nodded. "I'm okay, I'm okay. My knees buckled. I'm just…I'm overwhelmed, is all."

Dr. Whitman cleared his throat. "We need to discuss treatments before you two leave. If you are going to do it at all, it needs to be started immediately."

Isabella plopped down, the doctor's announcement knocking her back in her seat. His words wrapped around her throat like a massive hand strangling her life from her, leaving her breathless. Gurgling, she grasped her throat and gasped for air. She buried her hands in her face and nodded, mumbling, "Okay." Lifting her head, she dropped her hands to her lap, her arms limp. She quizzically furrowed her brow. "Okay, you said I would have a month or two more with treatment?" she asked, her voice frail and breathy.

"Yes." He nodded.

Isabella rubbed her forehead with the tips of her fingers, working out the tiny knots forming under the surface of her skin. "I need to think about it for a few days. I'll let you know." She dropped her hand to her side, stood to her feet, pulled her shoulders back, lifted her chin, and headed for the door. "Thank you, Dr. Whitman. I'll be in touch."

Isabella set her purse next to her nightstand and slipped off her shoes. Josh tiptoed in behind her and shut the bedroom door with a soft click, emptying the contents of his pockets on his nightstand. Isabella tilted her head at the sound of the door, glancing over her shoulder at her husband. Settling into the darkness of their bedroom, she put her hand to her lips and exhaled a deep breath. She felt like the air in her lungs had been pent up since sitting across from Dr. Whitman. She stood at the edge of the bed wordless—unable to speak, her expression unreadable in the darkness. She had held her composure, but now that she found them alone in their room, a single tear fell onto her freckled cheek. Josh tentatively edged his way around the bed and came up from behind her. He slipped his arms around her waist and pulled her torso next to his, holding her tightly. A torrent of hot tears stung her eyes, pouring from them. Wordless, he held her as she wept.

After several minutes of profuse sobbing, Isabella breathed in a deep, shuddery breath, wiping her hand over her tear-soaked face. Longing to speak words of comfort to her, Josh searched his heart for the proper expressions. His lips parted, but his throat closed, strangling his voice. He swallowed hard. His eyes roamed, scanning the room as he struggled to free his voice from his clenched throat.

Finally, clearing his throat, he pushed past the invisible vice grip around his neck. "Sweetheart, you're exhausted. Let's lie down for a little bit and take a much-needed nap. Neither of us can think straight right now. We need to rest." Isabella turned her body around and into his embrace. "I'll snuggle up with you." He traced his finger down her petite nose. Smiling, he cradled her head in his hand and gently pressed his lips against her forehead. "I love you."

Isabella smiled weakly, turned, and signaled for him to unzip her dress. The dress slid over her hourglass figure. As her dress hit the floor, she climbed into the bed and snuggle into the pillow. Josh slipped off his shoes and crawled in beside her. Draping his arm around her shoulder, he cuddled up close and closed his eyes, drifting off to sleep.

Minutes turned into an hour as Isabella lay in the bed curled up next to her husband. She listened to the cries of the train rushing through town. Just as she nodded off, the horn blared once again and jolted her awake, her eyes blinking wide. She lay curled in her husband's arms for another hour, scanning the room with her eyes. Her mind rifled through its files—searching for a way to organize the things she had to do before she could leave her children. Sleep eluded her. Fear of them growing up without her plagued her thoughts. She wanted to stay awake for the remainder of her time and relish every second she had left. Eternal sleep would come soon enough. As she lay awake thinking about her prognosis, she knew she wanted to enjoy the remainder of the time she had with her family. Treatment meant extreme sickness, and the reward was merely a month longer in this world, but it would be a month of doctor's offices and vomiting and her hair falling out. She would be too sick to enjoy the time she had left. No, she wanted to forego treatment and make every minute count.

Josh shook the memory of that day from his mind. Tears moistened his eyes. He turned the pages and read the entries over the three months after Isabella received the devastating news of her impending death. In those three months, she planned a second honeymoon, insisting Josh pretend it was nothing more than simply a second honeymoon. They spent a week together, just the two of them, in the Cayman Islands; it was something she had longed to do for years. As soon as they returned, they planned a family vacation to Tennessee during the Mardi Gras holidays since Caleb would have time off school. Isabella insisted they wait until they returned home to tell the children the news of her sickness. She wanted happiness during their trip. Once they were home, she spent an entire week in the kitchen cooking meals; she canned most of them and froze the remainder.

She labeled them all: *with love, Mommy Awesome.*

By mid-March, Isabella grew weak but insisted on one last trip to Tennessee with Josh, Ciara, and Josh

Junior, just the four of them. Despite the frailness of her body, she overflowed with joy during their outings on that trip. She gave Josh a list of things she desired to experience before leaving this world, and he fulfilled those wishes. A smile inched its way across his face as he read her musings from their last trip together. She had jotted down details he had forgotten about the trip. Chronicling each day in vivid detail, she described the aromas of the food she savored, the bouquets of nature she drank into her senses as they hiked through the mountains, the sounds of the water rushing towards the falls, and the music of the birds as they sang their love songs one to another.

Josh flipped the pages of her journal, accidentally going too far forward onto blank pages. He backed up to her last entry on April 16. A tear rolled down his cheek as he remembered the first blank page...

On April 17, Isabella woke up unable to lift her head to get out of bed. Josh creaked open the bedroom door to check on her. She opened her weary eyes, dark circles beneath them, and smiled wanly.

"Can I bring you some broth?" he asked.

"No," she mouthed, shaking her head. "My hair," she breathed. Josh made his way around the bed. Her hair was mussed up on one side from the length of time in bed.

Holding a wooden, soft-bristled brush, Josh exited the bathroom, shutting the door with a soft click. He had purchased the brush so he could pamper her and keep her hair soft and silky. He lifted her to a seated position, surrounding her with pillows for support.

Crawling into the bed behind her, he sat upright and worked the brush through her long tangles. "I'm going to miss this," she whispered.

Josh forced a smile past his pain. Tears stung the edges of his eyes, but he held them back and gently pulled the brush through. She winced with each stroke of the brush through her hair. Isabella tilted her head to the side, stretched her hand to grasp his, and gazed into his eyes. "Do you love me?" She breathed.

Josh set the brush on the bed and turned his wife's body to face him. He gently stroked her chin and lifted her head; their eyes met. "You know I do." He gently caressed her lips with his.

With each labored breath, Isabella counted the seconds, willing them to stretch in length. "Will you help me to the bay window?"

"Of course." Josh slid his arms under her and lifted her from the bed, setting her feet on the floor. He secured his arm around her and helped her to walk across the room to her favorite reading and writing spot.

She grabbed the cushioned bench built within the window and pointed towards her nightstand. Josh stepped in the direction she pointed. "Now, I want you...to get something...for me," she started, her breathing ragged. "I've been writing...my whole life, and...I want to share...it with you...I want you to have...all of it—" She gasped for breath. Her knees buckled, and blackness consumed her. Josh raced to her side and caught her before she hit the floor. "Oh," she breathed. She lifted her trembling hand

and traced her fingers over the side of Josh's face. The corners of her mouth turned up. "My hero. You're so...handsome." She inhaled a shuddery breath. "I've made so many...mistakes in my life...marrying you...was not one of them. Death...will not stop...me from...loving you." Her hand went slack and fell to her side. She inhaled a ragged breath. Releasing her spirit, she breathed out her last breath.

A pool of tears flooded Josh's eyes, spilling over the dams created by his lids. He pulled Isabella's body to his and wept. "Tink, no!" he wailed.

Crossroads

14

The Dirt Road
The Diary

Josh closed the journal and cradled it to his chest, weeping. "This is what she was trying to guide me to..." His voice broke into sobs. "She wanted me to have all her writings, her journals." He wanted to kick himself for allowing a year to pass before searching through her nightstand. "How could I not open this drawer until now? You're such an idiot, Josh," he fussed at himself.

When his crying subsided, he set the journal on the bed and ran his hands over his wet cheeks, soaking up his tears. Tilting the box, he dug past the layers of gift paper and found two five-year diaries, one pink and the other purple. Each diary sported a small envelope taped to the front. Josh picked up the pink diary. He pulled the envelope free, tugging on the tape. Dumping a small set of keys and a folded note into his cupped palm, he shook the envelope over his hand.

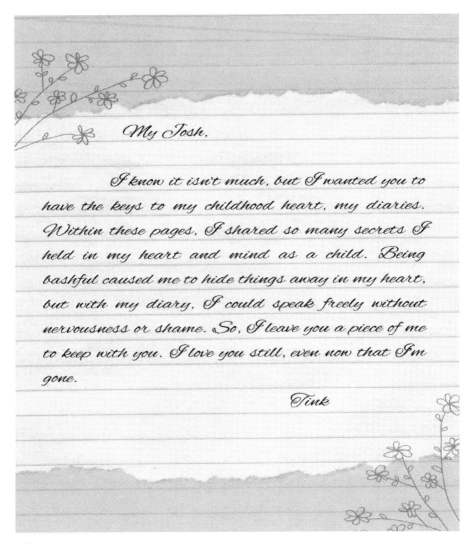

My Josh,

I know it isn't much, but I wanted you to have the keys to my childhood heart, my diaries. Within these pages, I shared so many secrets I held in my heart and mind as a child. Being bashful caused me to hide things away in my heart, but with my diary, I could speak freely without nervousness or shame. So, I leave you a piece of me to keep with you. I love you still, even now that I'm gone.

Tink

He opened the note and read Tink's address:

His hand trembled as he slid the minuscule key into the keyhole of the pink diary and twisted to the left. With a click, the latch sprang open. Josh dropped the ring of tiny keys back into the envelope and lifted the cover of Tink's diary. A smile twitched at the corners of his lips as his eyes skimmed over the first page.

Josh combed his eyes over the page, tracing the childlike handwriting with his fingertips, and smiled. Paging through the diary, he read her daily thoughts and dreams, each beginning, *Dear Diary*.

Dear diary...

Febuary 6, 1989

Dear Diary,

Today is my birftday. And my mommy and daddy got me u. I am happy to tell you all kinns of cool stuf me and Daniel get to do.

Tink

Dear diary...

March 24, 1989

Dear Diary,

Today I almos died! It was scary. Me and Daniel walked down the road to see Ms. Stevson. She is realy nice. A car almos hit me. But a nice man save my life! I got scratches from being throwed in the dich, but I am ok. Before almos dieing I road my bike to Joshs house to see if he was going skating. Aunt Ruth said she wood take us if he wood be there to wach us. He said he would keep an eye on us, but we had to make a deal. I wisht he wanted to couple skate with me. But he shoed me a trick. I laid on the skate floor and he skated fast and jumped over me! He is the best skater in the hole world! Waching Josh skate was the best.

Tink

Josh read page after page of Tink's heart as a child. It was filled with daydreams of him. She spent nearly the entire summer of '89 at her Aunt's home, so each day of June and July was filled with her walks and bicycle rides to his house to see him. She wrote how she watched him skate his heart out every Friday and Saturday night over that summer.

Dear diary...

July 29, 1989

Dear Diary,
Tomorow I go back home and get redy for the first day of school. I love school. But I don't have manee friends. Just two. Me and Daniel went skating again tonight. Josh did so many cool tricks. I really wisht I coold skate like him. His momma told me his name is Joshua Caleb. Itin it so pretty Diary?! I wisht he wood merry me. But I am not pretty. So he want. Diary, I wisht you coold make wishtst come true! You know wat Diary. I am going to name my first boy Caleb after him even if he never merries me. Waching Josh skate was the best, but a mean boy pict on me and made me cry. He runed my hole nite. Diary, you and Daniel are the only ones I will evar tell. It is our secrit.
Tink

Tink

♥'s

Josh

183

Crossroads

Josh spent hours reading through the five-year diary, covering her life from age nine to thirteen; he must have read every entry five times. He closed his eyes after reading each day's events and imagining her tiny frame running around doing everything she had written. Throughout the pages, she shared her love for him with her diary. Gasping and throwing his hand over his mouth, he blinked in surprise as he read her heart's desire (even as a little girl) to one day marry him. She had told him she named Caleb after him. While he knew that, reading her words in her little-girl handwriting made his heart swell with so much love he could barely contain it. A grin lingered on his lips as he flipped the pages back to her first mention of going to see him.

Stringing his thoughts together, he formed a plan to use her diary as his guide to her crossroads. He now understood why their honeymoon had not functioned as a portal back in time. Crossroads were those places and moments where choices were available, choices that had the power to lead the traveler down a different path. Their honeymoon, along with the other moments in time he attempted to travel back to, was a time when choices had already been finalized; there were no crossroads, no new decrees to be made at them, so he decided to use Tink's desires as a child and find those moments she wrote about in her diary to take him back to those places and convince himself to approach her. She clearly wrote her heart's desire in those moments. Yet, her bashfulness captured her tongue and held her lips closed on the matter, so if he could talk himself (the Josh from those moments) into seeing her as she would become in the future and not as the child she was in those years, maybe she would choose a different path, one that led to them always being together.

Josh stood in his parents' driveway and pulled the token from his pocket. Thumbing it across his fingers, he opened the pink diary to March 24, 1989. He closed his eyes, inhaled a deep breath, and spoke to the moonstone, "March 24, 1989." *Being more precise should help*, he thought to himself.

Opening his eyes, he stood stock-still, awaiting the inevitable dizziness that always accompanied time travel, but it never came. He turned his head from side to side, scanning the yard and the road for signs of change. He stepped to the edge of the drive, the paved road still beneath his feet, and craned his neck to peer down the street in both directions. Eyeing the road sign at the four-way crossing, he envisioned Tink rounding the corner on her yellow bicycle, his first trip back in time emblazoned in his memory. Without a thought, he started for the four-way stop, turning right onto McMartin Road. The wall of pines edging the road swayed as a gust of wind swept through, the trees shifting in odd ways. Limbs shrank back, pulling themselves towards their trunks like Stretch Armstrong's arms would slowly inch back to their normal position. The wind squalled and whirled around Josh, kicking up a large wisp of red dust, flurrying in a massive whirlwind around him. Woozy, he stumbled forward and found himself on all fours, his hands buried in a thick layer of red dirt.

Josh shook his head and tried hard to focus, shuffling his feet under himself to stand. Laughter floated through the air. Josh smiled, recognizing the voice. He started forward, briskly hiking toward the sound of Tink's voice. Sprinting onto Westley, he eyed two short figures at the end of the road and heard familiar giggles echoing in the distance. He increased his pace, his feet pounding on the hard, red clay. As he drew near to the two children, Tink skipped towards Royce Road. Daniel tagged along in her wake, pestering her and pulling her ponytail.

The dusty road climbed over a small, steep hill. The roar of a loud engine revving blasted from the east end of Royce Road. Josh recognized the noise as that of a sports car. Simultaneously, a memory burned in his thoughts; Tink almost died that day. She had written about it in her diary. A rush of adrenaline coursed through his veins, his heart pounding in his chest as he leaped to full speed. Inhaling deep, rapid breaths, he blew them out with such force that the intake of oxygen seemed to work as fuel for his body. Tink froze in the middle of the dirt road as the red car headed straight for her, swerving like a drunk driver. Josh lunged from the side of the road and reached out deftly, snatching her tiny frame and slinging her to the ditch. Tink let out an ear-piercing scream. The car's front end clipped Josh and flung him to the opposite side of the road. His head slammed into a rock and gushed blood.

The car slid into the ditch, pulled back out, gained speed, and disappeared down the road. Hurrying away, the driver spewed a thick cloud of red dust behind the car. Daniel raced to Tink's side, screaming and crying for help. She twisted onto her side and pushed herself to a seated position. Covered in red dirt, grass, and spatters of blood, she propped her arms on her raised, scuffed knees.

With a sidelong glance, she furtively cut her eyes across the road to the man lying unconscious. "Daniel, is he...dead?" Her chin trembled.

Looking in all directions, Daniel teetered across the lumpy road to the body left for dead by the Mustang. Beads of perspiration dewed at his temples. His heart pounded in his chest. As he drew near to the man's body, his stomach twisted into a mass of knots. Acid churned in his belly and threatened to spew forth. He stopped in his tracks and hovered over the man. Tink winced as she crouched forward and stood to her feet. Worried about the man who saved her life, she edged past Daniel. She stooped over the man, fearing his unmoving and bloodied body to be dead. She poked the man's face, but he didn't budge, so she laid her head on his chest and searched for a heartbeat. She exhaled, relieved the man wasn't dead.

"His heart's beating." She lifted her head and cast her eyes on Daniel. "Where's your canteen?"

His eyes grew wide, darting from side to side. "I...I think I dropped it."

"Go find it, please." She knit her brow.

Daniel jogged to the other side of the road where

they were just before the car nearly killed them. Plopping to his knees, he dug through the verdant growth that edged the road and sloped into the ditch. Grasping the canteen, he raced back to Tink's side.

"Squirt him," she insisted, her eyes going wide.

Daniel stood over him and flipped the canteen upside down. Water doused the man's face and chest. He jerked his head from side to side, spitting and gasping. Tink knelt down, inching her face closer and closer to the man's. Josh opened his eyes; a young girl's blurry face hovered over him. Blood rushed from his head, making him dizzy beyond the normal dizziness associated with time travel. As the young girl drew closer to Josh, everything slid back into focus. He noticed her gray eyes glimmering in the sunlight and her nose and cheeks smattered with sun-kissed freckles.

He rapidly blinked several times and groaned. "When am I?"

Tink raised her brows, her forehead wrinkling. "You're in Oak Ridge on Royce Road. You saved my life, Mister."

Josh reached for his head, rubbing his fingertips over the massive knot on the side of his head. Blood oozed onto his hand. "My head."

"You hit your head after the car hit you. You threw me outta the way, but it hit you." Tears rolled down her freckled cheeks. Tink narrowed her eyes and looked at the man, a question forming in the back of her mind. "You were at Josh's house earlier today, weren't you?"

Josh rubbed his eyes and pinched the bridge of his

nose. "Yeah, yeah, that was me," he said in his thick, tenor voice. He pushed himself up to a seated position. His head pounded like a hammer slamming into the side of his skull.

"What's your name?" Tink asked.

"My name is Jo…" He pressed the heel of his hand against the side of his head, "John," he stuttered. Josh pieced the events together in his mind, his eyes going wide as he realized the person driving the car was apparently drunk. "We should call the police." He scrambled to his feet and shoved his hand in his back pocket to fetch his cell phone. Blood dripped down his neck onto the front of his shirt. "Huh," he screeched at the sight of it. Pulling his Android from his pocket, he eyed the black screen and pressed the "on" button on the side of the device.

"What's that?" Daniel asked, knitting his brow.

Josh pressed the blank screen repeatedly. Realizing cell phones didn't exist yet, he folded his fingers over his phone and sighed. "Nothing. It's just a piece of junk now," he murmured. He shoved it back in his pocket. "Did either of you happen to see the license plate number on the car?"

Tink and Daniel stood ramrod straight, wringing their hands, and shook their heads no. "Oh, man," Josh muttered, grabbing his head. "My head is still bleeding."

Daniel slipped his t-shirt over his head. Wadding it up, he handed it to the man he knew as John. "Here, press this on it."

Josh smiled a half-smile. "Thanks, Daniel."

Daniel knit his brow. "How'd you know my name?"

Josh pressed past the pain of the pounding in his head to scan his mind for an answer to how he would know Daniel's name. "Ummm...I'm friends with Josh's dad. I was there when Tink came by earlier. She mentioned you." He shrugged his shoulders. "I just assumed."

"Oh, okay." Daniel rolled his eyes and shrugged back.

"Look, you two need to get home and get her doctored up. I'm going to find a phone and call the police."

Tink pointed in the direction of Mrs. Stevenson's house. "Mrs. Stevenson lives in the pink house down that road. She's nice. She'll let you use her phone."

Josh gazed at Tink, thankful she was safe. "You take care of yourself, Tink. You're a special little girl." He squatted in front of her and placed his hands on her shoulders. "And I know something I think will make you a happy little girl." A playful grin stretched across his face.

Tink's eyes brightened. "What's that?"

"Josh likes you." He winked at her.

As he walked towards Mrs. Stevenson's house to call the police, the realization that he was the man who saved Tink's life hit him. She had written about him in her childhood diary, which he had just read earlier that day, so he had already traveled back even then. He wondered if he could convince his younger self to marry her. Though he hoped to change the past, he doubted his power to alter time. As he strolled down the street and pondered the irony of it all, his head spun again; the trees blurred and slid out of focus. The red dirt road disappeared as time reverted back to 2021; the surrounding landscape changed as lanky saplings shot up, growing exponentially as their trunks expanded and their limbs stretched their massive arms over the verdant fields.

A stab of regret twisted in his gut as he realized she had slipped from his grasp once more, but he comforted himself with the victory of finding one of Isabella's crossroads. If choices concerning the direction one took in their journey were necessary for a crossroad to exist, he wondered what Tink's choice had been all those years ago.

What was it about that day that created a crossroads in her life? Had he always been destined to travel back to that day to save her? Did he already tell her that the Josh of that time liked her? Was that the pivotal decision she faced? Was Tink's choice at her crossroads about what to do after discovering he liked her? If he had already said those things to her in the past, she apparently decided not to be with him. Their lives had taken them down paths that separated them rather than bringing them together as children, but Josh was determined to do everything in his power to change that. He might not be able to get Tink to change her directions, but he could use her crossroads to get to himself and convince himself to wait on her.

Crossroads

15

The Wrong Turn
The Lies That Bind Us

Josh's head throbbed as he hobbled back to his truck. He pressed his hand gently against the side of his head and winced, blood oozing onto his hand. "Ahhh," he spit. "I really got hurt back there? And the injury followed me back to 2021?" he questioned, glaring at the blood dripping down his hand. Envisioning the driver of the red Mustang, he narrowed his eyes and clenched his teeth, his jaw working under his florid skin. Anger roiled in his belly like lava churning just before a volcanic rupture. "In my opinion, there's no statute of limitations on nearly running over a child. I will find out who you were and make you pay," he growled.

Inhaling a deep breath, he reined in the rage growing within him, settling his spirit and bringing the furious fiend inside him into submission. He had a more pressing issue at hand. Revenge (and even justice for drinking and driving and nearly killing a child) needed to be placed in the back of his mind, so he whispered a prayer for strength to keep the angry beast at bay and thrust the vivid images of Tink nearly dying to the back of his mind. Turning onto McMartin, he pondered the complexity and challenge of the dilemma now facing him.

"It worked. It worked! Tink's diary worked as a guide to her crossroads, but I was already...oh, oh, oh, I was actually already there! I've already traveled back in time. That was me she wrote about in her diary. I'm the one who saved her. Wait a minute...so, when I used my crossroads, had I already traveled back to those times as well?" His eyes widened as the reality of what had happened hit him. "That's why Tink was counting and saying something about my shirt at The Trail, and that's why my lemonade was already ordered at Vita Sapori, and on our wedding day, that's why she told me it's bad luck to see the bride before the ceremony. I was always meant to do all of this, and I must've told her my name was John even then because Tink never mentioned a man named Josh saving her. It's like she never knew the adult me saved her life that day."

He picked up his pace, lengthening his stride. "But, then again, she was only eight years old. She may not even remember what the man looked like. Wait a minute...since it's already happened, I've got to figure out how to make actual changes. I mean, if I already told her that Josh likes her, that information obviously didn't cause her to take a road that led to us sooner, but there's no way to know for certain that I did tell her that before, but I'm going to assume I did tell her Josh likes her. These are her crossroads, her choices, but I'm still there. I'm there at her crossroads, and if I've already had encounters with her, I can find a way to have encounters with myself by using her crossroads," he rambled on and on. "Geez, I feel like my brain is saying the same thing over and over. I've gotta get my head wrapped around all of this. I'm beginning to wonder if the future can be changed!"

Josh stopped in the middle of the street and craned his neck, taking in the vast differences time had created in his surroundings. Watching things change and grow slowly over nearly thirty years was nowhere near as startling as seeing the fields sparse with trees morphing into dark woods within minutes. His mouth dropped, agape, at the stark differences. "No, no, he argued with himself. Chadok told me that day in the graveyard that different paths could be taken at crossroads. That has to mean that the future can be changed. He even gave some sort of warning about it, didn't he?" He questioned himself, pressed the heel of his hand against the laceration on his head, and cringed; a knot pushed hard against his scalp, throbbing beneath the surface.

"Okay, I'm going to keep following Tink's crossroads, but I *need* to find a way to interact with myself." Josh rubbed the back of his neck and breathed hard before continuing, "But so many time travel theories say you mess up the space/time continuum if you interact with yourself, but I *have* to do it in order to change things. Tink's heart wants to marry me, even at the sweet age of eight. She's not going to turn down a different path at any of her crossroads; it's me (my younger self) who needs to be able to see her as my future. She already sees me as hers; she just doesn't have the confidence to tell me how she feels. I have to be the one to take the path that makes her wishes come true. I'll be careful not to let the teenage me touch me. I think I saw a movie that showed something about (if that happens) the two selves merging as one or something." He shook his head and threw his hands in the air, debating himself. "I don't know if it's real; I mean, two weeks ago, I would've told anyone saying they traveled through time that they were crazy, but I know it's possible. I've done it, so even if I don't know if that's real or not, I can't take a chance on it. I'll keep a certain distance, but I've gotta form a relationship with myself, or how else will I convince myself to marry her?" He rounded the corner onto Milner Drive and jogged to his truck.

Josh fired up the engine of his blue truck. It sputtered to life. He flipped the A/C knob on and cranked it up, cooling off the muggy cab. He cut his eyes to the pink diary lying in the passenger seat. Grasping the diary, he reclined his chair and opened the diary back up to Tink's entry for the day he just returned from in 1989.

His eyes skimmed over the day's events; everything remained the same. Flipping the page, he read through several accounts of her time during the summer of 1989. He turned the page to July 29, 1989, and read, "Watching Josh skate was the best, but a mean boy picked on me and made me cry. He ruined my whole night. Diary, you and Daniel are the only ones I will ever tell. It is our secret. Tink," he read her account of the events that day. He jabbed the inscription with his pointer finger. "This, this is it. Isabella told me she was picked on as a child, but she never told me about this particular instance, and I don't remember anything about it from that night, so I need to get back there and make friends with myself and be certain that I see what's going on." He shook his head and threw his hand in the air. "I know me, and the thirteen-year-old me always got into fights at school defending those picked on by bullies. If I would've had an inkling of a clue that Tink was being harassed and I was there, I would've beat the snot out of that bully." He tugged on his shirt and eyed the blood. He knew he couldn't head straight for the crossroad; he had to go home and clean up. It would seem odd if he showed up at the skating rink with a bloody shirt and a bleeding head.

Josh pulled in his drive and braced himself for the onslaught he expected his children to unleash upon him. Here he was coming home sporting a busted head and blood-spattered clothes after they recently pulled him into an intervention. He couldn't tell them what really happened, but they had raised their children to be honest, even if the honesty hurt.

"I can't; I can't do it." The father in him surrendered to the panic-stricken, time-traveling Josh.

Inhaling a sharp breath, he grabbed the pink diary, climbed out of the truck, shut the door behind him, and headed for the front door. His mind raced with stringing thoughts like puzzle pieces that fit on varying boards—the ends never matching up. Conflicted, he stiffened his shoulders. The keys jangled in his hand as he unlocked the door and let himself in the house, hoping and praying the children had made themselves busy.

Josh Junior met him at the door, nearly plowing over him. "Dad, Dad, Londyn's here. Londyn's here," he screeched. "She's staying the whole weekend and said she'd take me to practice driving tomorrow if it's okay with you."

Londyn rounded the corner from the children's side of the house. She smiled at her dad. "I'm bunking with Ciara for a few days. It'll be like old—" Her eyes flew wide open, and her jaw dropped (mouth agape). "Dad, what happened to you?" she yelped. "You're bleeding."

She rushed to his side, stretching her hand out to turn his head and examine his injury. He winced and pulled back as she touched the egg-like knot on the side of his head. "What happened to you, daddy?" Her chin trembled, fear of losing another parent gripping her heart.

Cringing, Josh grasped her wrist with his hand, pulling her away from his wound. "It's nothing. I was working down at your grandparents' house, and I tripped. Hit my head on somethin' hard." He swallowed hard, pushing down the lump of truth forming in his throat.

Londyn wrinkled her nose and inspected the gash. "I'd say. You sure did a good job of it."

She dropped her hand and started for the pantry. Isabella kept a fully stocked first-aid kit in the pantry. Londyn had utilized it on many occasions when she lived with her dad and stepmom, and she needed it more than she liked to admit when she was home for visits while in college and even after she graduated. She had a knack for clumsiness. She hated to admit to her ungainliness, but her moral standard bound her to honesty, and being honest meant she had to readily admit she fumbled the carving knife frequently, slicing herself every week. Her dad encouraged her to focus her artistic abilities on the less dangerous side of artwork, like pottery and painting. She loved them both, but pottery left her with several burns, and painting ended with having her eyes flushed out on more than one occasion. Paint in the eye hurt, so Isabella made sure to equip the first-aid kit with an eye cup and a bulb syringe, and Londyn had kept them frequently employed as an essential part of the kit.

Londyn patted the barstool, signaling for her dad to be seated. He plopped down on the stool, his shoulders slumped. She pressed the cold pack against the growing knot on the side of her dad's head. "I know I'm the last one with any right to ask anyone to be cautious, considering how I'm always hurting myself," she said, her eyes tearing, "but please, Daddy, please be careful." Her chin trembled, and her voice broke. "I...I don't...think...I could handle...losing...you." Tears rushed to the surface of her eyes, pouring onto her blotchy, red cheeks.

Josh sighed deeply and grasped her hand, pulling the pack away from his head and holding her hand in his. "I'm sorry, pumpkin. I promise I'll be more careful. It was just a little slip off the ladder. I'll wait until Caleb is in town to do any more ladder work and get him to help me, okay?" He glanced into her red-rimmed eyes and wiped the tears from her plump cheeks.

Londyn nodded infinitesimally. Tears continued to spill onto her cheeks. Josh brushed his thumbs over her face, soaking up the deluge of tears flowing. "I'm okay, sweetheart."

"Okay, daddy." She sniffled and chuckled. "I guess it's a good thing Caleb is moving back in for a while, huh?"

Wide-eyed, Josh sat up, shoulders rigid. "Caleb is moving back in? When did this come about?"

"I thought you knew. He said his professors let him take his finals early, and he withdrew from his summer courses. The Dean was supportive of his decision. He told him he could move back into the dorms for the fall semester." Londyn narrowed her eyes and tilted her head to the side. "He didn't mention it to you already?"

Josh dropped his head and pinched the bridge of his nose. "No, no, he didn't say anything," he mumbled, shaking his head. With a deep sigh, he stood. "I'm gonna go get cleaned up, sweetheart. I love you, pumpkin." Turning on his heels, he started for his bedroom. Just as he reached the threshold of his bedroom door, he halted and glanced back at her. "After I get cleaned up, would you like to go for a coffee with me? We can go to our old hangout on Old Ridge Road."

The corners of Londyn's lips turned up. Her smile stretched to her eyes, brightening them. "That'd be nice, dad."

Josh shut his bedroom door behind him, dropping Tink's diary on his neatly made bed. He picked up the framed 5x7 of the two of them and Ciara and Josh Junior from their last vacation together. Isabella wanted to go whitewater rafting. She had never been, and she wanted to experience the thrill of the rapids before she left the world, so the four of them took a memorable trip to Tennessee and booked a rafting trip down the Upper Pigeon River. The picture was perfectly timed, with water splashing over them. The huge smiles on all their faces made Josh tear up as he gazed at the image before placing it back on the nightstand. He stripped off his bloody clothes and donned a clean shirt and a fresh pair of jeans.

The aroma of Columbian Supreme coffee filled the seating area of a small coffee shop nestled between a bookstore and a ladies' boutique. Hints of the strong fragrance swept across the outdoor patio each time someone opened the door. Josh pulled the metal stool out from under the small table; it screeched across the patio pavement. Much of his daddy/daughter time with Londyn had been spent at Cup of Life Coffee Shop. It had been a while since they visited their favorite spot, and they needed a little time together.

Londyn sat across from her dad with her mug of coffee. Glancing up at the star-filled sky, she smiled. "So, what's your mug say, Daddy?" She leaned over the table, her long, thin nose hovering just above the steaming mug, and breathed in the rich aroma curling its way into the atmosphere. "Mmmmm...." She hummed.

Every mug at Cup of Life had a different wise saying about life or a scripture engraved on it. Josh and Londyn always started their visitation by reading and discussing the quotes. "'Honesty is the first chapter in the book of wisdom.' Thomas Jefferson," Josh said. He gulped and shifted his eyes to the ground. A tight knot formed in his throat, and the sharp pain of guilt stabbed his heart. He swallowed hard against the lump in his esophagus and cleared his throat. "So, what's yours say?"

She cast her large, round eyes on the mug. Clearing her throat, she read, "Sometimes we need someone to be an angel in our lives and to bring us a ray of hope." Schledia Phillips, *Plain Jane.*

"I like that one," Josh said. A half-smile slid across his face.

"Me too!" Londyn exclaimed, her crystal-blue eyes beaming. "I think Thomas Jefferson was saying (if we look at wisdom as a book and that book is filled with chapters) it takes every single chapter. Otherwise, wisdom isn't complete; it's missing pieces. That book must begin with honesty, so he's saying honesty is the foundation of wisdom. If you think about it, Dad, it's what you and

Isabella taught us. I guess that means you're at least as smart as Thomas Jefferson," she said, chortling and winking.

"Well, not too shabby. I'll take it." He winked back and grinned. "And the saying on your cup, I have to say that God has recently shown me that He can do just that. He can bring someone unexpected into our lives as an angel who gives us hope in our darkest hour."

"So, you feel like you have some hope again?" Her eyes picrced through his. She stretched her arm across the metal table and gently placed her hand on her dad's, folding her fingers around his palm.

Josh ever so slightly lifted his prominent chin. "Yes, I do. I know it may sound crazy to you kids, but I have found a way to keep your stepmom's memory alive in my heart, and it helps me."

Yanking her arm back across the table, Londyn sat ramrod straight, inhaled a deep breath (slowly releasing it), and rolled her eyes. Tisking, she asked, "Are you talking about all that nonsense stuff about time travel you mentioned last week?"

Josh's shoulders slumped. He sat silent for a brief moment, gagged by the white lies he'd been speaking in order to be with Tink again. Shifting his eyes to the table, he glanced at the saying on his cup of coffee. He quickly processed the importance of the foundation of honesty to wisdom, weighing it against having Isabella back in his arms. The white lies wrapped around his body and bound him to repeat them for the sake of his love. Realizing honesty, in this particular situation, led to being labeled insane and possibly being institutionalized, he made a swift decision that a white lie, in this instance, was the wisest decision he could make.

"No, sweetheart, that's not what I'm talking about. Look, I was angry and grieving last week and a little out of my mind." He exhaled a deep breath before righting himself, his back straight as a board. Bracing himself, he began, "I found her journal and read it. It may seem silly to y'all, but I go to the places where she was when she made her entries. I read her words and envision her there at that moment, so it's kind of like I'm traveling back in time to see her. My mind is back there in those times. It's my way of seeing her, talking to her, and simply being near her."

Londyn sighed. "Okay, Dad," she conceded, shaking her head. "I understand; I do, and I'm happy you've found a way to get through all this, but you can't be mad at us for worrying about you. She was our mom, and we lost her too." Tears pooled in her eyes, and light from the lamppost cast flickering star-like light in her tears. "She was more a mom to me than my own, and we all want her back."

A thin layer of tears glazed over Josh's eyes. A shaft of yellow light from the lamppost sent a wave of ripple caustics over his gray irises; the yellow flecks in his eyes seemed to sparkle. "I know, sweetheart. I know. I guess I've only been thinking of my own grief lately. I'll do better. I promise."

The front door creaked as Caleb pushed it open. A

swarm of gnats and mosquitos hovered around the doorway, hugging the porch light. Loaded down with several bags (and pulling his suitcase), Caleb crossed the threshold and announced, "I'm home for the summer!"

Caleb's voice echoed through the house. Josh Junior yanked his head up from the comic he was reading and tilted his ear to the right. Recognizing his brother's voice, he pounced to his bedroom floor and raced to the living room. "Caleb!" he yelled, sprinting across the room.

Caleb held his hand up for a high-five. Josh Junior leaped in the air as he neared his big brother, their hands slamming against one another with a loud splat. "Dude, you're so awesome. That one burned good," Caleb insisted, wincing. "Dog gone...that burned." He shook his hand as if it would cool the sting. "Where's C?" he asked through clenched teeth.

Josh Junior shrugged. "I don't know. I guess she's in her room. Londyn is here for the weekend, too, but she's out having coffee with Dad. She's gonna take me to practice driving tomorrow. Wanna come?"

Caleb scrunched his face and shrugged his shoulders. "Nah, I don't think so, not tomorrow."

Josh Junior's face fell into a pout. "Oh," he mumbled under his breath, his shoulders sagging.

"What's wrong, buddy?" Caleb asked, patting him on the shoulder.

"It's just...we have church on Sunday and family dinner after that, and I don't know...if I don't get to spend any time with you tomorrow, I won't get to hang out with you before you're gone, is all."

Caleb knit his brow. "Dude, I'm not here for the weekend. I'm here 'til the end of summer. We have plenty of time to hang. I just need a day to myself, okay?" His eyes met his little brother's chestnut-brown eyes.

"Okay." Josh Junior nodded. A smile stretched across his face, brightening his sad eyes.

"Alright, now, before I hit the sack, I need to talk to C." Caleb fist-bumped his brother and strode back to Ciara's room, knocking on the door.

"Come in," Ciara called.

The doorknob clicked as it turned, and the door creaked open. Caleb poked his head in the opening. The fresh scent of crisp linen breezed past Caleb's face. The difference between a girl's and a boy's room was stark. His sister's room was bright, light, airy, and smelled wonderful. He thought back to his dorm. It always smelled like dirty socks. He kept his dorm tidy, but he never could figure out how girls managed to make their rooms so fragrant. "I can't believe you didn't hear me when I came into the house."

Ciara sat on her bed with her legs crossed, bopping her head to the beat of the music playing in her earbuds. She pulled them from her ears and grinned at her brother. "What was that?"

Caleb rolled his eyes and shook his head. "Nothing. Can I come in?"

"Of course," Ciara said, patting the spot beside her on the bed.

Caleb plopped down beside her. "How's he doing?" he asked.

Ciara's smile faded. She sighed. "A little better, I think. He's out with Londyn for coffee, so that's good." She glanced up at her brother. "She said your professors let you take your finals early. That's great."

Caleb dropped his head and stared at the lavender carpet. "I lied, but it's just a little white lie." He blushed. "I couldn't be there any longer. I needed a break, and you guys needed me here." He lifted his head, their eyes meeting. A rush of guilt washed over him. He cut his eyes to the bed and picked at the purple ribbons woven in her comforter. "My grades were all high enough to take the loss. My GPA will reflect it, but I'll bust my butt next semester to start bringing it back up."

Ciara tilted her head to the side, furrowing her brow. "Caleb, what'd you do? We would've been okay."

He turned away from his sister; his eyes pooled with tears. "I know. I'm sorry. I feel horrible, but Dad can't know. He's already at a breaking point. He doesn't need to be disappointed in me on top of everything else. I've been telling myself that a little white lie is no big deal, but it doesn't feel any different from a big lie. A lie is a lie, but I've already said it, so now I'm bound to it." He sighed, closing his eyes.

Ciara turned her mouth down in a frown and placed her hand on her brother's, pulling his fingers away from the ribbons in her comforter. "I won't say anything," she started, "it's not my place, but you should pray about telling Dad the truth. Yeah, he'll be mad, but I think he'll understand. We've all been through a lot over the last year, and asking you to keep on with college at this point is a little much to ask. You need time to grieve over Mom just like the rest of us, and with everything going on with Dad, well, it has us all up in arms, freaking out." She scooted closer to her brother, wrapped her arms around him, and whispered in his ear, "Please tell me you'll pray about it."

The lie he had already told slithered around his chest and tightened itself like a boa constrictor, forcing his lungs to close. Unable to breathe or speak, he nodded and pulled away from his sister.

Josh pulled into the drive, throwing it in park. Londyn turned to open the door. Her hand released the knob as she glanced back at her dad. She picked up on the fact that the engine was still running. "Dad, are you coming in? It looks like Caleb's home."

Josh thought through his response, the lies he had already spoken binding him to keep them intact. "Not right now, sweetie. Before I go to bed, I need to go and spend some time with Tink. I'll be back soon. I'm just going down the road to the place she mentioned in her next entry. That's all."

"O...okay, dad." The corners of Londyn's mouth turned down. Josh read the disappointment in her countenance. "Go spend some time with her," she continued. "And tell her we all love and miss her, okay." She feigned a smile and opened the door. Climbing out of the truck, she turned back and looked her dad in the eyes. "I love you, daddy. You'll always be my hero." She shut the door and started for the front door.

16

The Road Less Traveled
The Rink

Stars flickered in the dark sky, and the waxing moon cast a blue hue onto the road. The hum of the truck engine hypnotized Josh. Frogs croaking and an owl hooting drew him back to his senses. His eyes grew heavy. He made a right onto Deer Track Road. He followed the narrow, winding road until it branched off to the left, creating a Y. Crickets joined the frogs, singing their nightly symphony; their voices filled the truck cab with their country lullaby, breaking the monotony of the persistent thrumming of the engine that sought to lull

Josh to sleep. He took the left fork and drove to an enormous metal building. Turning into the parking lot, he passed the Oak Ridge Country Cookin' sign. The empty parking lot was dark. A single streetlight illuminated the entrance into the parking lot with a faint yellow glow shining onto the black pavement of the street. The beams from his truck's headlights shined onto two darkened floodlights mounted onto the front of the building above the double front doors. The restaurant had closed for the evening, so he knew his timing to be perfect for time travel back to the skating rink from his childhood. With no customers in the restaurant, he needn't fear disappearing through the moonstone's portal in front of witnesses. He shoved his hand in his pocket and retrieved the token.

Holding the moonstone in his cupped palm, he spoke, "Take me to July 29, 1989." Worried the truck may hinder the portal from taking him back in time, he climbed out, placed his feet firmly on the black asphalt, and shut the door with a soft click. His head spun, sending him off kilter. He sought his balance and resisted the urge to close his eyes. He wanted to witness the portal for himself, to see every step of his travel back to 1989. His previous travels were mainly spent attempting to end the spinning in his mind and keep himself upright, giving him a glimpse here and there of the changes taking place around him as the wormhole opened and thrust him back to different years. The ground beneath his feet shifted. Attempting to catch himself, he stepped forward with one foot and glanced down at the asphalt as it shifted and broke apart into pebbles. Throwing his hand out to balance himself on the hood of his truck, his hand squashed into what felt like putty. He cut his eyes to his hand and watched as the cobalt blue goo that had once been metal disintegrated and disappeared. Yanking his head from side to side, he searched out his surroundings. The floodlights above the double doors of the metal building flickered on and off and on again, shining down upon a wooden sign just above the doors reading, *Skate World*.

Josh's eyes skimmed quickly over the empty parking lot. Shafts of moonlight lit up the rocky parking lot. As he sauntered to the double doors, small pebbles strewn amongst chunky rocks crunched under his feet. The locked door refused to budge. Tilting his head towards the night sky, he gazed upon the sliver of the moon illuminating the heavens. Stars sparkled against the blackness of the atmosphere. He couldn't remember ever witnessing so many of them filling what he could see of outer space from his tiny spot on Earth. He wondered why he never realized how magnificent the universe appeared from the Northern Hemisphere.

The loud click of the door unlocking let Josh know the skating rink was soon to open. Several cars drove through, dropping off young teenagers. The scent of heavy hairspray brushed over his face as a group of teenage girls pranced past him and headed into the rink. Two lights pierced through the darkness as Daniel's mom, Ruth, pulled into the pebbly parking lot. Josh squinted, cocked his head to the side, and peered through the windshield of the '82 Grand Prix, eyeing Daniel and Tink in the backseat. He slunk back into the shadows (on the side of the rink) and watched them climb out of the car, toting their skates over their shoulders. The roar of a motorcycle grew louder as it approached the parking lot. Josh knew his thirteen-year-old self would be pulling up momentarily. He patiently waited until he witnessed his younger self park his bike and enter the building before he stepped out from the shadows.

The sounds of Duran Duran flooded the rink. Josh crossed the threshold and dove into the music of the past. The melody swept him away, snatching him like a riptide to the depths of 1989. Seeking an opportunity to impress his younger self, Josh tightened the laces on his skates and skated onto the floor. Once he built up the proper speed needed, he spun his body around in a flying leap, landing backward perfectly. He craned his neck to watch for small children and increased his speed. Bending at the waist, he thrust his knees up under himself and twisted his body into a backflip, skidding to a stop as the wheels of his skates hit the hardwood floor.

Tink squealed, "Yee, Daniel, Daniel, did you see that?" She pointed to the adult Josh. "That was amaz...Hey, I think that's John. That's the guy who saved my life! Don't you remember?" She tugged on Daniel's shirt. "Isn't that the guy?"

Daniel narrowed his eyes, looking keenly at the man spinning around the rink like a professional. "I think you're right, and he's even better than Josh."

Thirteen-year-old Josh playfully swatted Daniel's shoulder as he tipped his skates forward and skidded to a stop between Daniel and Tink. "I heard that." He threw his arm out towards the man, palm up. "You can't make a comparison here. He's a grown man. He's had more practice." He folded his arms across his chest. "I wonder if he'll show me how he did that flip?" He skated off and headed straight for his adult self.

From the corner of his eyes, Josh saw his younger self approaching. Inwardly, he congratulated himself on a job well done. He knew himself, so he knew how to draw his own attention.

Thirteen-year-old Josh skidded to a halt next to the adult Josh. "Hey, you're friends with my dad, right?"

Josh nodded. "Yeah, I am."

"What's your name?"

"John."

"You're really good, Mr. John."

Josh folded his arms across his chest to keep himself from sticking his hand out for a shake. A handshake was a natural reflex, but he feared what may happen if the Josh of '89 touched the Josh of 2021. "Thanks. You can call me John. I can teach you a few tricks if you like."

Josh beamed. "Yeah, that'd be wicked!"

Wow, I forgot I used to say that, Josh thought to himself.

Josh instructed his younger self in the sequence he needed to carry out to pull off the backflip. The two of them skated out onto the floor and practiced propelling themselves off the floor until thirteen-year-old Josh managed (at least twelve times) to push himself high enough to pull off the flip. He gazed starry-eyed at his adult self and daydreamed of growing up to be just like the man coaching him.

Adult Josh kept Tink in his peripheral vision, searching for the bully she had written about in her diary. He talked his younger self into taking a break and getting a Coke from the concession area. They chatted about their love of roller skating while they sipped on their drinks. The adult Josh scanned the rink occasionally, spying out anyone who looked like trouble.

Tink and Daniel made their way to the skate floor and practiced skating backward. Marcus, an older boy, jumped and spun across the floor like an amateur figure skater. He whizzed past them and elbowed Tink in the ribs. Cackling, he spit, "Outta my way, freckle face."

Tink grabbed her side and winced, turning on her heels to skate forward. Tears pooled in her eyes, but she fought them back. Marcus glanced over his broad shoulders and looked down his aquiline nose at her. His shrewd eyes bore through her. She squirmed under his glower. Averting his ireful glare, she turned her gaze to Daniel, her eyes growing wide. Marcus kept his eyes focused on Tink as he rounded the rink. She felt his eyes following her, yet she kept her face forward and her eyes straight ahead. The feeling of someone watching her made her nervous. A chill shivered up her spine. The stench of cheap cologne wafted up behind her, growing stronger as he neared them both. She felt tangled in a web she didn't want to be in, trapped like a spider's prey waiting for his approach.

Coming on her again from behind, he skated next to her. His scathing voice snorted, "Hey, Ugly, you and your dorky friend need to give up and leave. Y'all suck."

Tink shrank back from the eyes that tracked her as he skated past. "Leave me alone," she choked out, her throat tightening around her words as she tried to speak to them.

Time-traveling Josh sat across from his thirteen-year-old self, keeping him engaged in conversation. Every few minutes, he cut his eyes to the skate floor to catch a glimpse of Tink from the corner of his eyes. As he demonstrated some of his favorite moves on skates, he skimmed over the rink, his eyes darting from one end to the other. He spied Tink's strained look as Marcus zipped past her and Daniel; worry gripped his heart. His heart pounded in his chest—forcing adrenaline through his veins, but this fight was for his younger self, so he breathed deep and conjured a plan to involve the Josh of '89.

Josh picked up his soda and slurped it dry. He intentionally turned his head towards the skate floor. "Hey, isn't that the girl who rode her bike to your house the day I was there? I think that the boy in the yellow shirt is bullying her. It looks like she's crying."

Slamming his drink onto the table, thirteen-year-old Josh yanked his head to the side, his eyes landing on Tink. He noticed her hand holding her side. His heart hammered against his ribcage, pushing blood that boiled with anger through his body. His hands visibly shook, and his instincts kicked into high gear. He shoved the table and jumped to his feet, landing ready on his wheels. He hurried across the concession floor and jumped onto the wooden skate floor, zipping to Tink's aide on the far side of the rink. Marcus made his way towards Tink, an evil glint in his eyes.

Josh sucked in a hard breath of air through clenched teeth. "Stay away from her," he seethed, his voice gruff and fierce.

Marcus whirled around and threw his arms in the air. "Stay away from who?" He returned to his conquest of jumps on the skate floor, showing off. He landed a turn and skated backward around the rink.

Josh skated up to Tink and Daniel. Gaining her attention, he placed his hand on her shoulder and asked, "Are you okay? Was he messing with you?"

Unable to shift her eyes from his, Tink stood stock still, a captive to his stare. Her heart leaped in her chest. Blood rushed to her face, flushing her cheeks. Forcing herself free from his gaze, she glanced at the floor and mumbled, "Yeah, he elbowed me and said mean things to me."

Anger churned in Josh's blood, scalding his face and ears. Tink lifted her head and stared past him, her eyes going wide. Josh felt a tight grip on his shoulder and yanked around in alarm to find Marcus grinning impishly, his fist flying toward his face. The impact sent him back against the metal railing that edged the skate floor. Marcus took advantage of Josh's position, turned, and cantered away; his chest puffed out in arrogance. As he skated past, he stuck out his arm and smacked Tink in the face. She threw her hand over her reddened cheek, clutching her face, and cried, her hair a disheveled mess. Immediately, commotion enveloped her as Josh sprang to his feet and dove for Marcus. The collision sent Marcus hurling to the floor. Josh flung him over onto his back and climbed on him, straddling his body. He balled up his fists and pummeled his face repeatedly. The owner rushed over and pulled Josh (kicking and flailing) off Marcus and held him in a vice grip. Marcus curled into a ball on the floor and gave a strangled groan.

Daniel and Tink yelled simultaneously, "It was Marcus; it was Marcus. He started it, Mr. Tony."

Mr. Tony released Josh. "What happened over here?"

Daniel and Tink began again, "Marcus hit him—"

"Shush, you two. I'm talking to Josh." He grasped Josh's shoulder and looked him in the eyes. "Why did you jump on that boy?"

Josh cleared his throat. "He was harassing Tink. I told him to leave her alone. He came around and punched me, but then he slapped her. That's when I jumped on him."

Mr. Tony glanced at Tink's red cheek. "That true?"

"Yes, Sir." She nodded. Her pointed chin trembled.

"Alright." He reached down and hauled Marcus to his feet. Dragging him across the floor by his arm, he headed to the front door. He opened the door and shoved

217

him out. "Don't come back," he spit.

Adult Josh grinned as Tink threw her arms around his younger self. Assured he had made the first step in changing their future (bringing them together while they were still young), he untied his skates and carried them to the front. Glancing over his shoulder, he waved bye to himself as he shoved open the front door and stepped out of the rink, preparing himself physically and mentally for the vortex that would take him back to the future. He fumbled through his pocket and retrieved the token. Gravel crunched under his feet as he sauntered across the parking lot. He couldn't help but laugh as the world around him spun in a maelstrom, sucking him back to what was now an unknown future.

17

The Byroad
The Purple Diary

The stars in the night sky shifted and reverted to their original positions on the evening Josh had driven to the restaurant that had once been Skate World. A grin spread across his face as he jogged to the truck that had magically materialized before his eyes as the wormhole propelled him back to 2021. The stench of a stinky grease trap brushed past his face. He crinkled his nose. Rustling leaves caught his attention. He eyed the limbs swaying in the wind, warning of a coming storm. He rolled his eyes at the thought of worry and cast his eyes on the truck door. Opening it, he jumped in, excited to see if he had accomplished his goal of changing the future. The engine roared to life as he turned the ignition. He glanced at the empty seat next to him and wondered if Tink was waiting at home for him. He sped down the back roads, watching the old metal building that had once been Skate World disappear in the rearview mirror.

Multicolored, dim lights flickered in the living room, shining blue, green, and red hues across the white walls. The blue truck idled as Josh watched through the windows as the colors flashed across the living room wall. Apprehension gripped his heart, his chest rising and falling rapidly. He closed his eyes and inhaled a deep breath, slowly releasing it as he turned off the truck. The sound of crickets and cicadas chirping filled the night. Josh mustered up the strength to climb out of the truck and enter the unknown future he had possibly created by changing a simple path at one of Isabella's crossroads. The ramifications of his intervention, while yet unknown, may have made an enormous impact. His heart pounded against his chest in anticipation. Inhaling a deep breath, he ambled across the lawn, fumbling the keys through his fingers in search of the house key.

The front door creaked open as Josh stepped into the darkness of his home. The television lights shimmered through the room, bathing the white fireplace in multiple colors. A cascade of colors tinged the 11x14 wedding photograph of Isabella and Josh that hung above the fireplace. Josh's mouth turned down in a frown as he eyed the picture; neither their wedding location nor their wedding attire had changed. Everything seemed to be the same. He cut his eyes to the bundle of covers on the couch. Hoping and praying Tink lay beneath them, he gently pulled the patchwork quilt back to find Caleb snoring with the remote still in his hand. He slipped the remote from his son's palm and turned off the television. An array of sympathy cards covered the coffee table. His heart sank in his chest; the weight of grief forced all the oxygen from his lungs. His shoulders drooped as he turned on his heels and moped towards the bedroom he now knew to be empty. He hadn't changed anything, at least not anything he could see visibly. They were still married at the same time of year, which told him he had not accomplished getting them together at a younger age by prompting his thirteen-year-old self to fight in her defense, and she was still gone, so cancer had still taken her away from them all.

"Her diary," he whispered, setting his mind to read it through again to see if he could find differences. "Something had to change," he said, insisting to himself convincingly. He had become used to conversations with himself over time travel.

He shut his bedroom door with a soft click and locked it. Plopping down on the edge of his side of the bed, he picked up the pink diary, opening it to July 29, 1989.

July 29, 1989

Dear diary...

Tomorow I go back home and get redy for the first day of school. I love school. But I don't have manee friends. Just two. Me and Daniel went skating again tonight. Josh did so many cool tricks. I really wisht I coold skate like him. His name is Joshua Caleb. It is so pretty. You know wat Diary. I am going to name my first boy Caleb after him. Waching Josh skate was the best, but a mean boy pict on me and made me cry. He tryed to runen my hole nite, but he made my nite instead. Josh saw him hit me, and he beated him up. I wisht you coold make wishtst come true! I woold wisht for Josh to merry me. Diary, you are the only ones I will evar tell. It is our secrit.

Tink

♥'s

Josh

Tears pooled in Josh's eyes as he read her entry. "I changed things. I did. Even her entry is different. She still says she loves me and wants to marry me, but I didn't manage to get her to take a path that would lead to her telling me how she felt; she didn't take a different path. I've got to get the younger me to do something more drastic."

Josh flipped to the next entry, reading her young heart's desire to one day marry him, written in note after note in her diary. Searching for a clue or sign as to why her path never changed, his eyes skimmed over the letters she had written in her diary. His eyes shimmered with a thin layer of tears, and his heart swelled as he read her entry for May 9, 1993.

May 9, 1993

Dear diary...

This morning, I finally gave in and accepted Josh's invitation to church. My family has never been really big on church attendance, so I've been reluctant to go, but I figured if I ever hope to be seen by him as someone he could date, I should at least give it a try. He said he's been going with his grandma all his life, but he had an experience at church a while back that made God real to him. He seems so different. I've never been in a church that was so happy. Mostly, I've caught the church bus that drives through my neighborhood, but the people there are different. This church was exciting! I don't really understand everything, but I liked how it made me feel, so I'm going back with him next Sunday. I wish I could tell him how I feel, but I'm scared. What if he rejects me? What if he laughs at the idea of it? I don't think I could handle it. It's still our secret, Diary.

Tink

The five-year diary had many changes within its pages, yet none led to them being together. Frustrated, Josh flung the pink diary across the bed; it toppled onto

Isabella's nightstand and knocked over the lamp. Josh jerked his head around at the sound of the lamp crashing to the floor with a loud clatter, glass shattering over the floor. He shook his head in defeat and headed for the shower to wash away the frustrations of the multiple days he had visited in one single day.

Sunlight trickled through the thin slats of the blinds, creating lines of light across the bedroom wall. A sliver of light pierced Josh's eyelids; he squeezed them tight, crinkling them in response to the unwanted invasion. Tink's voice surrounded his mind and whispered, "The purple diary. You haven't read the purple diary."

Josh pounced to the floor and scurried around the room. He came to an abrupt halt as he rounded the end of the bed and eyed the shattered lightbulb scattered over the floor. He hurried to the kitchen to grab a broom and dustpan. He swept up as much as he could and emptied it into a box he labeled broken glass. Pulling the vacuum from the hall closet, he cleaned up the remaining minuscule shards of broken glass. He picked up the pink diary from the floor, folding back the bent pages from his outburst of anger and frustration the previous night. Holding it in his hand, he used his other hand to open the nightstand drawer, pulling out the box it had been stored in by his wife. Slipping it back in, he grabbed the purple diary—a diary he had yet to read through.

The purple five-year diary began on Isabella's fourteenth birthday.

February 6, 1994

Dear Diary,

Today is my fourteenth birthday! I asked my parents if I could invite the youth group from church to my party. They said yes! That means Josh got to come to my party! It was the best birthday ever! Josh gave me a leather Bible with my name engraved in it. It's so beautiful! He's my best friend, but I wish he could see me as more than a friend. Well, maybe one day he will look at me and think I'm beautiful.

Tink

226

Josh read page after page of entries detailing how close the two of them had become after he fought to defend her from Marcus. He became her personal bodyguard, always looking out for her. "Why didn't we marry?" He threw the diary on the bed and pinched the bridge of his nose in frustration. "I made one minor alteration to the past. After that, so many things changed. Before I went back and prompted myself to fight in her defense, she never went to church with me, and we weren't best buddies. If we were that close, why, oh, why did I not marry her? We always hung out together, and we went to church together. What happened?"

Josh glanced at the nightstand (the drawer still hanging open) and eyed a brown leather bible with Tink engraved on it. The edges were bent and worn, showing its age. Tears flooded his eyes, spilling onto his cheeks. He stretched forth his hand and grabbed it, opening it to the presentation page, and read:

This

Holy

Bible

Is Presented to:

Tink

By

Your best buddy, Josh

On

February 6, 1994

Crossroads

"Well, it seems that being best buddies still left me in the dark about her name," he chuckled, drying the tears from his face with his hand. Flipping through the pages, he eyed the pink and yellow highlighted scriptures throughout. Tink had put his gift to great use.

Setting the bible back in the drawer, he slid the drawer shut with a soft click. He fluffed his pillows against the headboard, settled in snuggly against them, and grabbed the purple diary—returning to his investigation. The patter of footsteps and whispering in the kitchen caught his attention. He tilted his head to his door, expecting Londyn or Ciara to pop in at any moment to ask for breakfast, but no one knocked. Shrugging, he opened the diary to where he had left off, turning the page to read the next entry. After reading through a week's worth of letters to Tink's diary, the tantalizing scent of bacon frying seeped through the crack under his door. His stomach growled, tempting him to set aside his detective work for the time being, but he muscled through the craving for bacon, eggs, and grits and continued reading Tink's thoughts through her teenage years. Most of Tink's entries were a few lines here, a paragraph there, and maybe two paragraphs on a day full of adventure, but when he flipped over to September 17, 1994, he noticed the length of her entry was much longer than usual, so he began to read it from the beginning.

September 17, 1994

Dear Diary,

Today was the worst day of my life. The way it began gave me hope, but the way it ended has left me wanting to die!

Josh read Tink's description in vivid details of that day...

⟶♡⟵

Isabella's mom pulled into the Parker's driveway. Tink leaned over and kissed her mom on the cheek. "Thanks for bringing me, Mom, and for allowing me to go out with the youth."

"You're welcome, honey, and you're sure Josh is okay with bringing you home?"

"Yes, ma'am, his dad is letting him use his van; he's taking a bunch of teenagers home tonight."

"Alright, you be safe on that horse."

"I will, Mom." Tink grabbed her fishing pole and tackle box, which her dad bought her, from the back of the truck and headed to Josh's back patio.

Crossroads

Walking through the garage, she approached the door to the back patio. As she turned the doorknob, she heard Josh defending her once again. "Tink is much prettier than Samantha, Dale," Josh said.

Tink's breath caught in her throat. She stopped short of opening the door and stood frozen in time with her hand still clinging to the knob. Releasing her pent-up breath, she inched closer to the door and pressed her head against the cool metal door.

"That's irrelevant. You're eighteen; she's fourteen. She's off limits," he retorted, anger tinging his tone.

"You seriously came over here to get up in my business and tell me who to date and who to leave alone?"

"I've seen the way Tink looks at you, and I know she's going on this church thing with you guys today, so just in case she gets up the courage to tell you she likes you, I'm here to make sure you know to keep your hands off. The age difference is too different."

"What makes you think I don't already know that? I'm not stupid. I'm her friend, and I look out for her. That's it!"

Tink's heart sank at those words, so she focused on what she heard him say when she first walked up—she was prettier than Samantha. She knew Samantha had a crush on Josh. All the girls in the church had a crush on him. He was gorgeous, but he was her friend, her protector. She smiled at the thought of him thinking she was pretty. She rounded the corner as Dale's silhouette disappeared through the back fence.

Tink shoved open the door that led out to the back

patio. "Hey, Josh," she said as soon as he came into view.

Josh yanked his head around at the sound of the heavy door closing shut with a loud clunk. "Oh, hey, Tink. How long have you been here?"

"Oh, my mom just dropped me off. Daddy bought me a fishing pole and some tackle. I haven't been fishing since I was like eight years old, so I may need help with the tackle."

"Sure thing," he said, walking over and holding his hand out for the tackle box and the rod, "I'll put those in the back of the van with mine."

"Okay," Tink responded, handing him her things. Her cheeks flushed pink.

Josh drove several of the teenagers out to the pastor's ranch for the church's annual back-to-school adventure day filled with fishing, hayrides, horseback riding, rowboats, and ending in a bonfire. Josh swung by Samantha's house and picked her up. Tink cut her eyes to look at her. Jealousy tried to grip her heart, but then she remembered hearing Josh's words earlier. He said she was prettier than Samantha.

Several teenagers climbed in small boats and went fishing while Tink, Josh, Samantha, Willie, and Jonathan mounted the horses for a ride. Josh helped Tink mount, ensuring she was secure before assisting Samantha with her horse. The five of them road through the trails around the ranch, spending over an hour on horseback. They eventually made their way back to the stables, dismounting. Tink spent time brushing Cinnamon, the horse she picked to ride. While she groomed and fed her *horse, the others went fishing.*

Hoping she wasn't too late to join Josh in a boat, Tink jogged up to the edge of the pond. She stood on the bank of the pond, tall grass shooting up around her (nearly swallowing her tiny frame) while gnats and mosquitos ate her alive, making a feast on her legs and ankles. She ignored their bites as best she could, swatting at them occasionally as she gazed over the glistening water. The sunlight glimmered like diamonds embedded in the currents on the water's surface. She wondered how such beauty could be teeming with so many swarming minions. Narrowing her eyes, she skimmed over the pond in search of the boat with Josh in it. Following along the edge of the bank, she made her way into the tree line. Underbrush crunched under the weight of her steps as she inched closer to the edge, her eyes finally landing on the boat she longed to find, but what she found shattered her young heart. Josh sat in an aluminum boat with Samantha. He braced his left hand on the seat as he leaned over to grab his fishing rod with his right. Tink watched as Samantha grasped his hand in hers. Josh turned his head to face her, his eyes questioning her intentions. Making her intentions clear, Samantha leaned forward and pressed her lips against his.

Tink threw her hand over her mouth and whimpered. She stepped backward through the undergrowth and caught her leg on a thorny briar. Slicing her ankle, she turned and darted through the trees. Tears streamed down her face as she hurried from the woods and sprinted towards the pastor's home. Drying her face as best she could with her dirty hands, she knocked on the back door and asked to use the phone.

Tink sat in her bathtub, her arms folded around her knees, crying. As the piping hot water cooled to barely lukewarm, she stood to her feet and grabbed a towel, wrapping it around herself. She donned her nightgown and sat on the edge of her bed, combing her long, brunette hair. As she finished a French braid, she tied it off and curled it into a ball under her covers. She brushed the tears from her raw, reddened cheeks and cried herself to sleep.

After reading Isabella's account of the worst day of her life, Josh closed the purple diary. "That's it. That's the moment that kept everything the same. This is Tink's crossroad. This is the moment a different path can be chosen."

Crossroads

18

The Turning Point
The Church Gathering

Josh climbed from the bed and went to his closet. He pulled out a nice pullover shirt and slipped it over his head. "That's the day I need to change," he said, his voice muffled by the shirt. He poked his head through the neck hole and slid his arms through the sleeves. "Somehow, I have to convince myself to wait on Tink that she's worth waiting on."

The aroma of breakfast saturated his room. Shoving his feet into his shoes, he opened his bedroom door and entered the kitchen. Londyn, Caleb, Ciara, and

Crossroads

Josh Junior sat at the bar eating. "Good morning, guys!"

Josh Junior dropped his fork and scuttled across the floor to his dad, flinging his arms around him. "Dad, you're up. Come have breakfast with us," he insisted, tugging his dad's shirt.

Josh grinned and followed Josh Junior's lead. Ciara glanced up from her plate of food. "We figured you'd still sleep another couple of hours, so we didn't prepare you a plate."

Josh waved her off with a tisk. "I'm sorry. I have been sleeping in lately, haven't I?" He grabbed a bowl and spoon and meandered to the bar. The stool screeched across the floor as he pulled it out to sit. Nestling next to Caleb, he scooped a large heap of grits into his bowl. "So, son, what's this I hear about you being home for the summer?"

Caleb cut his eyes and glared at Londyn. "I was planning on talking to you about it myself, but I guess I should have done that sooner." He narrowed his eyes at her.

Londyn widened her eyes and shrugged. *Sorry,* she mouthed.

"I think it's a good idea, son. You need a little time off to be with your family. I'm glad you're home." Josh patted Caleb on the back of his shoulder.

Caleb tilted his head towards his stepdad and smiled a half smile. "Thanks for understanding. It means a lot."

Josh shoved a spoonful of grits in his mouth and closed his eyes. "Mmmmm..." he sighed. Ciara set a cup of coffee in front of him. He breathed deep, inhaling the aroma, and opened his eyes, picking up the cup and sipping the hot beverage. "So, what's on everyone's agenda for today?"

Josh Junior perked up, grinning, and responded, "Londyn is taking me and Ciara to practice driving today in her car!"

Josh raised his brow and nodded, "Okay," he mumbled as he swallowed his grits.

Londyn glanced at her dad, her eyes going wide. "If that's okay with you, that is. I'll take them down Wellington Road; no one ever drives down there. We'll be safe."

"Yeah, that's fine, sweetie." Patting Caleb on the back, he asked, "What about you, son? What's on your agenda for the day?"

Caleb's mouth turned down in a frown, his eyes darting to the floor. "Honestly, I'm exhausted. I want to lounge around the house today before filling my schedule with events. I hope that's okay."

"Of course."

"Well," he said, looking at the girls and Josh Junior, "I have a couple of things I need to do this morning, but after we all get home, how about we rent a couple of movies, order pizza, and pop some popcorn?"

"Sounds great, Dad," they all responded in unison. Smiles slid across their faces, and their eyes glimmered with the hope of some sense of normalcy returning to their lives.

Josh excused himself, making his way to his room.

Crossroads

He grabbed the purple diary off the bed, snatched his keys and the token from his nightstand, and shoved them in his pocket before heading to his truck. The bright late-morning sunlight sent waves of heat past Josh. He inhaled a deep breath and searched for oxygen. On the Gulf Coast, the heat of summer seemed to suck it out of the atmosphere. He climbed in his truck and slipped on his Oakleys. As he drove to his parents' home, he concocted a plan to convince the Josh from 1994 to give Tink time to grow up. Driving down the street, he mulled over his plan to influence himself at eighteen. He threw the truck in park, turned off the ignition, climbed out, and pounced onto the driveway. He shut the door with a loud clunk and shoved his hand in his pocket to retrieve the coin that transported him back in time.

Holding the moonstone in his line of sight, he spoke to it, "Take me to September 17, 1994."

As the vortex opened, it swirled around him in a whirlpool of time. Colors blended together and altered themselves, trees shrunk in stature and girth, the ground shifted, his truck disintegrated (altering its composition into a putty-like goo before fragmenting and disappearing), and matter reallocated, altering his surroundings. He steadied himself—paying closer attention to the changes in time as objects spun past him and disappeared into oblivion.

He closed his eyes for a brief moment in order to regain his equilibrium. When he blinked his eyes open,

238

his dad's old truck and van sat in the driveway. Nostalgia swept over him. He traced his hands over the old van he used in his teenage years to transport his friends back and forth to church. A half-smile crept across his face. Time travel had been a precious gift, bestowing him with childhood memories he had forgotten.

Chadok has to be an angel. There's just no other way, he thought to himself.

Voices echoed from the back patio. Josh followed the sound, making his way around the side of the house. Awaiting the exact moment when he needed to make his entrance, he pressed his back against the orange and brown mottled brick, listening for the conversation Tink overheard and had written about in her purple diary.

"I came here to tell you to stay away from my little cousin," Dale barked.

"What? What are you talking about?"

"My little brother fessed up about Tink and you," Dale spit.

"I don't know what Daniel told you, but Tink is like family to me; we go to church together, and I teach her how to skate. That's it, Dale."

"Yeah, well, Daniel tells me she's crazy about you. Apparently, you won her heart when you beat up Marcus, but that doesn't matter. She's too young. Samantha's your age. She goes to church with you. She told me that she's head over heels for you, and dude, look at her; she's hot! Leave Tink alone and date Samantha."

"Huh, Tink is much prettier than Samantha, Dale," Josh said.

Crossroads

"That's irrelevant. You're eighteen; Tink's fourteen. She's off limits," he retorted, anger tinging his tone.

"You seriously came over here to get up in my business and tell me who to date and who to leave alone?"

"I've seen the way Tink looks at you, and I know she's going on this church thing with you guys today, so just in case she gets up the courage to tell you she likes you, I'm here to make sure you know to keep your hands off. The age difference is too different."

"What makes you think I don't already know that? I'm not stupid. I'm her friend, and I look out for her. That's it!"

The crunching of leaves and twigs told the Josh of 2021 that Dale had marched off the property.

"Hey, Josh," Tink's small, dainty voice echoed. The adult Josh pressed the back of his head against the brick wall, glanced up at the sunlight piercing the treetops in thin shafts of light, and smiled at the sound of his deceased wife's young voice.

"Oh, hey, Tink. How long have you been here?" Eighteen-year-old Josh asked, his voice tainted with worry.

"Oh, my mom just dropped me off. Daddy bought me a fishing pole and some tackle. I haven't been fishing since I was like eight years old, so I may need help with the tackle."

The Josh of 2021 stepped out from the side of the house. "Hey, Josh, how are you doing?"

Eighteen-year-old Josh turned his head towards the voice coming from the other end of the house and

240

narrowed his eyes to see the man clearly. "J...John?" he stuttered.

The older Josh pulled back his shoulders, stiffening them confidently, and walked toward his younger self. "Yeah," he answered.

"Wow, it's been a while since we've seen you. Man, I hate you came all this way. Dad's not here. He's working the swing shift, so he's on second shift today."

Tink yanked her head around. Darting to his side, she flung her arms around the man who had saved her life. "John, it's you! I never got to thank you for saving my life that day." She pulled back from her impulsive embrace.

Josh smiled down at Tink. "No need to thank me, young lady. I'm glad to see you doing so well. You've grown up so much since that day. Wow, you'll be a young woman in just a few short years." He cut his eyes to his younger self and then glanced back down at Tink. "Do you mind if I have a short conversation with Josh here in private?"

Tink cut her eyes to Josh and then back to John. "Oh, okay," glancing back to Josh, she asked, "Can I wait in the house?"

"Of course." Josh walked to the back door and opened it for her. Tink set her tackle box on the patio and leaned her fishing rod against the house. "I'll be inside in a sec," Josh added.

"Alright," she mumbled as she crossed the threshold.

Josh slid the sliding door shut and turned back to

the man he knew as John. He extended his hand and signaled for John to sit at the patio table. The metal chair screeched across the concrete. Shivers ran up both their spines simultaneously.

"What's going on?" Eighteen-year-old Josh asked.

"Well," the Josh of 2021 folded his arms across his chest and leaned back in the chair. Harrumphing, he settled his mind on how best to approach the subject matter. "I know you don't really know me. Yeah, we've talked a few times, but to you, I'm just a guy who happens to be friends with your dad."

Young Josh shrugged his shoulders. "I respect your advice. I mean, you pointed out Tink being bullied, and you saved her life when that drunk driver nearly ran her over. You have my respect." Josh smiled a half-smile and chuckled. "Besides, I admire you for your skate skills alone." He gave the man he knew as John a thumbs up and tisked.

Josh chortled and leaned forward, propping his arms on the glass patio table. "I should probably start by admitting I overheard your conversation with the guy who was just here, and I feel like I need to share a story from my life with you. Is that okay?"

Eighteen-year-old Josh blushed. Rubbing his crinkled forehead, he slumped back in his seat and nodded. "Yeah, okay."

"I recently lost my wife to cancer," Josh started.

The young Josh dropped his hand to his side and turned his mouth down in a frown. "Aww...man, I'm sorry to hear that."

Josh glanced down at the table and shook his head. His eyes filled with tears. Glancing across the table, he locked his eyes on those of his younger self. "I only had ten short years of her being my wife, mainly because I was too dumb to see how crazy in love with me she was when we were children." He leaned forward, propping his elbows on the table and folding his hands together. "See, I'd known her most of my life, and much like the conversation I just overheard, I was older than her, so I brushed off the idea of her as a possibility for me, even though I secretly had feelings for her. I mean, she was beautiful, and she was a friend. I cared about her, but I knew the age difference wasn't right, so I pursued a relationship with a girl who attended my church. We were also friends. The difference was she was my age."

The Josh of 2021 threw his hands out (with an over-exaggerated shoulder shrug) and tilted his head to the side. "We were both seniors in high school. She was a good Christian girl. I knew she'd make a good wife and mother. I graduated and went to college, and we married a few months later. Eventually, she left me...and our two children." He leaned back in his chair, folding his arms across his chest. With a deep sigh, he continued, "Then, one day, I met this woman, and it turns out we knew each other as children. I hadn't seen her since she was a young girl. We became quick friends. It seemed that we fell in love even faster. I married her, and God gave us ten beautiful, wonderful years together, but if I had been smart when I was young, I could've married her in the beginning, and then I would've had all those years with her."

The Josh of '94 sat straight, his shoulders rigid, and knit his brow. He jerked his head around, facing the sliding glass door. His eyes shifted back and forth from the door to the man he knew as John. "Are...are you saying I should date Tink? The girl who just went in the house?"

Josh shook his head; the corners of his mouth turned down in a frown. Slightly disappointed in his own tone, he gathered his thoughts before continuing. "No, Josh, I'm not saying that," he started slowly into his explanation, "She's obviously too young for you...right now, but what I am saying is five years is not a long time in the whole scheme of things. That young lady," Josh pointed towards the sliding glass door, "will not be a little girl in just a few short years. You, you will be kicking yourself in the backside if you don't exercise patience and give her a chance to grow into the beautiful young woman she *will* be in a few short years. Trust me. I live with regret daily because I didn't wait for the young girl that God made to complete me to grow into the woman she needed to be in order to make me whole."

Young Josh squirmed in his seat. "Tink is like family to me, and I do love her." He dropped his head and stared at the concrete slab. Blood rushed to his face, burning his ears. He interlaced his fingers and wrung his hands together. "To be honest with you, Tink's age is the only reason I haven't allowed myself to consider her an option. That would be wrong."

"It would be wrong." Josh nodded and leaned

forward, cautious not to get too close to his younger self. Like a shock collar, the fear of messing with the space-time continuum restrained him from moving past a certain point—the point of no return for him. He feared what messing with it might cause. "But waiting for her to grow up is not wrong. Right now, be what you have been to her, a friend and a protector. You'll be amazed at how quickly time passes, and Samantha," Josh rolled his eyes, "yes, she's a friend, and you two may attend the same church, but that doesn't mean she's the one God made for you."

"So, you believe that God has one particular person in mind for me...like someone made just for me?" The young Josh folded his hands together and contemplated the idea behind his question.

"I do, but I also believe that (more often than not) we don't listen to His voice when He speaks to us, and as a result, most people end up marrying the person they chose for themselves. I call it God's permissive will. He permits it and will even bless the marriage, but it wasn't in His perfect will for that individual's life."

The Josh of 1994 rubbed his jaw between his thumb and closed fingers, nearly pinching himself. "When it comes to something as serious as marriage, I don't want to make a mistake."

"Then I advise you to focus on your education and career. Don't date right now. Why do you need to anyway?" The adult Josh shrugged, "And most definitely don't date someone simply because you think she's a logical choice." Josh folded his hands together behind his head and leaned back in the metal chair. "Tell me this...how long is this culinary school you want to attend?"

"The program is two years for a degree in Culinary Arts. I'm moving to Birmingham in January to attend classes there. They have an internship program. If I'm chosen for it, I'll work under a chef, hopefully at Bella Veranda, for a year, but there are a couple of options. I don't get to choose. It's chosen for me. In the end, I'll be gone for three years if I'm accepted. If not, I guess I'll decide where to go from there."

Josh dropped his hands to his side and sat up straight. "Well, there you have it. In three years, you'll be twenty-one, and she'll be, what, sixteen, seventeen?"

"Seventeen."

"So, you come home in three years and see where it goes from there." Josh stood to his feet. "Anyway, I need to get on. I'll come by to see your dad later. Think about what we talked about. I'll see you again. Oh, the girl that guy was encouraging you to date...if she likes you as much as he says she does, you don't need to put yourself in a position where she has the opportunity to be forward. Just because she's a church girl doesn't mean she won't make a move, and that, my friend, just might ruin your opportunity." He turned on his heels, waved goodbye, and headed back around the side of the house. As he rounded the corner, he pulled the token from his pocket and watched as the number twenty-one materialized within the veins of the moonstone.

The Right Turn
The Watermelon Festival

The sun's rays shined through the windshield of Josh's truck, heating the inside of his cab. Josh opened the driver's door, allowing the pent-up heat to escape, and climbed in. The sweltering heat of Oak Ridge had a personality (and a musty smell) of its own. The oxygen-depleted cab sucked the moisture from his lungs. He gasped for air and grabbed the purple diary off the passenger seat. Sweat immediately beaded up all over his body—as if the atmosphere commanded the water within him to rise to the surface. Cranking the truck, he twisted

247

the air conditioning knob to full blast. Cold air whooshed across his face. He wiped the sweat from his brow, opened the diary, and flipped through the pages, turning to the entry for the day he had just returned from in 1994 and read:

September 17, 1994

Dear Diary,

Today was one of the best days of my life. Mom dropped me off at Josh's for the back-to-school adventure the church holds each year. It was my first time going. When I got to Josh's house, I walked up on him talking to Dale. By the way, Daniel is on my list. He betrayed me to Dale. He told Dale what I said to him the other day about Josh. I guess I learned that you're the only one I can trust with that secret, except it's not a secret anymore. Ughh... Anyway, Dale went there to tell Josh to stay away from me because he thinks I'm too young, and he told Josh he needed to date Samantha, but I heard Josh tell Dale that he believes that I'm prettier than Samantha. I thought my heart was gonna beat out of my chest! He thinks I'm pretty, but he also thinks I'm too young. I wanted to cry when I heard him say that, but I was so happy to hear him say that I'm pretty that I focused on that instead. Anyway, we rode horses together, and we went fishing together. He even roasted my marshmallows for me; I kept dropping mine in the fire. Knowing that he knows that I like him made it kinda hard being around him, but I pretended I didn't hear anything Dale said to him. Samantha tried to get his attention all day, asking him to help her get on her horse and pretending she was scared to touch the fish she caught, but I don't think he fell for any of her tricks. Today was the best!

Tink

Josh smiled as he read her account of the day. "I did it. I changed the day that broke her heart," he whispered to himself. Shivering, he slightly bumped up the air conditioner's thermostat.

He thumbed through the pages and read her record of events throughout her teenage years, and he had indeed changed the outcome. Their relationship stayed relatively the same, yet it changed in minuscule ways as the months passed. The two of them were like family to each other. He came home from culinary school for the occasional weekend visit (as well as) the holidays, and he was always sure to pick her up for church on his weekends home. She filled her diary (page after page) with stories of his time in town. With each trip home, he invited her to his home after church to enjoy a new recipe he wanted to try. She was always his food critic.

A half-smile crept across Josh's face when he read how he had been accepted into the apprenticeship program at Bella Veranda, where he had been studying under their chef for a year. Reading through her diary, he enjoyed her writings and the occasional love poem—exposing her heart and love for him. It felt as if he was watching Tink grow into a young woman. He was thankful he had her writings and musings because time travel had not added new memories for him from the newly created timelines. His memories only held the first timeline—how things had been before he began his many journeys through the vortex created by the moonstone. A part of him wished time travel allowed the collective memory of all the timelines he had now witnessed to be retained in his thoughts. Still, he imagined things may get confusing if that were the case, so he quickly brushed those thoughts aside and turned his attention once again to her diary, reading her entry for the twenty-third of May:

May 23, 1997

Dear Diary,

Do I have a story for you, Diary! Josh drove home for the weekend to be here for my graduation. He called me as soon as he got back in town and asked me if I wanted to go skating tonight, so, of course, I said yes. He picked me up and took me to Skate World. It's been a while since we went skating. When they called for couple-skating only, I skated off to the concession stand, but he came up from behind me and asked me to couple-skate with him. I thought my heart would burst. I've longed for that since I was eight years old! While we were skating, he told me he wanted us to be skate partners and learn how to skate dance together. Of course, I told him I would love to learn how to dance on skates. After he brought me home, he told me he had a graduation present for me. It was a charm bracelet with three charms, a skate charm, a graduation cap, and a heart. He pointed out what each one was and told me that the heart was his heart because he was giving it to me. Then he asked me if I would date him once I turned eighteen. Oh, Diary, I couldn't help myself. I told him right then and there that I had loved him since I was a little girl and would absolutely date him once I turned eighteen. Then he walked me to the door, leaned over, and kissed my forehead. I thought I was going to faint. I can't believe tonight actually happened. That was the best graduation present a girl could ask for.

Tink

Josh's eyes welled with tears as he read Isabella's description of their confession of love. "I can't believe I did it," he cried. Flipping the page, he continued to read about how their love developed. When he reached July of 1998, he read her account of his proposal at the Watermelon Festival.

"This I have to see for myself," he said, shifting the truck into reverse and backing out of his parents' driveway.

Heading for The Trail—the place seared in his memories as the location where he ran into Tink after fifteen years, the place where they had their first "friend" date, the place where he had shared his secret affection for her by showing her the carving he made as a teenager on the backside of the tree—Josh shifted into drive and pressed the accelerator. He wondered if the carving in the old tree would still be there with all the changes he had managed to make. Anxious to find out, he slammed his foot to the floor, accelerating. An unnerved feeling settled in his heart. He didn't understand it, but he couldn't shake it.

Swerving into the parking lot, he skidded to a stop across two parking spaces and threw the truck into park. He turned off the ignition, opened the door, and pounced to the ground. Running at a clipped pace, he hurried down the trail to the open field where the large oak grew. Nervousness consumed his curiosity. Panting, he stopped short of the tree. He slowly inched his way to the massive oak. He placed his hand on the trunk and traced his fingertips over the rough bark as he made his way to the backside of the tree. He cracked a half-smile when he found his carving safe and sound. He had made the changes he desired, but those changes affected a piece of his life he hoped to remain the same, which overwhelmed him with worry and anxiety, frustrating him. Shaking his head, he dismissed the doubt creeping into his heart and mind.

Josh shoved his hand in his pocket and pulled out the moonstone. Pulling it in his line of vision, he spoke, "Take me to July 4, 1998."

As the veins in the moonstone shifted, bringing the number 98 to the surface, he closed his large palm around the coin and squeezed it tight. He stepped towards the tree line, feeling it would be a more secure location when the moonstone delivered him to the watermelon festival. The musty scent of the woods caught his breath. Crinkling his nose, he gasped. Knowing the vortex would thrust him into the past, he sought to hide from the crowds. He stepped into the woods, walking through the brambles and shrubs. Leaves and twigs crunched under his footfalls. The ground shifted beneath his feet. The fragrant bouquet of pine, oak, and creek water spun around him; shrubs disappeared and reappeared in different areas. The trees around him swirled, shrinking in stature. Josh's head spun as the time he lived in vanished in a spinning maelstrom. He anchored himself to a tree, narrowing his eyes to peer into the empty field where the large oak dwindled in size. A gaseous-looking haze covered the park. Josh watched as sound equipment appeared in the pavilion. A concession stand emerged on one side of it, and an ice cream stand morphed into view on the other side. His eyes grew wide as people materialized before him.

The haze dissipated as he stepped from the wooded area into the meadow bustling with people from 1998. The aroma of candied apples caught Josh's attention, drawing him towards the throngs of people gathered for the town's yearly celebration. He pressed his way through the crowds, searching for Tink and his twenty-two-year-old self. He made his way to the bridge where he and Isabella had caught up after so many years without seeing one another. Before creating alternate timelines, that day had been their confession day, the day they shared their secret affection for ¬one another from childhood. He had a new confession day now—Tink's high school graduation, but it was a confession he had been unable to hold in his memories.

As he stood staring at the bridge (envisioning Isabella standing in that spot at twenty-nine years old, looking like an angel), a voice called from behind him. "John," the dainty voice called.

Recognizing the voice, he glanced back over his shoulder. His eyes met those of eighteen-year-old Tink. Josh smiled. "Hey, Tink."

Tink rushed over to the man she knew as John and threw her arms around him. A bright smile stretched across her delicate face. Pulling free from their embrace, she placed her tiny hands on his cheeks. "Wow, you haven't aged a day since I saw you last."

He ran his fingers through his salt-and-pepper hair. The temporary color he used when he first began his journeys faded, revealing his actual age. "Thanks, I inherited good genes," he laughed.

Tink dropped her hands in front of her heart and interlaced her fingers. "You were right, you know." She grinned sheepishly, biting her bottom lip. "You may not remember this, but when I was nine, you told me that Josh liked me." Wide-eyed, she continued, "We're dating now, Josh and me. We told each other how we felt a little over a year ago, and we started officially dating in February when I turned eighteen." Her face beamed, blushing with excitement and love.

"That's wonderful. I'm so happy for you two." Josh returned her smile.

"You know, we might not be together right now had you not told me that. It made me hope, and, well, I never wanted to date any other boy because I held onto that hope."

"Well," Josh chuckled, "I'm glad I could be of service."

Tink grabbed Josh's hand. "Come on, Josh will be so happy to see you." She tugged on his arm and pulled him behind her as she weaved her way through the crowds, heading towards the pavilion.

As they neared the front of the festival, Josh eyed the newly built pavilion. His mind drifted back to 2009 when he sat at a keyboard on that same platform. It was the first time he played for Isabella to sing at the gospel singing, a gospel singing that had not been thought of in

1998. He remembered the sound of her voice as she sang the old hymn they picked out just moments beforehand. He heard the nervousness in her voice as they practiced together before stepping onto the platform to play before everyone. His eyes filled with tears as he realized that memory was just that, a memory that existed only in his mind now.

A mass of people flocked around the pavilion as if it were a rock concert. Josh and eighteen-year-old Tink zigzagged through them, making their way to the front. Fingers swiftly moved across a keyboard in a beautiful melody. Tink stopped dead in her tracks and dropped Josh's hand. It was the man she loved on the keyboard, and she knew it. She knew him. She knew how he played the piano. She had been listening to him play since she was a small child.

"What's he doing up there?" she whispered to herself. "John," she grasped Josh's shoulder and shook him, "that's him. That's Josh on the keyboard!"

Josh glanced down at her and smiled a half-smile.

"Good afternoon," the Josh of '98 said as he played a soft melody on the keyboard. "I've been given permission to start the celebration with a song I wrote. I wrote this song for an extraordinary young woman in my life. She's the reason I want to be a better man. Tink, could you come up here, please?"

Tink looked over her shoulder at the man she knew as John and grinned. *I better go*, she mouthed. The crowd before her stepped to the side, creating a narrow path to the platform for her to follow. As she stepped onto the stage, she came to a standstill in front of the keyboard. Grinning, she widened her eyes and raised her brows. She folded her hands together, propped her chin on them, and swayed to the melody.

Josh played the introduction to the song he had written and sang:

"There comes a time,
In the life of every man,
When time stands still,
And he can see God's plan.
And the one He made
To make him whole
She's the flesh of his flesh,
And the heart of his soul.
You, you are the one,
The one God made for me.
You are the one,
To help me see,
All that God
Has called me to be.
There comes a time,
In the life of every man.
When he gets on one knee,
Asking if she'll have his hand.
She's the one God made
To make him whole
She's the flesh of his flesh
And the heart of his soul.
You, you are the one

The one God made for me.
You are the one,
To help me see
All that God
Has called me to be."

Tears streamed down Isabella's cheeks. Josh pushed away from the keyboard, stood before Tink, knelt on one knee, and pulled a ring from his jacket pocket. "Tink, I love you. I think I always have. I was just afraid to allow myself to admit what I felt. I promise to be the best man I know how to be, and I promise to love you as long as I live. Will you marry me?"

Tink brushed her fingers over her tear-soaked cheeks, soaking up the moisture, and grinned. "Yes, yes, I'll marry you."

Josh stood to his feet and slipped the ring on her finger. Leaning forward, he gently kissed her forehead and wrapped his arms around her, pulling her into his embrace. The Josh of 2021 smiled. His eyes welled with tears. He had accomplished his mission. He had changed his past, and because of the moonstone, he had been given the opportunity to witness those changes, but he wanted to see more; he wanted to see their wedding. He had no recollection of their wedding day. His memories were inundated with the original timeline, so he only remembered marrying Tink when they were in their late twenties and early thirties. He wanted to share his new memories. He needed to be at their wedding.

Crossroads

The Beautiful Journey
The Wedding

People (young and old) bustled about The Trail, munching on slices of watermelon and slurping down frozen sodas. Josh edged through the swarm of people gathered in the park, making his way to the tree line. With his back to the woods, he slowly stepped into the shadows and disappeared behind the trees. He pulled out the token and eyed the moonstone. His head swam with a mixture of black dots and flickers of light beaming through the tree crowns in thin shafts. The veins of the moonstone snaked to the surface, forming the number twenty-one. He braced his torso against a tree trunk, preparing for the portal to suck him back through to his time. As nature's particles and matter whirled around him, breaking up their structures and reallocating themselves to the time difference, the kaleidoscopic flow of colors and growth sent his mind into a spinning frenzy. Changing his stance, he spread his feet apart and bent his knees.

Josh had made many trips through the gateway-in-time that had been opened by the moonstone. They had taught him much about what to expect when the portal propelled him into the future. Despite all he had learned thus far, nothing could prepare him for the quagmire created under his feet as matter fluctuated under the force created by the wormhole. Try as he might, as the ground gave way beneath his feet, his knees buckled. He threw his hands out to break his fall; his fingers sank into the putty-like terrain. He hauled himself to his feet and swiped the gooey earth fragments from his hands. The particles altered as he rubbed his hands together to remove the mushy dirt. He watched as rich soil spattered to the ground.

The spinning madness around Josh stopped. Midafternoon sunlight beamed through the trees in thin, sweltering shafts. Josh shielded his eyes with his hand, squinting, as he stepped out of the tree line and eyed the aging pavilion, the paint peeling and splintered wood cracking. He had returned to 2021 on a mission, a mission in search of a wedding date, the day he hoped to watch their beautiful journey together at its inception.

Josh started for his truck, nippily hiking the trail that gave the local park its name. The wooden planks of the bridge creaked under his heavy footfalls as he raced across it. Anxious to find a location and a date for his wedding to Isabella, he flipped through the pages of her diary, searching for an announcement as to when and where their nuptials took place. His stomach twisted in knots as he combed through the only connection he had to the alterations he had made in his own life, variations in his lifeline that would never be a part of his memories. As he pursued a clue as to where and when he needed to go, he turned to the page dated August 14, 1998. Joy rushed through his body like adrenaline as he read Isabella's account of the family meeting to plan their wedding. Their parents joined Tink and Josh in a premarital counseling session with Pastor Reynald. As Josh imagined they would, they both desired to marry in their church. Elation washed over him as he read where Isabella wrote down the date when they all decided to begin their beautiful journey together through life. Despite all the adjustments made to the timeline, he still knew himself, and he knew Isabella. The love they both had for God was undeniable. Josh thanked God that the shifts he had made to their lives led to Isabella living for God at a much younger age than in their original timeframe.

Josh folded the diary shut, the lock softly clicking in place. He turned the ignition and revved the engine with a destination in mind. The truck tires spun, spewing dirt and gravel, as he pulled onto the road and headed to their church. Josh pulled into the church parking lot and parked. Climbing out of the truck, he pounced to the ground and jogged to the front door. Pulling the heavy glass door open, he stepped onto the marble entranceway flooring. As he rounded the corner into the hallway, Pastor Denison stepped out of his office.

Josh turned the doorknob to the men's prayer room. Pastor Denison tilted to the side, attempting to see more than the back of the man's head. Narrowing his eyes, he scrutinized the side profile of the man in his church. "Josh, Josh Parker, is that you?" he called out from behind the man, his voice tainted with confusion.

Josh released the doorknob, dropping his hand to his side, and turned to face his Pastor and friend. "Yeah, Brother, it's me." He stepped forward with his hand extended for a shake. "I was just coming to utilize the men's prayer room for a time."

Pastor Denison knit his brow and took measured steps closer to Josh. His eyes darted from Josh's extended hand to his jubilant face. His brow relaxed, and a bright smile slid across Pastor Denison's face as he grasped Josh's hand in a firm shake. "Yeah, absolutely. How've you been, Josh? It's been...well...."

"Yeah, I'm making it." Josh halted the shake, still hanging onto his Pastor's hand, and tilted his head infinitesimally to the side. "Actually, I'm...I'm doing great considering everything. Just working hard to change my future."

"Well, that's great, Josh. I'll let you have your time

with the Lord. Call me if you need me." Pastor Denison dropped his hand. Turning on his heels, he headed back to his office.

The door to the men's prayer room creaked open. The scent of citrus brushed past Josh's face as he stepped over the threshold and shut the door behind him with a soft click. Shoving his hand in his pocket, he retrieved the moonstone. "Take me to December 18, 1999," he said. Josh knelt at the altar. Steadying himself, he leaned over it. "Jesus, thank you for sending Chadok to me that day in the graveyard. Thank you for changing my life and giving me a way to Tink." As he prayed, the altar disintegrated. His eyes blinked wide open as he crashed to the floor.

The doorknob turned, drawing Josh's attention; he hauled himself to his feet. The door slowly creaked open. Josh's eyes shifted side to side over the room as memories of his days spent praying for God's guidance as a young man flooded his mind.

The Josh of 1999 flung the door wide open. "No one's supposed to be in here," he commanded, his voice stern.

The Josh of 2021 turned on his heels and faced his younger self. "Josh," he said.

"John," the Josh of 1999 called. He darted across the room to embrace his old friend.

Josh held his hand out to stop his younger self from approaching. "I'm not feeling well," The young Josh halted immediately, his eyes going wide, "you don't want to be sick on your honeymoon."

"Yeah, you're right." Josh tugged on his bowtie and cracked a half-smile.

"I had to come see this for myself. I'm so happy for you."

Josh took several cautious steps back. "I'm so glad you were able to make it. We didn't know how to get you an invitation. How'd you find out?"

A half-smile slid across Josh's face. "Oh, I have my ways. I try to keep up with you two as best I can. I kinda feel responsible for the two of you being together."

"You are, man. I waited for her just like you suggested, and here we are today; she's about to be my wife. I'm so excited I can barely contain myself. You're staying for the ceremony, aren't you?"

"Of course, I am. I came a long way to be here to see this day. I'll sit in back so as not to expose anyone to anything."

"Yeah, yeah, oh, man, Tink's gonna be so happy to see you. She said you were there when I proposed," he said, in a questioning way rather than a mere statement, knitting his brow as he spoke.

"Yeah, I was. You did a very romantic thing that day. Good job, son. Good job."

Josh quietly slipped out of the prayer room and stepped into the sanctuary. He watched as droves of friends and family members filed in, seating themselves either on his or Isabella's side of the church. While they waited, the projector screen in front of the baptismal dropped down, and a video of Isabella as she grew up, blended with clips of Josh as a young boy maturing into a man, played on the screen. Tears welled in Josh's eyes as he witnessed pictures and video clips of the two of them while dating. It differed from his memories, yet it still seemed so familiar; it was as if they experienced the same dates and interactions—only while younger.

The video ended, and the screen lifted. Pastor Reynald and the Josh of 1999 stepped through the side door, making their way to the front of the sanctuary. Josh wiped his hand over his tear-soaked cheeks and smiled. Soft music played as the bridal party emerged from the back of the church and made their way to their designated areas at the front. The Josh of 2021 stood to his feet as the bridal march played. Turning to the side, he faced the center aisle. His eyes fell upon young Isabella draped in a white, satin gown covered in lace. Isabella tilted her head to the side, her eyes landing on the man she knew as John. A soft smile inched across her face.

Josh folded his hands together in front of himself, interlacing his fingers. A bright smile stretched across his face as tears streamed down his cheeks. *You look beautiful*, he mouthed.

"Thank you," Isabella whispered, her smile extending.

Isabella wound her hand tight around the bouquet she held and turned her gaze to the front of the church where the man she had loved since she was a little girl stood...waiting! She took slow, soft steps toward him and the beautiful journey they were embarking on together.

Crossroads

Once they made it to the front of the sanctuary, her father took her hand, kissed it, and placed it in Josh's hand. Isabella gazed lovingly into Josh's eyes as she stepped towards him. Hand in hand, they exchanged their vows.

"Isabella, my Tink, when I was a little boy, my momma used to tell me to always be nice to little girls because one day those little girls will grow up. I'm so thankful my momma taught me that lesson, and I'm thankful I waited for you (the little girl I knew) to grow up. You've always been like family to me. Now, you will be the flesh of my flesh and bone of my bone. You complete me. You make me desire to be a better man. I promise to always love you, to always be there for you, and to be your skate partner forever." Josh winked and grinned. He slipped Isabella's ring on her finger. "With this ring, I thee wed."

"Josh," Isabella sniffled. A tear made its way past the barrier of her lashes. "I've loved you for as long as I can remember. You're the only one for me, and I'm thankful God created me with you in mind. You were my first kiss, and you'll be my last. I promise to always love and honor you, to always be there for you, to be your taste tester, and to be your skate partner forever." Isabella's eyes glimmered, her face beaming with joy. She slipped Josh's ring on his finger. "With this ring, I thee wed."

Pastor Reynald cleared his throat and said, "I now pronounce you man and wife. You may now kiss the bride."

Josh leaned forward and pulled Isabella into his

arms, placing his hand on the small of her back. His lips gently brushed against hers, caressing them ever so softly. Isabella wanted to melt into his arms, but now was not the time for that, so she took a step back. Josh released her from his grasp, and they both turned to face their guests.

Pastor Reynald announced, "I introduce Mr. and Mrs. Joshua Caleb Parker."

As the music started, Josh grasped Isabella's hand, interlacing his fingers with hers. Hand in hand, they walked down the aisle. Before they stepped through the double doors at the back of the church, Isabella dropped her husband's hand and stepped to the back pew. Wrapping her arms around the man she knew as John, she whispered, "Thank you for saving my life in so many ways. You didn't just save my physical life. Because of you, I believed Josh could love me, and because of you, I waited for him to fall in love with me. You are the reason we're here today." Isabella kissed him on the cheek before joining her husband and stepping through the double doors.

Crossroads

21

The Bump in the Road
The Announcement

Josh leaned back in the pew as the wedding guests exited the sanctuary and headed to the fellowship hall behind the newly married couple. Once the room cleared, he made his way to the Sunday school room he had used when traveling back in time. Void of all memories of the new life created for himself by changing the timeline, he longed to visit the special moments they had created together in their new life. He nervously fidgeted, pacing back and forth from one side of the room to the other. Shoving his twiddling hand in his pocket, he wrapped his fingers around the token and fumbled it through his fingers. He needed to get back to Tink's diary—their memories together—so he could experience them for himself. Holding the token in his line of sight, he watched as the veins of the moonstone morphed into the number twenty-one. He closed his eyes and dropped to his knees as the room spun around him; particles and matter shifted and altered themselves. Josh squeezed his eyes and prayed for the swirling maelstrom to settle quickly.

The late afternoon sun shifted westward in the sky, painting the heavens in beautiful yellow, orange, and brown hues. Josh stood outside his truck (for a brief moment) and eyed the scenery, captivated by God's artistry. A smile slid across one side of his face as he climbed into the cab of his truck. He picked up the diary lying on the seat and unlocked it. He flipped through the pages, finding the last entry on February 5, 1999, the day before her twentieth birthday. "What?" he grumbled. "Her five years are up in this thing," he barked as he slung the diary across the front seat, cranked the engine, and slammed his foot to the floor.

Angry, he spun out of the church parking lot and headed home to search for clues to their life. He heaved as the realization of his anger punched him, knocking the wind from his lungs. Anger consumed him before he began crossing through the vortex in time; it was as if fury imprisoned him, surrounding him with enraging thoughts and irritants. Trapped in that emotion, he couldn't seem to lift his foot to move forward, but since the beginning of his journeys, the anger within him seemed to settle.

"I can't go back to all the rage," he mumbled through a clenched jaw. As he turned onto his street, he hit a bump in the road, knocking Tink's purple diary onto the floorboard.

The sun hid below the horizon and cast shadows across the skies. Josh unlocked the front door and stepped into the darkness of his living room. He eyed the new wedding photo set on the mantle in the same exact spot Isabella had chosen for their original wedding portrait. A half-smile slipped across one side of his face, and warmth rushed through his chest. It felt nice to know Isabella had always been his in this timeline, yet she was still the same woman he knew and loved in the original timeline. It amazed him that such a small thing as the placement of a photograph spoke to him and gave him a sense of peace.

Pouring a cup of coffee, he eyed the island that once held two stoves. Now, only one stove sat in the center of the ten-foot island. When he married Tink in the original timeline, he remodeled the island so that they could have a dueling kitchen, but now the kitchen looked just as it had before he married her. He sipped on his coffee, slipped off his shoes, and nestled comfortably in his recliner, dozing off.

Josh's eyes blinked open. His body felt stiff and stove up like he had been asleep for days. His stomach growled and twisted within him, insinuating he had slept far longer than he needed to. He bolted upright and yanked his head from side to side, searching for his whereabouts. He sighed in relief when he realized he was home. Darkness consumed the house. Sauntering over the cold, hard tile, he entered the darkness of his bedroom. Feeling his way around, he found the bathroom door and shut it behind him. He stepped into the shower and rinsed the chaos of what he thought to be the day away. The day he spent using the moonstone at Tink's crossroads had been exhilarating and wonderful. He had traveled through time (visiting three different years in the past), talked the young Josh into waiting for the girl he loved to grow up, witnessed the Josh of 1998 propose to Isabella at the Watermelon Festival, and watched her walk down the aisle to Josh while he stood anxiously next to the pastor from their youth. It all had taken a toll on his physical body. As fantastic as all those experiences were, time travel exhausted him. It did something to not only the physical body but to the mind. Even though all of his memories existed in the original time frame, he soaked up every ounce of information he could grasp from the altered timeline he had created. Using either Isabella's diaries or simply traveling back in time to experience the changes for himself, he gathered the collection of events in hopes of adding them to his memories. Yet he found separating the compilation of experiences and occasions chaotic in his thoughts and exhausting him even further.

Josh collapsed onto his bed and found himself dreaming of Isabella...

Josh walked through the front door to find the house

seemingly empty. Typically, smells of sautéed peppers and onions saturated their house when he arrived home after a long day at work. He breathed in deep breaths, longing for the savory scents of his wife's cooking, so when he realized Isabella had not been in the kitchen preparing a meal for the family, he stepped cautiously through the living room and into the kitchen, searching for his wife. Listening closely for any signs of life in his home, he leaned his ear towards the children's bedrooms. Nothing. He breezed across the kitchen and heard sniffling. He stepped into the hallway, making sure his footfalls fell softly. He edged his way to his bedroom door and pressed his ear against it. Faint sobs echoed through the thick, wooden door. Behind the door, Isabella sat on the edge of the bed and ran her hand over her cheeks, soaking up the dampness left by the tears. The door slowly creaked open. Josh made his way to the bed and sat next to her.

"What's wrong, sweetheart?" he asked. Gently stroking her face, he pulled her tear-soaked hair behind her ear.

Her chin trembled as she turned to look her husband in the eyes. "I lost the baby," she cried.

Josh scooped his wife into his arms and cradled her. "I'm so sorry." He rocked her back and forth. "Why didn't you call me at work?"

She nestled her head against his chest and answered, "I didn't want to bother you with it. You have enough stress as it is."

Josh stopped rocking, lifted her chin, and gently kissed her forehead. "Sweetheart," he whispered, "I'm your partner. We're in this together, and our baby, well, our baby could never be a bother."

Isabella closed her eyes. *"I'm just so tired. This is the second baby we've lost, Josh. I so desperately want to have your child, but it doesn't seem like it's the road God has planned for us."*

"Sweetie, this is just another bump in the road. That's all. We may not understand it now, but there will come a time when we can see the whole picture and know why we lost our babies. Have you thought about writing about it? You're such a gifted writer, and it would be therapeutic. Why don't you make a baby book for them? You can put little memories in it like the pregnancy tests and the papers filled with possible names."

"That's a good idea," Isabella sniffled. *"I love you, Josh,"* she whispered. *Turning her face to his, she pressed her lips gently against his.*

Early morning sunlight trickled through the blinds, dancing across Josh's face. His eyes flicked open. He bolted from the bed and searched the closet for the album Isabella had created for the babies they lost. "There has to be a reason I had that dream. It was a memory coming to the surface for a reason. Maybe I can find our baby books."

He rummaged through the boxes in their closet and found an album titled Our Babies. Flipping through the pages, he found a pregnancy test labeled: Taken March 5, 2000. Under the test was a note written by Isabella:

As Josh flipped through the album, he found an album titled Our Babies. Flipping through the pages, he found a pregnancy test labeled: Taken March 5, 2000. Under the test was a note written by Isabella:

Date *March 5 2000*

My Precious Baby

My precious baby not meant to be.
My precious child. I hope to one
day see.
In my arms, I long to hold you
and cuddle you so tight.
And hear you whisper: I love you
mommy goodnight.
My precious baby. I love you so
dear.
My precious child. I wish you
were here.
Love Mommy

Crossroads

As Josh flipped through the album, he found another loss in 2003 and another in 2005. He turned the page again, and a picture fell out, a 4D photograph of their baby. An arrow pointed to the baby, stating, "It's a girl!" Imprinted in the top right corner was the baby's due date of May 25, 2007. Josh held the picture in his hand. Tears filled his eyes as he gazed at their daughter. He turned over the picture and read in Isabella's handwriting, Finley Adaline Parker, ultrasound taken March 3, 2007. Josh flipped the picture back over and stared in amazement at their baby. Awestruck by the details of her features he was able to see, he imagined how she must have appeared at birth. With the date, time, and hospital stamped on the picture, he knew his next crossroad.

He quickly donned his clothes and made his way to the bathroom to dress for the day. Standing in front of the mirror, he eyed the mostly gray beard growing on his face. "How long was I asleep?" he mumbled, rubbing his hand over his chin. "It looks like two days' worth of growth, and I shave daily." He pondered the effects time travel had on his body. It completely zapped all of his energy. "I must've slept right through an entire day or more," he said to himself. He picked up his razor and brought it to his jawline. He stopped just before placing it against his skin and set the razor down. "Think this through, Josh. You're about to see Tink and yourself in 2007. Those two have been seeing you since 1989." He nodded and shrugged, reaching his hand to his head and running his fingers through his salt-and-pepper hair.

"Well, at least you still had color in your hair when you returned to '89. That took at least ten years off your age." He thought about the times he had seen them and the years that had passed between his visits to the past. "They've gotta see me aging somewhat. Tink just mentioned that I hadn't aged a day, so you need to leave the beard, old man," he said to himself, pointing to his reflection. Picking up the brush, he ran it through his hair and headed to Oak Hills Hospital to see Isabella. He longed to see her pregnant belly and hold her in his arms.

The forty-five-minute drive outside of Oak Ridge, Alabama, to the hospital seemed to take forever as the minutes passed at a snail's pace. The warmth of late spring's early mornings filled the cab of his truck and wrapped around him like a thin blanket. Parking by the highway, he jogged across the bridge. A paddling of ducks glided across the glistening waters of the pond (chattering and quacking) as if they were holding an understandable conversation with each other. Josh smiled as he made his way past them at a clipped pace. He rushed through the revolving door of the hospital. Panting, he breathed deeply, making his way around the corner and down the hall to the restroom. He practically lived at Oak Hills Hospital when Isabella was dying, so he knew the terrain well. He pulled out the moonstone and spoke to it, "March 3, 2007."

The coin, in a swirling frenzy, unleashed the wormhole. Josh threw his arms out to the side and used the stall walls to steady himself. The lights flickered in and out as the portal swept around him, carrying him back in time to the day Isabella and his younger self had their appointment to see a 4D ultrasound of their baby. When his fingers dipped into the metal walls creating the stall, he swiftly yanked his hands away. He opened his eyes and watched a kaleidoscope of colors eddy over the walls as if the walls were moving liquid. With widened eyes, he stared in amazement as they reassembled themselves into the standard hospital-blue walls he had seen when he was younger.

Still dizzy from the wormhole thrusting him back in time, he staggered from the restroom. Josh leaned against the wall next to the bathroom entrance and ran his fingers through his hair, grooming himself. He wiped his hands over his face and gained his composure before starting down the hall. Rounding the corner, he strode through the lobby and entered the gift shop.

As he crossed the threshold, the dinging bell announced his entrance. A young woman in her early twenties stepped out from the backroom and asked, "Can I help you?"

"I'm here to see some friends who are having a baby. I'd like to get an outfit for her to go home in," he responded.

The young lady came out from behind the counter and escorted him to the side of the store with newborn clothing. He browsed through the outfits and chose an adorable pink and white dress. As he started for the checkout, he remembered they would find out today that they were having a girl, so he stepped back to the rack and rifled through the outfits for baby boys to avoid suspicion. Checking out, he thanked the lady for her assistance. He paced back and forth through the lobby, waiting for his younger self and Isabella to walk through. Excitement rushed through his veins, sending his heart into a frenzy as he marched from one side of the room to the other. With each ding of the elevator, he swung his body around to face the elevator doors. After the third ring, he turned to face himself as a younger man and a glowing Isabella. Elation washed over his countenance; a smile slid across his face, lifting his bright eyes into a smile of their own. Overtaken by her beauty, he gasped and stood, gazing across the room at the woman he loved. Isabella already had her children when they married in the timeline his memories occupied, so he had never witnessed her pregnant. Her beauty astounded him.

Shaking himself free of his dazed admiration, he breezed across the lobby. Laughing, Isabella and Josh stared at the picture she held in her hand as they strolled across the lobby toward the glowing exit sign hanging above the revolving door on the far side of the room. The Josh of 2021 stepped out before them and called, "Josh, Isabella?"

Isabella dropped her hand to her side and looked up. The Josh of 2007 stepped in front of his wife before making eye contact with his future self. "John," he said as Isabella pushed past his arm and threw her arms around the older Josh's neck.

"John," she squealed. "I can't believe we ran into

279

you today of all days. This is wonderful." She kissed him on the cheek and dropped her arms down to her side. "This is amazing, isn't it, sweetheart?" She turned her gaze upon her husband.

"Yeah, absolutely," Josh proclaimed.

"We have great news; we're having a baby." Isabella handed him the 4D photograph of their daughter. "We're naming her Finley Adaline. Isn't she beautiful?" She smiled at the picture before glancing back up at the man she knew to be John. "You know," she glanced from John to Josh, "you look like you're related. I never noticed before, but you two look so much alike."

The Josh of 2021 took an infinitesimal step back. While he had been more concerned with making sure he seemed to age as they were aging, he figured this day would come—the day when the resemblance was noticed. With a raised brow, he quickly thought through his response, remembering his mother has a cousin named John. "We are actually...related, that is. Yeah, Tom and I are friends, but," he turned his gaze upon Josh, "your mom, Evelyn, is my cousin. Your great-grandpa Dewey has a sister named Gloria. She's my grandmother."

"Oh, yeah, I've heard mom mention great-aunt Gloria, but she lives in Upper Michigan, so I've never met her. Well, that explains why I've always felt a kinship with you," Josh said.

Isabella tapped her husband on the shoulder. "See, I told you that you look like your mom's side of the family." She turned to the Josh of 2021 and added, "His brother keeps telling him that he looks like his dad, but

I've always insisted he looks like his momma. There's not an ounce of his daddy in him."

The Josh of 2007 held his hand out to his older self for a shake, but the Josh of 2021 placed one of the gift boxes in his hand instead.

"This is for you. I spoke to your dad earlier, and he told me the news, so I hoped to catch you two here before I have to head back out of town. I wanted to give you something for the baby to wear home from the hospital." He handed the other box to Isabella and shrugged. "Two of them since I had no way of knowing it was a girl until seeing the ultrasound picture."

"Aww...thank you, John. That's so sweet," Tink said, opening the gift box and pulling out a newborn dress trimmed in white lace. Tiny mauve flowers lined the smocked neckline. "It's beautiful," Isabella whispered, pulling the dress to her face and breathing in the scent of new material. Somehow, the fragrance of a baby saturated the linen dress.

Isabella folded the dress and placed it back in the box, closing it. She threw her arms around the man she called John and hugged him tightly. "Thank you again, John. You'll never know how special you are to us both."

Josh pulled away from her embrace and cupped the side of her face in his hand. "You are the most beautiful pregnant woman I've ever laid my eyes on." He cut his eyes to his younger self, locking eyes with him. "And you are the most blessed young man I've ever known. Never take her for granted," he insisted.

"Oh, I won't," the Josh of 2007 assured him.

Crossroads

Tink brushed her fingertips down Josh's arm. "I hate that we have to run, but we have another appointment in fifteen minutes. Finley will wear this dress home from the hospital; I promise." She lifted herself on her tiptoes and kissed the older Josh's cheek. "We would love to have you here for her birth," she said as she linked her arm with her husband's and sauntered towards the revolving door.

The Hard Road
The Due Date

The frigid hospital environment melted away with Isabella's embrace. Josh closed his eyes and savored the feeling of having his arms around a pregnant Tink. After reminiscing with Isabella and doting on her beauty as a pregnant woman, he turned on his heels and started for the restroom he had used to travel to March of 2007. He locked the bathroom stall, pulled out the moonstone, and said, "Take me to May 25, 2007."

The token unleashed the whirling maelstrom, thrusting Josh two and a half months forward in time to Finley's due date. The floor beneath his feet gave way; its particles broke apart and moved in waves under him before realigning themselves and solidifying. A kaleidoscope of colors swirled around him as time zipped past him at an incredible pace. Within a matter of seconds, the shifting of time came to an abrupt halt. Josh discovered that the longer the time travel process took, the farther back or forward in time that the moonstone took him. He wondered if the colors that circled around him through the vortex were moments in time rushing past him, or maybe (just maybe) he was the one moving at a high velocity through the wormhole as it snaked its way through time.

Josh blinked his eyes several times and stumbled from the bathroom stall. He steadied himself against the door before heading into the hall. Shuffling his feet over the blue and white tile flooring, he staggered to the gift shop tucked away in the hospital lobby. Rubbing his eyes and pinching the bridge of his nose, he squeezed his eyes tight before blinking away the blur. He stood before the floral cooler, searching for the perfect bouquet of flowers for his wife, the new mother. Bouncing on the balls of his feet, he grinned as his eyes skimmed over the array of choices before him.

"From the look on your face, I'd say you're about to be a father," said the young girl behind the counter.

"You'd be correct," Josh said, tilting his head to glance back at the bubbly, young auburn-haired girl. She looked to be no more than twenty years old. "What gave it away?" He chuckled.

"Oh, the huge grin on your face and the spring in your step." She winked. A smile stretched across her face. "I love watching the excited dads. My little boy's daddy didn't even show up when I went into labor." Her smile faded.

Josh dropped the corners of his lips, turning them down. "I'm sorry to hear that. He obviously wasn't the right man for you. The right one will come along. It may take a while; it took years for my wife and I to find our way back to one another, but we did...with God's help, of course. That's what you need, God's help. He will make sure the right person steps into your life and your son's."

One corner of the young woman's mouth turned up. "You think so?"

"Oh, I know so, and when that person steps into your life, it is essential that they be the right person to be the father your son needs, just as much as the right person to be a husband."

The young lady dropped her head and stared at the notepad on the counter. She picked up a pen and began doodling on the pad. "Sometimes I worry that a good man (one that would be a good father and husband) wouldn't want someone like me. I mean, I had a child out of wedlock, and I know lots of girls do nowadays, but it wasn't the person I wanted to be. I wanted to marry and then have children." She looked up and glanced across the room at Josh. "I was raised in the church, you know, but I went astray, and now I worry I'll never be able to go back."

Crossroads

Josh picked out a vase filled with purple delphiniums, violets, tulips, and sweet peas with white calla lilies sprinkled amongst the purple arrangement. He carried it to the front counter without saying so much as a word. Setting it down in front of the young girl, he looked her in the eyes. "What's your name, young lady?"

"Amelia."

"Amelia, the first thing you need to know is that God loves you, and He is literally standing at the edge of the road waiting for you to turn the corner and run back to Him. Literally." Josh pushed the vase to the side and grabbed Amelia's hand, sliding the pen out from her fingers and setting it to the side. "The next thing you need to know is that you are a beautiful young woman; any good man would be lucky to have you. You know, my wife and I met when we were children. We were so young, and she always loved me, but I was older, and I ended up going off to culinary school and getting married to a girl I dated in high school. We had two beautiful children together, but she wasn't the one God had made for me, so we ended up going through a divorce. Yeah, God knew all along that I would marry her, but He also knew the girl He had formed with me in mind. I believe that. Just like God formed Eve for Adam, He forms every young woman with a particular young man in mind. We don't always wait for God to guide us to that person; sometimes, we don't see it when He places them in our path. After my divorce, I thought I was doomed to be alone for the rest of my life. I knew the sacredness of marriage and thought I couldn't remarry, but God had other plans for me. He caused Isabella's path to cross mine, and we fell madly in love, and guess what…she had been married and divorced and had two children of her own, but that didn't matter. Sure, we both had been damaged in life, but neither of us was damaged goods, nor are you. Don't you listen to Satan's lies. You are worthy of a good man; you will find him."

Amelia's eyes pooled with tears. "Thank you." She glanced at the bouquet and rang it up. "The flowers are elegant. I'm sure your wife will love them." Amelia traced her fingertips under her eyes, catching the tears. "That'll be forty-two dollars."

Josh pulled out his wallet and handed her the cash. "You have a wonderful day, Amelia."

Exiting the gift shop, Josh strode to the elevator and pushed the button for the fourth floor. He tapped his foot at a quick, steady pace while waiting. The numbers above the elevator doors glowed, lighting the number six. As the light shifted to the number five, he rubbed his free hand over the nape of his neck; the world seemed to be moving in slow motion. He wished the elevator would hurry up. When the L finally lit up, he jumped at the dinging of the doors opening.

Josh fidgeted in the elevator, rolling one of the flower's stems between his fingertips. As the glowing numbers inched up the panel, nervous knots tightened in the pit of his belly. When the button numbered four lit up, Josh jerked his hand from the stem and dropped it to his side; the door opened with a ding. Stepping out of the elevator onto the maternity floor, he carried the bouquet of flowers and headed to the waiting area. A long line of fluorescent lights cast a yellowish glow down the hallway, almost as if the glow guided him to his destination. One of the lights flickered, creating a strobe effect on the blue-tiled flooring. An eerie sensation swept over him. As he entered the waiting area, he eyed his younger self, pacing back and forth across the room, tears streaming down his face. His heart sank in his chest, and the corners of his mouth slid down his cheeks. "Josh, what's wrong?" he called from the far side of the room. Knitting his brow, he took measured steps towards himself, being cautious to keep a safe distance. He was desperate not to upset the space-time continuum.

Young Josh dropped his hand from his reddened, weary eyes and faced the man he knew as John. "John, I'm so glad you're here. They made me leave. They said there were some complications, and they may have to do a C-section. I'm scared; I'm really scared, John." 8

The Josh of 2021 stood silent. Shock overcame his excitement over the birth of his child. He stared at himself (mouth agape) and wondered what to say. *What would I want someone to say to me right now?* He questioned himself. Reflexively, Josh started across the room to console his younger self. Remembering the space-time continuum at the last moment, he stopped, stiffening his arms and back. As he came to an abrupt halt, the doctor trundled through the door. His face (flushed a deep scarlet) wore a fixed, unreadable expression; he dropped his head and slumped his shoulders as he took slow, cautious steps toward the younger Josh.

"Mr. Parker…" he said, clearing his throat. He opened his mouth, but no words came.

"Is my wife alright? Josh cried.

"Yes, Sir, your wife is resting, but—" The fixed expression he held as he entered the room wavered. His chin quivered. "Your daughter…well, there were complications. On the monitor, well, we couldn't find her heartbeat. We searched for it while the ultrasound tech rushed to the room with the equipment. As we searched for her heartbeat, we found that her placenta was covering the cervix, so we had to do an emergency C-section." He swallowed the hard knot rising in his throat. "The cord had wrapped around the baby's neck and cut off her blood flow. She…she didn't make it. We did everything we could, Josh. I'm so sorry."

Josh squared his shoulders and inhaled a deep breath. "Does Isabella know?"

"We felt it best to inform you first. Isabella's still asleep from the surgery. I thought you'd like to be there when she wakes up." Dr. DeMond gently placed his hand on Josh's shoulder and gave him three short pats. "I'm so sorry for your loss, Josh."

As the words left Dr. DeMond's lips, the Josh of 2007 burst into tears. His squared shoulders collapsed, and he crumpled forward, hanging onto the doctor and burying his face in his shoulder.

The Josh of 2021 stepped backward, faltering and slamming into the door; it creaked open and sent him toppling onto the hallway floor. The bouquet of flowers landed next to him. His chest tightened, and his breathing escalated into rapid breaths. He inhaled several large gulps of air, his lungs repeatedly searching for oxygen. The hall spun around, sending him into a dizzy frenzy. He quickly realized the madness around him was not that of time travel; he was in shock. He needed to get out. Hurling himself to his feet, he scooped up the flowers and staggered down the hall and around the corner. Hot tears stung his eyes as they pushed themselves in an endless surge over his cheeks. Gasping for air, he clung to the wall, keeping himself upright, as he stumbled forward down the hall.

As he neared the elevator, the doors opened with a ding. Clay Denison—his friend and pastor—stepped off the elevator and eyed him. "Josh..." he stuttered. "Is everything okay?"

Josh tilted his head to look at the man calling his name.

Pastor Denison narrowed his eyes and scrutinized Josh's features. "Oh, I'm sorry. You actually look a lot like one of my church members, but he's a good bit younger than you." He knit his brow. "I'm actually on my way here to see him. His wife is having a baby."

Josh cleared his throat. "Ye..yes, I know. I'm...I'm re...lated," he said, his voice breaking.

"Are you okay?" Pastor Denison asked, placing his hand gently on Josh's shoulder.

"The baby...she was stillborn," Josh cried, burying his face in his hands. Tipping forward, he crumpled into his friend and pastor. The warmth and comfort of arms wrapped around him. Breaking, he sobbed into the shoulder of his friend and minister.

Clay Denison held the stranger, patting him on the back. "I'm so sorry. Can I pray with you?" He pulled from the embrace and placed his hands firmly on Josh's shoulders. "What's your name, Sir? We'll pray together right now."

Sniffling, Josh wiped his cheeks (drying his tears) and glanced into Pastor Denison's eyes. "John. My name is John."

"Okay, John, let's go to the Lord together." Pastor Denison closed his eyes, his hands remaining on Josh's shoulders. "Father God, we come to You today, lifting up John and his family. I ask You to speak peace into their lives. Pull this family close to You, under the shadow of Your wings. Send Your Holy Spirit to bring comfort to them. In Jesus' name, I pray, Amen."

Josh wrapped his arms around Pastor Denison. "Thank you. Your prayers mean the world to me."

"You're welcome. I hate to run off having just met you, but I think I need to make my way down to see Josh and Isabella. They need me right now more than ever."

"Yes, yes, they do, Pastor. I need to head back home now anyway. See you again soon, I hope." Josh glanced down at the bouquet of flowers still in his hand. "Will you..." he held the bouquet out for Pastor Denison to take, "Take these with you? I was so overwhelmed I forgot them."

Pastor Denison took the bouquet and smiled. "They're beautiful. I'll pass them on. Hope to see you again. Come visit us at church sometimes, why don't ya," he requested as he pulled a card from his wallet, scribbled a scripture on it, and handed it to him. He forced a strained smile as he turned on his heel to walk down the hall to the waiting room. Waving, he called, "I'm sorry to have met you under these circumstances."

Josh glanced down at the card, reading the passage he'd written, and waved back. "Thank you for being a wonderful friend to Josh. He needs you right now," Josh called down the hall to Pastor Denison.

With that, Josh dropped his hand to his side and pushed the down button on the elevator pad. Stepping into the elevator, he mashed the button for the lobby floor. As the heavy metal doors clicked shut, he found himself utterly alone. Heartbroken over the loss of another child with Isabella, he shoved his back against the corner of the wall and slid down to the floor. He buried his face in his hands and sobbed. "God, I just don't understand why my life has to be filled with so much loss. What did I do to deserve all this? I'm sorry; I wish I could be like Horatio Spafford, who lost his wife and children and still wrote that beautiful hymn, "It is Well with My Soul". But I'm not strong. Not right now. I'm broken and desperate. Help me, Lord."

With a ding, the elevator doors opened. Josh hauled himself to his feet and stumbled from the elevator. Shuffling down the hallway, he made his way to the restroom. Longing for sleep, peace, and the year 2021, Josh pulled open the heavy wooden door and stepped inside the icy-cold room. Pulling the moonstone into his line of sight, he realized he was homesick. He sighed in relief as the number twenty-one emerged in the smoky stone.

Crossroads

The Unexpected Turn
The New Timeline

Josh fell into the lavatory as the moonstone thrust him forward in time. Exhausted, he fumbled forward. His head slammed against the mirror hanging above the sink. Blood dripped down the bridge of his nose. He blinked several times, grabbed a wad of paper towels from the dispenser, and dabbed it on his forehead. Once the blood clotted, he cleaned his forehead as best he could. Running his fingers through his hair, he pulled some of his bangs down (rearranging his hair) to camouflage his injury.

When he turned off the ignition, he stared at his home through his windshield—a home that differed from the one he remembered—and sighed. His changes made led him to an unexpected turn on his journey through Crossroads. A starburst of sunlight glimmered through the windshield and pierced his eyes. Blinded by the rays, he squinted and covered his eyes with his hand. He shuffled his way to the front door, picked up the newspaper at his feet, and unlocked the door. His home suffered from a lack of attention; he hadn't noticed it when he left that morning. He'd been so anxious to see what the future held for him after he changed the past that he only noticed things he purposely sought out, like their wedding portrait hanging above the mantle. Their home needed a new paint job. When he stepped over the threshold, his pupils dilated, adjusting to the darkness of the living room. Blinds held back the sun's rays from piercing through the windows, and dark, heavy curtains smothered out any hint of brightness that sought to edge its way through the wooden slats serving as prison bars to the sun and all her beauty and warmth. A dank chill hovered in the room.

Josh locked the door behind him and started for his bedroom. He glanced at the 16 x 20 wedding photo hanging above the fireplace and smiled. Isabella's dress draped over her slender frame, hugging her tiny waist. "Isabella," he mumbled. "Maybe I haven't lost her." He started for their bedroom and flung the newspaper onto the kitchen counter as he passed through. "Tink, Tink," he called. The door flung open with the flick of his wrist, and darkness seemed to swallow him. His shoulders slumped as he heaved a heavy sigh, releasing the pent-up hope he had gathered that she may still be with him. He eyed a heap of wrinkled clothes at the foot of his unkempt bed. He skimmed over the room with his eyes, tilting his head from side to side. He stepped to the edge of the pile of clothes and grabbed a shirt from it. Bringing it to his face, he breathed in the scent of lavender. "They're clean?" he wondered aloud. "Have I become a total slob?" He dropped the clothes back into the pile and stumbled to the side of the bed. Exhausted from the day and the drain time travel had taken on his body, he collapsed in the bed and fell fast asleep.

Josh flicked open his eyes and scanned over his bedroom, taking in the changes made to his room through the alterations in the timeline. Stretching, he pulled the kinks from his back and neck. A nap was precisely what he needed to get his emotions in check. He dropped his feet to the floor and headed to the bathroom to wash away the grime and devastation of the day. He listened for the sounds of his children as he donned his clothes. Silence. He stepped into the living room and called for them. "Josh, Ciara." He remembered Caleb coming home for the summer and added, "Caleb!" Silence. "Where are they?" he mumbled under his breath.

As he made his way past the kitchen, he eyed the newspaper he had brought in before his nap; picking it up, he read the date, "Saturday, May 29, 2021. Okay, I'm in the right year." Jerking his head around, he stared at the island with a single stove as its centerpiece. "The island was like this last night, too. Why? Why wouldn't we have created a dual kitchen?" he wondered. Standing at the edge of the living room, he took slow, deliberate steps back toward the hallway. His heart pounded against his ribcage; he inhaled short, quick breaths of air, his lungs closing in on him. "I made so many changes, and they don't seem to be for the best," he mumbled under his breath.

With a tilt of his head, he glanced into the dark hallway. Fear coiled its claws around his throat. "The children," he breathed, his voice strangled. Panic joined fear (his companion), swathing Josh's chest with his heavy shroud. "What have I done?" he cried.

He turned on his heels and raced down the hallway to Josh Junior's room. Flinging the door open, he stepped into the room. His jaw dropped, mouth agape. His eyes darted from one wall to the next. A white baby bed stood against the far wall. Above the white dresser hung glittery, wooden letters painted yellow that spelled out the name of the baby he had just lost—at least, it felt to him as if he had just lost her. He understood they had lost Finley in 2007, but he had experienced it only hours earlier. His raw emotions crept up his throat, pushing their way out through a blood-curdling scream! "No! No, no, no, no, her room is still here, just like Tink is ready to give birth any day. I don't understand. That was so long ago, and what about Josh? This was his room. Josh, Josh," he cried.

Josh threw his hand over his mouth and gasped

for breath. Jerking around, he ran down the hallway to Ciara's room, yelling, "Ciara, Ciara." He slung her bedroom door open and stared into what now seemed to be his office. "What? No, no, this can't be happening. What have I done to my children?"

Shoving his hand in his pocket, he pulled out his cell phone and dialed Londyn's number. "Hello," a female voice answered the phone.

Relief washed over him. He inhaled a slow, calming breath. *Maybe I didn't erase them after all,* he thought to himself. "Oh, sweetie, I'm so glad you answered. I'm so confused right now. I can't seem to find your brother and sister."

"What? My brother and sister are missing! Who is this?"

"It's your dad. Who...do you...think it is?" He pulled the cell phone away from his ear and stared at it, his eyes going wide.

The young woman's voice escalated to a decibel Josh could hear clearly without having the phone to his ear. "I don't know who you think you are, but this is a sick joke. My dad left us when I was six. Now, who are you, and what has happened to my brother and sister?"

Josh slowly brought the phone back to the side of his face. "I'm sorry, I was trying to reach my daughter, Londyn."

"Whew, Okay, Mister, you dialed the wrong number. My name's Bonita, not Londyn. For a minute there, you had me scared. I thought something had happened to Seth and Lynelle. I hope you reach her." She ended the call.

Josh stared at his phone screen; it read call ended. He pressed the green phone icon. Clicking on the *recents* icon, the screen brought up his most recent calls. He read Londyn Parker clear as day. "Why would it still list her as having this number?" He rubbed his temples and paced back and forth down the hallway. "Okay, my phone has always been with me when I've used the moonstone, so maybe the phone wasn't affected by the changes I made? Everything else around here has changed, so that's got to be it. It has to be because I've had it on me."

Josh immediately went into his contacts, found Caleb, and called him. The phone immediately sprang into a message from the carrier. An automated voice answered, "Welcome to Americalls. We're sorry, the number you have dialed has calling restrictions that do not allow your call to be completed."

Josh's face flushed a deep red. He curled his lips over his teeth, clenched his jaw, and chunked the phone across the room. Smashing against the wall with a loud smack, it dented the sheetrock before dropping to the floor and sliding under his desk. He grasped the hair on the side of his head and paced back and forth down the hallway. "What am I supposed to do? I think I erased my children. What happened to Tink in this new timeline?" He darted into the living room and rummaged through their things, tossing every item to the side and creating a huge mess that covered the living room. Searching for signs of Isabella, he yanked open the drawer under the coffee table. He pulled out a photo album and flipped through the pages. His breathing calmed as he settled on the floor, leaning back against the couch with the album in his lap. Hot tears stung his raw cheeks as he scanned through the album, seeing their life together in the new timeline he had created. Lost in memories that were never his, he found himself smiling at what he could only imagine was going on in his mind during the different shots of him and Isabella throughout the years on holidays and at church events. "That's it; Clay Denison is my friend. He can help me to piece all of my life together." He folded the album closed and shoved it back in the drawer. Glancing around the room, disappointed in himself over the mess he had made of his home, he grasped the coffee table and pushed himself to his feet.

The sun shone down from its noon-time station, beating vehemently against Josh's truck. Creating a shield from the sun, Josh held his hand flat above his brow and dashed across the lawn toward the vehicle. Fumbling for the key, he unlocked the door and opened it, quickly removing his hand from the scalding hot door handle. He climbed in, cranked the truck, and immediately rolled down the window to allow the pent-up heat a way to escape.

He drove like a madman to the church and busted through the double doors like his life depended on seeing his friend and pastor, and to him, it did. He charged into Pastor Denison's office. "Hi, Sister Brandi, he'll see me," he said, holding his hand up in a stop signal to prevent her from bothering with standing or detaining him.

"But...he...asked...not to...be disturbed," Brandi

responded, her voice fading with each word she spoke.

"It's okay. We're friends, and this is an emergency."

Sister Brandi's face contorted into a mask of confusion as she inched herself back into her seat. Josh pushed the heavy wooden door open and stepped into the office. Pastor Denison looked up from the book he read and pulled his glasses from his face, setting them on the opened book.

"Clay..." Josh started, "You're my friend, and I need your help. I can't find my family—my wife and my children. I think I erased my kids. I have to figure out how to get them back, but please, please help me find Isabella." He marched across the floor of Pastor Denison's office. "I mean, I know Isabella just died in the original timeline. I only had ten years of being her husband back then, but I was hoping that maybe (because I changed everything and married her when we were young) she would still be here, but I can't find any sign of her being in our home in years. I mean, our photo albums ended over ten years ago. Where is she?" He rubbed the nape of his neck and shook his head. "I wouldn't blame her if she left me. Apparently, I'm a slob in this timeline," he mumbled under his breath. "But I'll change. I'm willing to change. I just want her back."

Josh wrung his hands together, twisting them so hard that his skin turned white. He paced back and forth in front of Clay Denison's desk, his chest rising and falling with each labored breath he took. "And what about our children? Josh Junior's room is now Finley's nursery. I think I blotted Josh Junior out of existence, and...and I need help figuring out how to get him back. What about the children we would've had after Finley? Ciara's room is an office, and Caleb's phone number gave me some weird I can't call this number message, and Londyn, well, her number belongs to a girl named Bonita, but hers and Caleb's numbers are still in my phone as their numbers." Josh knit his brow, wrinkles furrowing over his forehead. Perspiration beaded over his brow and dripped down the side of his face.

The persistent squeaking of Josh's tennis shoes grated as he strode from one side of the room to the other, sending a shiver up Pastor Denison's spine; he cringed. "Josh," he held his hand out, pointing to the leather, high-back chair on the far side of his desk, "sit down, please."

Josh halted his pacing and turned to face his friend. He pulled the chair away from the desk and plopped down, burying his face in his hands.

"I'm glad you came back. I've been praying for you since I saw you in here yesterday," Josh peeked from behind the barrier created by his hands, "when you came to use the prayer room," Pastor Denison continued, making eye contact with him.

Josh sprang to life and seated himself on the edge of the chair; his leg shook nervously. "Yeah, yeah, thank you for allowing me to use the room."

"That's what the prayer room is there for, Josh. Now, to answer these questions you've thrown my way. I want to speak to you about it without upsetting you, and you seem to be on edge." His countenance stayed calm.

"On edge?" Josh widened his eyes, crinkling his forehead. "Wouldn't you be on edge if your children suddenly disappeared without a trace of even having existed? And you're faced with the reality that it's your fault, that you caused them to never be born because of your decisions."

Clay nodded curtly, working hard to maintain a facial expression that hid his worry. "Well, that's sort of the thing, Josh. The only child that has ever existed that you mentioned to me is Finley, and she died in childbirth. I was there that day. You cried on my shoulder. You've never had a child named Josh Junior...or Ciara...or Caleb...or even Londyn, for that matter."

Pastor Denison stood to his feet and rounded his desk. He knelt down in front of Josh, extending his hand to him. Josh's face fell. He retracted his hand, pulling it to his chest, and shook his head 'no.' "But I did have them. It was in the other timeline, and I caused them not to be borne by changing the past and marrying Isabella when we were young. My first wife was Samantha, and Isabella was married to Dean."

Pastor Denison shook his head and sighed. The mask of worry he had held back covered the peaceful countenance he had worn during Josh's tirade against himself. He wondered if his friend had finally snapped and lost his mind completely. "Josh, I'm confused. I'm honestly worried about you right now. What are you talking about? What *other* timeline? Isabella is the *only* wife you've had."

Josh dropped his hand from his chest and grasped

Pastor Denison's hand, squeezing it with all his might. With his reddened, watery eyes, Josh stared into his pastor's troubled eyes. "Clay, I need you to hear me out, and I need you to believe me. Isabella passed away in April of last year from cancer."

Clay tugged on his hand, trying to release it from Josh's grasp. "Josh, you're not making any sense."

Josh set his face in a hard mask, tightened his grasp on his friend's hand, and locked eyes with him. "Just hear me out, please, Clay."

Clay sighed and dropped his head, staring at the floor. "Okay, okay, I'll hear you out, but on one condition."

"What's that?" Josh knit his brow.

"After I hear you out, please allow me to call one of my friends? She may be able to help you through what's going on."

"Like a psychiatrist?"

"Well, yeah, she is a psychiatrist, but she's also a believer, and she understands grief better than most. She's experienced a lot of it herself. She lost her husband and their three children in a car accident the week after she laid her father to rest. She will do you some good."

Josh shook his head and let out a deep breath of air, rolling his eyes. "Okay, if I can't convince you of the truth, I'll see your friend." He released Clay's hand and mumbled, "Maybe she'll believe me."

Propping his arms on his legs, he made himself comfortable and set his thoughts on the best way to begin. "For me, the Josh you see, sitting before you, Tink died last year. I wasn't taking it well, and I was angry. It all happened so fast. She had cancer. By the time we found out, it was too far gone. My anger was out of control. In my anger, I claimed I had no reason left to live." He glanced up at Clay. "You scolded me for that and told me my children heard me say it, and you insisted they gave me plenty of reason to live. You even said that if I lost them, then and only then would I be utterly alone, and well, now I am. I lost them. I erased them from existence." He tilted his head and gazed at Pastor Denison's bookshelf. His eyes skimmed over the titles, landing upon a book titled *Learning to Speak Life* by Schledia Anderson. With his eyes locked on the book, he mumbled, "My whole life, I've heard people say that we speak things into existence. I never understood that until now. My words that day...I didn't mean...I only thought I didn't have a reason to keep going." He turned his head and stared into Pastor Denison's eyes, "And then add your words to that mix. I truly am utterly alone now, Clay."

Clay's countenance fell, the corners of his mouth turning down. "Okay, well, how exactly did you manage to do that? You spoke some stuff, and I spoke some things, and now (all of a sudden) you woke up, and everything has changed? How come nothing has changed for me? Explain that."

Frustrated, Josh yanked his hand free from his friend's. Bitterness tinged his tone as he spit, "No, I didn't just wake up, and things were different, and things did change for you, but you don't remember it. I changed things through time travel."

Clay jerked to his feet and rounded his desk, grabbing his phone. "That's it. I'm calling Lucy."

Josh shoved the chair out from under him and sent it screeching across the wood floor. "No, Clay, stop. I can prove it. I saw you at the hospital when Isabella lost Finley."

Pastor Denison slammed the phone receiver down. "Yes, I know you saw me that day. You cried on my shoulder, and I cried with you."

"No, not the other me. Not the me from that time. This me. Don't you remember? You ran into me at the elevator, even called me Josh, but I couldn't have you thinkin' I was a crazy person, so I told you I was related, and my name was John."

Clay set the phone back on his desk and stared at his friend. He tried hard to remember that day. It had been fourteen years, but the story sounded familiar to him. Josh saw the look in Clay's eyes. He almost had him convinced, but he needed a bit more of a nudge. He thought through how he could convince him he was telling the truth. He shoved his hand in his pocket to retrieve the moonstone and felt his wallet. Holding his finger up, he asked Clay to give him a minute. He grasped his wallet, plucked it from his pocket, and opened it. Slipping out a crisp, new business card, he held it up, eyeing the old emblem of Living Life church. He flipped the card over and read aloud the handwritten passage, "Matthew 11:28-30, 'Come to me, all ye that labour and are heavy laden, and I will give you rest. Take my yoke upon you and learn of me, for I am meek and lowly in heart, and ye shall find rest unto your souls. For my yoke is easy and my burden is light.'"

Tears pooled in Josh's eyes as he read the passage. He passed the card across the desk to Pastor Denison. "Here, you gave me this card and wrote this passage of scripture on it when you invited me to come to service."

Clay held the card in his fingers and pulled it into his line of sight. "This card is brand new." He narrowed his eyes and rubbed the card between his fingers. "And this is our old logo. How?" His eyes darted from the card to Josh. "I don't understand." Clay plopped down in his chair and covered his mouth with his free hand. "I remember seeing you that day. I do, but how?"

"It was this," Josh answered. He pulled the moonstone from his pocket and handed it to his pastor. "After you rebuked me for the stuff I was saying that day, you told me to go to the graveyard and talk with Tink and God, so I did, and this old man walked up and told me I could have her back. He gave me this. It's a moonstone; it uses what Chadok—that's the old man's name—calls crossroads. Apparently, crossroads are places in a person's life where decisions are made to either stay on one path or change to another, and because that's the moment of choice, the moonstone can take you to those intersections. I thought the old man was crazy, to be quite honest, but I accidentally used it and went back to when I was a child, and I saw her; I saw Tink as a little girl. After that, I found Chadok and asked him to explain it. He warned me that taking different paths had consequences. He gave me a totem of sorts that had three of my crossroads carved on it. I used 'em, and I got to see her again. I even realized I had already done it all. The first time Tink and I met to talk and get to know one another again, she commented about my shirt and how it was warm outside. Turns out it's because I had been there just a few minutes before..." Josh's eyes widened, "wearing a different shirt, Clay. It's mind-boggling."

Josh pulled his arms across his chest, stretching the knots in his back. Anxious to continue, he sat on the edge of the chair. "It felt so good to see her and relive those moments in life with her, but when I realized the portal to those moments was gone, I kind of went crazy. I used up my crossroads with her. I thought I could find more of them, but I never found any, so I decided to seek out her crossroads, moments I thought may have been decision-making moments in her life, and I went back to them, all the way back to when she was a little girl. I decided then that if I could convince the younger me that she was the one, I'd save her and me both all the heartache we went through in life. But apparently, all I did was erase our children. I never wanted to erase our babies. I just didn't think it all through. I've been so consumed with grief over losing her that all I've been able to see is my own pain. It's almost like my pain had me blindfolded. I couldn't see."

Clay sat across the desk, mouth agape, staring at Josh. "Josh, I don't believe it, but..." His eyes darted to the card he held in one hand and then to the moonstone he held in the other, "how can I deny that this card does not look like it's been in your wallet for fourteen years. The ink hasn't faded a bit." He bent the card. "It's as stiff as a brand-new business card. I don't get it." He dropped the card on his desk and threw his hands in the air, shrugging his shoulders.

"That's because you wrote it earlier today...for me."

"I may need to call Lucy for myself after today, but I believe you, Josh. I believe you."

The Wrong Way Stuck in Grief

Josh pulled the chair back towards the desk and plopped down into it. He leaned back against the cushiony highback, closed his eyes, and inhaled a deep breath of relief. Opening his eyes, he glanced at the ceiling and whispered, "Thank you, God." He dropped his head and eyed Pastor Denison. "Clay, help me piece together my life in this alternate reality and tell me where Tink is. Did she pass away last year? Is that still the same?"

Clay Denison closed his eyes. As he shook his head *no*, his mouth turned down in a frown.

He opened his mouth to explain his response, but

before he could speak a word, Josh pounced to his feet and threw his hands in the air. "Yes, yes, okay, so I got her back like Chadok said. She's alive." A grin spread quickly across his face.

Clay stood to his feet and held his hand out for his friend to sit. "Josh, you need to let me finish."

Josh jerked his head around and eyed Clay Denison, seeing the mask of concern covering his friend's face. "Yeah, yeah," he uttered. A thin layer of tears covered his gray eyes. "Yeah, you're right. There are no signs of her at home. We must not be together, but at least I can make it right. I can fix it."

"Josh, please sit and allow me to help you. Allow me to tell you about your life since I've known you."

Josh eased himself into his chair, hovering at the edge, and leaned his body forward, propping his arms on the desk. "I'm sorry. Go on. Tell me where Tink is."

"Josh, you and Isabella married when y'all were in your early twenties. The two of you were faithful to this church. I came here as pastor two years after y'all were married. We became quick friends. Almost immediately, my wife, Christy, and Isabella were inseparable. You two were madly in love, and you both wanted children. Isabella had several miscarriages, and each loss compounded. My wife was constantly by her side, but with the loss of each child, Isabella's grief deepened. It was as if she relived the previous losses each time she miscarried."

A tear broke past the barrier created by Josh's eyelid and trickled down his cheek. "Yeah, we lost a child in my timeline. It was hard on us both, but we both already had children, so we set our focus on them and figured maybe it wasn't in God's plan for us to have children together. We struggled with the loss, grieving heavily, but we found our place of acceptance."

"Well, in this timeline, finding acceptance was a bit more difficult for the two of you. You both grieved heavily, but Isabella suffered on a different level. She began struggling with depression, nearly losing her will to live at times. Then, in late 2006, came the news that she was pregnant again. This time, you insisted Isabella stay in bed during her first trimester. Christy and I were the only ones who knew anything about her pregnancy. The two of you decided not to announce it until she made it past the first trimester. We prayed with you both for a healthy pregnancy carried to full term."

Clay rubbed his forehead, relieving the tension building in his head, and sighed. "Isabella managed to carry Finley full term. We were all so excited, but then there were complications during delivery. The doctor said it was unrelated to her past issues with being able to carry a baby." Tears rushed to the surface of Clay's eyes as he recalled the events of that day. "She was a...perfectly...healthy baby, but...the cord..." his voice broke as he explained what Josh and Isabella had been through.

Clay scanned the room, searching for something to look at besides his grieving friend. Josh stood, rounded the desk, stood in front of him, and locked eyes with him, forcing him to look at him as he continued. "Please don't look away from me like that while you're telling me about my life. I need you to look me in the eyes, Clay."

Pastor Denison sighed. "I'm sorry, Josh. It's just hard to talk about it knowing how the you that I know took everything."

"But I'm not the same Josh that you know. I can take it. I need to know how the Josh in this timeline responded to everything so I can fix it."

With a deep sigh, Clay resigned himself to complete the story while keeping his eyes fixed on his friend. Locking his eyes on Josh's, he continued, "After the loss of Finley, Isabella went from a place of extreme pain to feeling as if it was her fault somehow, and that threw her into the depths of depression." Clay broke eye contact and glanced (for a brief moment) at the wooden planks stretching across the floor. Gathering his thoughts and how to say the rest, he closed his eyes and inhaled a deep breath. Exhaling, he whispered a prayer, "God help me say what I need to say."

Blinking his eyes open, he tilted his head and looked into Josh's morose eyes. His sullen countenance warned Josh the rest of his story would be even more unpleasant than all he had already shared. Josh braced himself, making his way back around the desk, seating himself, and squeezing the arm rails of the chair.

"Isabella was never the same, Josh. No matter how many prayers she received, she simply sank deeper and deeper into an endless well of depression. She never recovered. The two of you started to fall apart. You went from being in extreme pain over the loss to anger and even rage. In the beginning, your anger was towards God and only God, but as Isabella sank deeper into her depression, your anger shifted to her. I expected you to show up at any moment and tell me you'd left her."

"I left her?" Josh dropped his head, shaking it. Rubbing his forehead, he mumbled, "I'm such an idiot. This is not going to be easy to fix."

"Josh, you didn't leave Isabella."

Josh jerked his head back up and stared across the desk, waiting for the rest of Clay's story. Relief washed over his countenance.

"That's not what happened. I thought you were going to, and you probably would have eventually, but..." Clay inhaled a deep breath, releasing it slowly. "Isabella passed away, Josh.

Josh threw his hand over his mouth and crumpled back into the chair, sobbing. Clay stood to his feet and rounded his desk, kneeling in front of him. "I'm so sorry, Josh. That was one of the hardest things I've ever had to say."

After several minutes of profuse sobbing, Josh inhaled a deep, cleansing breath. Sniffling, he said, "Earlier, you said...you said she didn't pass away last April from cancer."

"She didn't. That's why I asked you to please allow me to finish. I needed you to understand what happened, how it happened, and why." Clay squinted and scratched the side of his head. "Josh, she passed in January of 2010 of something the doctor called takotsubo cardiomyopathy."

"What?" Josh furrowed his brow. "I don't understand. Tink didn't have heart problems. How could marrying her earlier in life change that kind of stuff?"

Clay placed his hand on Josh's. "It's the medical term for a broken heart."

Josh crinkled his face in disbelief. "People don't die from broken hearts, Clay."

James tilted his head and widened his eyes. "Apparently, they do. The doctor explained that while it's rare to die from it, it does happen."

"So, she went into such a deep depression from losing all our babies that she literally died from a broken heart?"

"All the loss she had endured played a big part, but you, well, you blamed yourself for her death. The two of you had a harsh argument that night. When the doctor explained what happened to her, you turned to me and cried, saying you were to blame, that you'd broken her heart. You poured your heart out, telling me in detail about that night and all that led up to it...

Josh sat in his truck with it still running. He'd had a bad day, and the last thing he needed was to walk through the door and find Isabella in the bed, sleeping her life away while the house fell apart around them. Rubbing his hands over his face, he massaged away the stress and mustered the strength to face whatever he would find behind the front door. He turned off the ignition and slammed the truck door. Unlocking the front door, he braced himself. As he stepped over the threshold, he scanned the room and searched for Isabella.

A foul odor smacked him in the face. He strode into the living room, stepping over a pile of garbage. "What in the...?" he grumbled, glaring at the garbage can and the pile of trash at his feet. "Buckey," he growled.

Isabella stirred and stretched in the bed at the sound of the rage in Josh's voice as he called for her dog. She dropped her legs to the floor, unsteadily stood to her feet, staggering to the bedroom door. Buckey, a 60-pound American Pitt he'd bought as a puppy for Isabella to help bring her out of her depression after losing Finley, trotted into the living room. His massive paws backed away from the pile of trash strewn across the floor. Buckey glanced up at his master. Josh's face flushed bright red. Isabella rounded the corner as Josh picked up a wooden candlestick from the coffee table.

Isabella screamed, "No!"

Stunned by her scream, Josh jerked, yanking his body around. As he whipped around, the bottom corner of the candlestick hit Buckey in the side of the head. Tears poured down Isabella's cheeks. Buckey stumbled to the side and toppled to the floor. Isabella rushed to his side, kneeling down next to him. Tilting his head, he stared into her eyes. The light in his eyes faded to an empty void as she held his bloody head in her hands. Weeping, she cradled him in her arms. She jerked her head around, narrowed her tear-filled eyes, and glared at Josh. "I hate you! I'll never forgive you for this," she spit. "Leave; get out of my sight. I never want to see you again."

Shocked at where his rage had taken him, Josh

dropped the candlestick and threw his hand over his mouth. "I'm sorry, Tink. I'm so sorry. I didn't mean to. I wasn't actually going to hit him. I just wanted to scare him, and then you screamed, and it caught me off guard."

"I don't care." An all too familiar pain shot through Isabella's heart. As the ache spread through her chest, an invisible force seemed to wrap its cold claw around her lungs, cutting off her supply of oxygen. Tink threw her hand over her heart, grasping it. She gasped for air in short, rapid, shallow breaths. Her face crumpled in pain. She hauled herself to her feet, toppling back to the floor.

Josh rushed to her side. "Are you okay?"

Tink tilted her head, glanced into his eyes, and shook her head no. "Some...thing's...wrong," she heaved.

Slipping his arms under her, Josh helped her to her feet. Her knees buckled, giving out from beneath her. Josh hoisted her up, cradling her to his chest. She draped her weak arms around his neck and did her best to hold onto him. "I'm scared," she breathed, burrowing her head in his neck.

"I've got you. You're gonna be okay. We're going to the hospital."

"Josh...I'm not...going to...make it." Isabella lifted her weak head and gazed into Josh's eyes. "I'm sorry. I'm...sorry...for giving...up, and I'm...sorry for saying...I hate you." She placed her frail hand on the side of his face, gently stroking his cheek. "I don't...hate you. I've...loved you...since...I was...a little...girl."

Josh's face scrunched into a mask of pain and shock. Tears rushed to the surface, making their way over *his lids and onto his cheeks. "Tink, no, don't leave me."*

Isabella stared off into the distance. A bright smile inched across her face. "Finley," she breathed, "Josh." She shook his arm. "It's Finley. She's...so...beautiful." She closed her eyes and gently laid her head back on his shoulder. She inhaled a deep breath and slowly released her spirit.

Crossroads

The Road Back Home
The Labyrinth

A pool of tears welled in Josh's gray eyes. He sat in the chair, his shoulders slumped and his jaw slack. "That's...that's our story, our legacy? I literally broke her heart?"

Clay Denison made his way back to his desk chair and sat down. "I'm sorry, Josh, but you needed to know what happened. When I stopped in to check on you after the funeral, your anger consumed you. Until you came here to use the prayer room yesterday, you haven't stepped foot in this church in eleven years, Josh."

Josh buried his face in his hands. "How could I?"

he mumbled, his voice muffled under his large hands. Sliding his hands over his face and back through his hair, he lifted his head and stared at his friend with bloodshot, puffy eyes. "I don't understand. That's not me; that's not the kind of person I am. How could I become so angry that I would do such a thing? And to turn my back on God?"

Clay folded his hands together and propped himself against the edge of his desk. "Josh, grief is a complicated labyrinth of a process, filled with varying emotions; the layout of that web of grief is different for everyone, but hopefully, every person going through it will find themselves on the pathway to acceptance. You just never found yourself on that path. You were lost in the maze, wandering around in one of the many traps Satan sets within the junctions of grief. He tricked you into a spiral."

Josh stood to his feet and paced back and forth across the office. "But I love Isabella. I've been devastated since losing her. She was everything to me. Why would I take anything out on her?"

Clay rubbed his chin and considered the best way to explain the grieving process. He stood to his feet and went to the closet door on the far side of the room. Opening the door, he retrieved a maze he, himself, had built. His obsession with mazes led him to use them in object lessons often, and he had made this one for grief counseling sessions. As a pastor, he had found all sorts of counseling to be part of his job. Shutting the door back, he called over his shoulder, "Josh, God made us to love, right?"

Josh nodded. "Yeah."

"Well, because God made us for the purpose of love, loss of any type thrusts us into a maze," he started, turning to face Josh and tilting the maze in his hands towards him, "where we have to navigate ourselves through all the emotions that stem from a piece of our heart being cut out. That's what loss is—the piece of our soul intertwined with the one we lost has been either slowly removed over time through an expected loss or ripped out by an unexpected turn of events. The network of emotions we travel through helps us to stitch together the gaping wound that remains." Pastor Denison rounded his desk. "There's no time limit on it. As I said, each maze is designed for each individual, and how the loved one left this world is as well."

Josh made his way back to the chair, grasping the back of it and bracing himself against it. Clay set the wooden maze on his desk and sat back in his chair. Shifting his weight to one side, he propped himself on the arm of the chair. "There's a path through the convoluted labyrinth that takes us directly to the exit where we find that we've accepted what life has handed us. It's possible for people to find their way through the maze of grief just that easy, but all too often, Josh, we find ourselves turning down a blind alley and heading down a dark path that leads us to a dead end where there is no exit, and while we're on that path our emotional state, our mental state, and even our body may be experiencing the same darkness in the form of shock. It's almost like we walk down that tunnel of emptiness and feel nothing."

Crossroads

Clay picked up a pen and used it as a pointer, running it along a dead-end path with solid black walls. "Most of us begin our grief process, going down this corridor. We meander blindly along the way, aimless, drained of any resemblance of life, and when we hit the dead-end, we numbly turn ourselves around and make our way back to where we started, turning down yet another wrong trail, and when we take that route, the lights are suddenly turned on." He flipped over his pen and pushed a button on the side, turning on a small flashlight at the top of his pen. The light shined over the walls of the path painted with pictures of a couple walking together, a couple standing in front of a house, and then a couple holding a baby. The images shifted in nature, revealing fights between the once-loving couple. He often used the maze in marriage counseling sessions as well. "The tunnel becomes like a movie screen filled with images of our loss with the audio on repeat and the levels peaking, distorting the sounds of things we said and playing it over and over again, antagonizing us with the constant reminders, and then there're the moments of the numbing silence of those things we never said. All we can see and hear is our loss, so we become angry— angry at ourselves for what we didn't do (or maybe even the things we did), angry at the person we lost for the choices they made that led to an early death, angry at everyone else around us for not understanding what we're going through, and yes, even angry at God. I truly believe you've been entombed in the passageway of anger, and you haven't known how to get out."

Josh rounded the chair and seated himself. "It sounds like you're right about me from this timeline, and I guess I did turn onto that same path back before I changed everything. I was becoming angry. I think you realized it. You had the church make a bunch of food and bring it to my home. Everybody came over to encourage the kids and me. It was the anniversary of losing her. You knew I wasn't doing well, so you were reaching out. I ended up snapping and saying some horrible things. You followed me to my office and gave me a good lecture. I was pretty mad at you that day, but I had enough respect for you to listen to what you said I needed to do." Josh arched his brow and widened his eyes, rolling them. Throwing his hands in the air, he continued, "It's what led me to where I met Chadok."

Stiffness settled into Clay's back and shoulders. He stretched his arms and rubbed the nape of his neck. "Right now, you may not be glad you listened to me, but I have to believe that all things work together for the good of those who love God, Josh, so there must be a reason you're here in this reality."

Josh turned his head to gaze out the window. "Clay, I don't understand how Isabella could end up so depressed that she completely shut down. The Isabella I know was a fighter; she fought 'til the end."

Clay widened his eyes and tilted his head to the side, shrugging. "Well, sometimes we veer onto a path shrouded in darkness but covered with pits of quicksand waiting to engulf us. That particular path is inundated with the shadows of regret that haunt us as we stumble

325

through the dreary passageway feeling hopeless. Then, all of a sudden, we become overwhelmed by an unseen force, a demon, that drains the life force from us, and the specter of depression sucks all the oxygen from the alleyway, leaving us unable to breathe."

He pointed to a path in the maze with shadow creatures painted on the walls with patches of wet-looking sand glued in several spots along the tunnel floor. "Once you get to the point that you have no strength (and you can't breathe), you give up, and unless someone comes along and helps you find your way out of that dank fortress of a tunnel, you'll die there. Isabella found herself imprisoned there, and despite the fact that you tried, I tried, and my wife tried, the blackness of the path blinded her; she simply couldn't see our extended hands reaching to pull her up and out of the quicksand swallowing her."

Clay leaned forward, propping his arms on his desk and looking Josh in the eyes, pointing to a particular portion of the maze. "What I'm hoping for right now is that you've finally crossed into the bottleneck of the maze. That's where we struggle with all the questions, besieged by the whys. Everyone who makes it through the grieving process passes through this portion of grief. It's when we've reached the point where we start crossing paths with others making their way through the maze, and we reach out to them, sharing our experience, our loss, and then over time, we reach the end, coming out from the network of passageways and accepting our loss."

Josh rubbed his forehead, distraught and confused at how different of a man he became through the changes he had made in time. Perplexed, he pinched the bridge of his nose and shook his head. "Of course, I want to come out of this, but you've gotta understand, I can't be okay with losing Tink. I just can't."

Clay closed the bible he had open on his desk and slid it over towards Josh. "Here, take it. It's yours anyway. You gave it to me the last time you came to talk to me after Isabella passed away. You said you didn't need it anymore, but I have a feeling it's time for you to take it back."

Josh took the bible in his hands and flipped it open, reading the inscription on the front page. Isabella had given it to him on their first anniversary. Tears welled in his eyes, streaming down his face. Clay settled back in his seat. "Now, don't get me wrong, Josh, accepting your loss doesn't mean you have to be happy about it, and it certainly doesn't mean that we don't miss the person. It simply means we've taken months, sometimes years even, to heal the part of our soul that was torn away, and I'm not saying you're at the end of that path just yet. I just think it's time for you to begin the healing process. I'm not sure what all that entails for you, but I do think it's time. You may not have lived this timeline, but you've seen the results of changing your decisions in life. It seems to me that you were only allotted ten years with your precious wife because that's all you got then and now."

Clay shrugged his shoulders. "It seems like maybe some things are set and can't be changed, almost like she was always meant to be yours, but only for an allotted time. Maybe no matter which path you took in life God's plan was to have her be yours because He made her for you specifically. It could be that ten years and no more was always the time frame set for the two of you. I don't know."

Clay rolled the pen he used as a pointer between his fingers. "Josh, I wish I could help you get her back, and I wish I had the answers for you on how to change it all back and get back your children, but I don't, but maybe, just maybe, you need to go back to where it all began."

Josh pounced to his feet, sending the chair screeching across the wood floor. "That's it!" he exclaimed. "I need to see Chadok." He rounded the desk and threw his arms around his friend and pastor, Clay Denison. "Thank you, man. I don't know how I could've made it without your friendship." Pulling free from the embrace, he scurried hurriedly across the office, shutting the door behind him as he left.

Josh climbed out of his truck, easing the door shut with a soft click, and made his way down the dusty road. Tall grass and weeds shot up throughout the burial plot. Shame washed over him at the condition of their gravesites. Standing at Isabella's grave, he read the inscription: Isabella "Tink" Parker, born February 6, 1980: died January 12, 2010. He turned his head to the side, his eyes landing on a much smaller headstone that read Finley Adaline Parker Born: May 25, 2007: Died: May 25, 2007. Josh's breath caught in his throat. His lungs constricted, holding back a groan growing within his soul. His chest began rising and falling in short, rapid breaths until he fell to his knees at the foot of their graves. A terrible moan broke free from deep within his spirit and pushed its way to the surface, forcing its way through his clenched throat. "Ahhhhhhhhh…" he groaned. Sobbing, he buried his face in his hands and folded his torso over his thighs.

Rocking back and forth, he bawled until his throat was raw from his groaning. He sat upright and opened his mouth to pray, but the words were stuck in his itchy, swollen throat. Swallowing, he pushed past the pain and cried out to God. "Jesus, I don't understand the whys to any of this," he prayed, his voice cracking, "but I know Clay Denison was right that day in my office. I wasn't alone. I had plenty of reasons to live. You gave me my children and Tink's children, but I was so consumed with my own pain that I couldn't see, but now, I'm utterly alone. What I created, through my selfishness of chasing after Tink and trying to get her back without even considering the consequences, is not what I ever truly wanted. I want my family back. I'm not yet in a place where I can accept losing Isabella. I just lost her a year ago. I need more time, but please forgive me for erasing my children, God, and give them back to me. They're the only ones who can help me navigate this crazy maze of grief. I need them, and I need you, Jesus. I need you in my life now more than ever. Please don't let me become the man I am in this reality. Give me another chance, please, God. Please."

Crossroads

Heavy footfalls clomped down the red-clay road in front of the burial lot. The clomping (along with the sound of the occasional twig snapping) grew faint as the footsteps moved farther and farther down the narrow road. Josh ignored the nearby presence. Sobbing, he cried out to God all the more, "Please, God, please give me another chance. Don't punish my children for my mistake." Wiping his hands over his face, he dried his tear-soaked cheeks. He hauled himself to his feet and turned, facing the direction of the footsteps.

The elderly man looked back over his shoulder at Josh and smiled, his green eyes glistening. "Chadok?" Josh muttered under his breath.

Chadok hollered, "You'll find your Crossroads; time will reveal 'em. Remember, your grief will be turned into joy." Josh stood mouth agape, wrinkling his forehead. Perplexed, he stood frozen for a solid minute. Feeling something cupped in his hand, he glanced down and opened his palm to find the moonstone Chadok had given him that fateful day. He had left it in Clay Denison's office, and he knew it. He narrowed his eyes and stared at the token, trying desperately to piece together what had just happened and how he wound up with the moonstone in his hand.

Josh jerked his head upward to see Chadok turn off the road near a sarcophagus. As Chadok disappeared behind the tombstone, a gentle hand grazed Josh's shoulder, and a soft female voice whispered, "Dad, are you okay? You've been out here a really long time."

Immediate recognition washed over Josh, swathing

every inch of his body in goosebumps. A chuckle broke forth from his chest and passed his lips, bringing a deluge of tears. He spun on his heels to find his daughter, Londyn, standing behind him.

"Londyn," he breathed, throwing his arms around her shoulders and squeezing her with all his might. His heart pounded in his chest, and his breath caught in his throat. Releasing his daughter, he whipped his head around to fix his eyes on the headstones he had read moments earlier. The grass had been neatly trimmed. Finley's tiny headstone had disappeared, and a mound of hard dirt (with sprigs of grass growing over it in patches) covered Isabella's gravesite. Gasping for air, he breathed deep, his jaw dropping. He clutched his chest, hoping to keep his heart from bursting through the walls encasing it. "Isabella Yvonne Parker, Born February 6, 1980: died April 17, 2020," he read the inscription, repeating it over (and over) again to assure himself of his present reality.

Josh threw his hand over his mouth. "When am I? How?" he whimpered, dissolving into joyous laughter. He turned his head toward the sarcophagus and glanced back at the token he held. Swallowing hard, he pushed down the lump in his throat and pulled his daughter into another tight embrace. "You're here. You're really here. I can't believe it. He heard my prayer."

"I'm here, Dad." Heaving, she added, "Can...'t...bre...athe..."

Josh loosened his hold on his daughter and placed his hands on her shoulders. Tears welled in his glistening, gray eyes. Pulling her close, he gently placed his lips on her forehead and kissed her. "I love you so much, Londyn. I couldn't have made it without you. Please don't leave me."

Londyn smiled and rolled her eyes in a light, playful manner. "Don't be silly, Dad. I'm not going anywhere."

Josh smiled in return. "Can you give me a moment more with Tink?"

"Of course, Dad. I'll be by the car." She stood on her tiptoes and kissed his cheek. "Love you."

Josh eyed the bouquet of yellow and white calla lilies dancing in the wind as he approached Isabella's headstone. He brought the moonstone to his lips and kissed it. Placing it on her headstone, he sniffled, "A gift for you. I don't need it. I won't change anything, even though I miss you dearly. I've learned that crossroads are to be left alone. God knew every choice we would make before we got to the intersection. He used the crossroads in your life to create the woman I love, and He blessed me with ten wonderful, beautiful years with you, Tink."

Josh glanced over his shoulder at Londyn, who was leaning against the hood of her car and jangling her keys in her hands. "I understand it now. What Chadok said about turning my grief into joy because joy doesn't even adequately describe what I felt when I heard her voice, Tink." He brushed his fingers over his eyes, wiping the tears away. "I'll never stop loving you; thank you for the words you left me in your journal and thank you for the gift you left me through your children, my children."

Josh walked at a clipped pace towards the green car parked behind his truck. Londyn scrolled through the newsfeed of her favorite social media app on her phone. As Josh approached her, he threw his arms around her shoulder and whispered, "Let's go home, sweetheart."

Jeremiah 31:13, "...for I will turn their mourning into joy, and will comfort them, and make them rejoice from their sorrow."

Schledia Phillips grew up on the Mississippi
Gulf Coast. Inspired by the beauty of her home
state and her present home in the state of
Alabama, she imbues her novels with the
magnificence of the South and its breathtaking
scenery. Ms. Phillips is the author of Young
Adult companion novels Pretty Boy and Plain
Jane, the New Adult Romance novel

Crossroads

Wildflowers, the Contemporary/Speculative Romance novel Crossroads, and B.A.S.I.C. Training (Becoming Armed Soldiers in Christ), a Biblical teaching on spiritual warfare. Writing in multiple genres, she engages the intellect and soul by way of her Biblical teachings. Schledia challenges her readers with awareness and understanding through her fiction novels, which touch on a wide variety of emotional and physical struggles her characters face, such as bullying, abuse, depression, grief, domestic violence, and suicide. She is presently exploring her imagination through a YA fantasy series. Her most significant accomplishments to date are having her novel, *Plain Jane*, placed on a "to read" list in a college course on mental health and having her novel, *Wildflowers*, made into a movie!

Schledia presently lives in Alabama with her loving husband, two of her children, and one grandchild. She is the mother of five, a stepmother of four, and a grandmother to two girls. She has served as a children's minister, youth minister, women's minister, and a Sunday school teacher. As a motivational speaker, she has been the Keynote Speaker for the Key Club International, a guest speaker in schools, and an inspirational speaker for women. She is a full-time teacher, mother, and caregiver.